a novel

THE WORMWOOD ULTIMATUM

By L.D. Nelson

Order this book online at www.trafford.com
or email orders@trafford.com

Most Trafford titles are also available at major online book retailers.

Printed in Victoria, BC, Canada.

ISBN: 978-1-4269-2715-7 (sc)
ISBN: 978-1-4269-2716-4 (hc)

Library of Congress Control Number: 2010902139

*Our mission is to efficiently provide the world's finest, most comprehensive book publishing
service, enabling every author to experience success. To find out how to publish your book, your
way, and have it available worldwide, visit us online at www.trafford.com*

Trafford rev. 3/23/10

Trafford PUBLISHING® www.trafford.com

North America & international
toll-free: 1 888 232 4444 (USA & Canada)
phone: 250 383 6864 ✦ fax: 812 355 4082

PROLOGUE

W HEN I BEGAN TO write this book, I had determined to present this story with all the known facts as they were revealed to me. I had researched all the information as it came to me and was determined to get this story out to the public with all the intricate details and let them decide if they wanted to believe it or not, since it seems to be so unbelievable. In telling this story I had to be cognizant of all the classified information I had received and how to use that information without becoming a person that would elicit an intelligence investigation into my own life by either the United States or Russian Governments.

Much of the classified information that was used in telling the story could possibly compromise the United States and the Russian Intelligence Services. I also had to use some fictitious names of key persons to get their full co-operation in telling the story to protect their privacy. However upon the near completion of my manuscript I lost control of it to some unnamed persons, when my house was broken into and my laptop was taken, with my unfinished manuscript in it, and somehow made it's way to The United States State Department.

Four weeks after my laptop with my unfinished manuscript was stolen from my house I received a Special Delivery package at my home in Moscow, there was no return address on it but inside I discovered to my dismay it was from the U.S. State Department, it contained an introduction and a lengthy letter from a person I shall call Rudy. It also contained my incomplete manuscript typed out on plain white copying paper, but my laptop was not returned. The letter was written with a very forceful tone, which in part strongly suggested that I obscure and change the locations and even the names of some of the cities that I had depicted in my manuscript. Also it said to change the names of all the primary characters, it was even strongly suggested that I destroy my manuscript altogether, and not submit it to any publisher; and to do so and have it published I may be compromising the national security interests of the whole Western world. However, if I cooperate I will be fully compensated for all my efforts thus far. But if I do seek to have it published without making the changes the letter suggested they will prevent the publication of my manuscript in any of the Western or European countries, and the world court may even consider legal action against me.

I am vehemently against all kinds of Government imposed censorship. However I understood by their letter that I had to comply with their directive if I wanted to get this story out to the general public. And now that I have obscured some of the locations, and changed the names of some of the cities, it has changed the genre of my book from a factual Novel, which was well documented into a book of fiction. It is still mostly true. I will leave it to my readers to decide.

As I tell the story I urge my readers to keep in mind that after many extensive interviews with the primary character's of which this story portrays, it was impossible to know what some of the intermediate characters had said or had thought. So in order to create a story that was both harmonious and interesting I, as the author took literary license to fill in with some conjecture what I was unable to discover from the intermediate characters. I can assure you that these various conjectures on my part were carefully and consistently used through learning of the character and circumstances pertaining to each of the intermediate characters after many extensive interviews with those who are still alive.

CHAPTER 1

A S THE EARLY MORNING sun rose lazily over the horizon on that crisp cold October morning, it appeared as a thin crescent of fire lying on the valley floor, to the driver of the big black sedan as he cautiously ambled down the side of the mountain road. A lone passenger in the rear seat was looking out the window with a deliberate gaze toward the mountains, as if he was expecting to see something that his driver was not aware of. The passenger was Erik Roskov, and he could not in a thousand lifetimes have imagined the chain of events that was about to take place, that would alter his life and so many others forever.

Erik's gaze out of the window was broken by a soft voice from his driver, "boss I can see the smoke from the cabin it looks like we are about five and a half kilometers away". Erik leaned forward to get a better look down the mountain road, and said "Pull the car over to the side Sid, I want to take a look around before anyone discovers we are here". Sid, the driver abruptly steered the sedan over to the side of the road and stopped, he knew when his boss gave an order that it was not a suggestion, and it was to be carried out promptly.

Erik opened the passenger side of the rear of the sedan and paused without getting out, he began to scan the horizon on his side of the mountain; and as though talking softly to an unseen person he said *"they have got to know we are here by now"*.

Erik had received a phone call the night before informing him that Mrs. Gertrude (Greta) Burkov, one of the principle members of the secret project that he was sent from England to investigate was in a cabin in the mountains just two hours from Moscow. He sent an agent to watch the cabin to make sure she was there all night.

He then made arrangements to be at the cabin first thing in the morning and take her into custody and send her to England, with one of his agents for questioning. It was a cold crisp morning in the mountains and he would have rather stayed in bed until about eight and then get up and have his morning coffee and toast and head to His office downtown, but he was rather excited to finally begin to unravel this mysterious project, known only as Wormwood by his superiors in the Intelligence Department in London.

The call that he received from London the night before was urgent and cautioned him that the Russian Military may also try and abduct the target to keep her from falling into the hands of British Intelligence. So here he was in the mountains with his driver Sid whom he had instructed to pick him up at 5:00 a.m. and drive him to the cabin.

This was Sid's passenger whom he respectfully referred to as "Boss". Erik Roskov was about six feet tall with red hair that was so tightly woven into small curls it could be easily mistaken as a manufactured hairpiece. He was not movie star handsome, and he was rugged in his appearance. He had full thick red eyebrows, and furrows carved in his brow like they had been drawn with a wide black marking pen. He had laugh lines which were prominent on his light complexioned face, which gave him the look of a father who had caught his teen age son smoking behind the barn. To which he gave a scowling look of displeasure and disappointment combined. He was so serious one had to wonder why he had laugh lines at all. He so seldom even smiled, and when he did arrange a rare smile his face appeared to be in severe pain.

His camouflage military jacket lay on the seat next to him, he was dressed in full camouflage military fatigues with a leather holster strapped just below his left arm pit resting snuggly against his massive rib cage, and inside the holster was a Russian-made 38 caliber automatic pistol in a 45 frame, a weapon of choice that he always had with him since his uncle Jerrod Stevens gave it to him when he turned eighteen years old. At that time he was living with his uncle in England, where he was attending school. Lying beside him on his jacket were two full clips of live ammunition.

4

Cautiously putting one foot outside on the ground and raising a pair of binoculars he held in one hand, he turned and stood erect while placing his forearms on the top of the sedan for support of the binoculars, then in one quick motion placed his other foot outside the car and firmed it up on the ground; now he was standing in a spread eagle position carefully scanning every inch of the horizon over the mountains, and down the road into the valley, Erik could now see the plumes of light gray smoke curling up from the mountain cabin that was yet just outside his range of vision but he did not see any sign of the Russian military.

Erik climbed back inside the car and closed the door, then he said to Sid his driver, "Continue driving down the road for another three or four kilometers and try to find a place to pull the car off the road, so it will be hidden from the air, and from anyone driving by on the road". Sid said, "I know just the place, did you hear that explosion boss "? "Yes I heard it too, it was probably someone blasting for minerals in the mountains" Sid pulled the sedan back onto the road and continued down toward the cabin.

Sid then pulled a small slim cigar from his shirt pocket and placed it in his mouth, as he engaged the cigar lighter in the car, and he heard Erik from the rear seat say; "If you're going to smoke that stinking thing roll up the glass between us, and turn on the circulating air". Sid had momentarily forgot after these five years he had served his boss that he could not tolerate the smell of a cigar, and he quickly engaged the air and rolled up the glass that separated the driver's seat of the sedan from the rear passengers seat, and spoke into the car's intercom in an apologetic voice; "Sorry boss I wasn't thinking".

Sid Kachinski was opposite in almost every way to Erik, Sid was born to very poor parents in the Russian city of Minsk, he never completed elementary school and lacked the social skills of the lowest class of the Russian citizenry. His father had left him and his mother when he was only five years old and they never saw or heard from him again.

When Sid was twelve years old he and his mother moved to the city of Moscow and shared a small one-room apartment with a black man who she called Ray. Ray and Sid did not get along from the very beginning, Ray was an American and that may have been the cause of much of their troubles; and when Sid was fifteen years old he left his mother's apartment and lived on the streets of Moscow. He ran small errands for some undesirable people that he met just to earn a few rubles to eat on. After two years on the streets he was "streetwise", he began to hang around the bars and the "Pleasure rooms". He was not in the least a handsome man he was small framed, slender and about five feet eight inches tall. He had very little hair on top of his head, and the little hair he had was combed neatly across the top of his head in a cornrow fashion, and there was a narrow band of jet black hair curling around his head from one ear to the other, only slightly widening at the back of his head where it sloped down to the top of his collar like a farmers hill that had been recently graded.

Contrast that with Erik Roskov the man now sitting in the rear seat of the sedan, with whom Sid had worked for, and been a close companion for the last five years. Erik was born into an affluent family and a member of Soviet aristocracy who enjoyed all the privileges that most Russian families could only dream of.

Erik was educated in a private military school in England and then attended Oxford University where he received degrees in both chemistry and political science. He graduated at the top of his class in only three years. His father was a member of the Politburo and held several high offices in the Soviet government and he was also a retired three star general in the Soviet military.

Erik was slightly younger than Sid. He was twenty eight while Sid was thirty four. Erik's rugged good looks and full head of curly red hair attracted many women, but he was not interested in any kind of a relationship. He was totally committed to his work, and had been all the five years Sid had known him.

As Sid drove the sedan slowly down the mountain road he glanced up into the rearview mirror only to see his boss carefully perusing a crude map that he held on his lap. Erik glanced up and made a gesture with his right hand as though he was fanning unseen tobacco smoke away from his face and Sid knew he had better get rid of his cigar. He rolled down his window about half way and tossed a nearly full cigar out onto the roadway and rolled it up again. Then without thinking he made a grimacing face and scowled as he raised his eyes to the rearview mirror, and just as quickly he reshaped his face to normal hoping his boss was still looking down at his map. He was, and thank God he didn't see him.

While sitting in the rear seat of his limo on a deserted mountain road studying the map that had led him to this mountain road, on which the small cabin lay just ahead of him, Erik turned his thoughts to his beloved mother.

CHAPTER 2

E RIK'S MOTHER HAD BEEN diagnosed with a terminal cancer just as he
was leaving Oxford University in England when he was just twenty
years old. He had completed his high school and vocational education at
a private English military school located in the city of Sussex. Then he
attended Oxford University, where he majored in, both Political Science,
and Chemistry.

He was sent to England when he was twelve years old, and he could
well remember that day when his mother and father bid farewell to him
at the air terminal in St. Petersburg Russia. He could remember thinking
why? why must he leave his home in Russia to go and live with an uncle
in England whom he had never met.

Were there no good private military schools in Russia that he could
attend and be close to his beloved mother and father? He remembered
that he never asked that question then or sense then. He knew his father
always made all the decisions in the family and no one, not he or his
mother would ever say or do anything that would question a decision his
father made.

His mother chose to remain in the main terminal area of the airport
that day, and after saying goodbye and giving him a tight hug and kissed
him; he and his father walked hand-in-hand toward the boarding gate.

As they arrived at the gate he tried to hold back tears as he said goodbye
to his father, but as the boarding began he found it was impossible to do,

and a small stream of tiny tears began to make their way out of his eyes, and began slowly cascading down his little boy cheeks. Though he tried very hard to hold them back he was unable too.

His father turned and looked into his little boy's face and he saw the look of embarrassment, without uttering a word he took his little boy's face into his massive strong hands and brushed back the tears. Then his father said "It will be fun and a good experience for you to live with your uncle Jerrod while you attend school in England". With those last words his father took him by the hand and they walked together up the boarding ramp into the plane.

His father was right it was fun living with his uncle, but for those eight years he missed being with his mother and father so very much, and he looked forward to the few visits he had with his father when he would travel to England on state business, and his father would always reserve at least a couple of days to stop in and visit with his son at the military school in Sussex and when he moved into Oxford University he did the same, but he longed to see his beloved mother whom he had not seen for the entire eight years he was in England.

Erik was twenty years old now and he remembered as though it was yesterday when he returned to his uncle's house from Oxford. It was two days before graduation,and his uncle gave him the telegram he had received that morning from his father in Russia which said, **"Mama diagnosed with cancer, she's okay, attend graduation ceremonies and return home", "Stop" "She can't wait to see you", "Stop" "Get money from uncle Jerrod and I will repay", "Stop" "Book the next flight home after graduation", "Stop" "Love Mama and Papa", The end.**

Erik was glad he had finished his exams, because he couldn't focus his mind on studying after he got the news about his mother. He attended his graduation ceremony as his father had instructed, said goodbye to a few close friends and with a very emotional parting from his uncle Jerrod he boarded a plane at the London Heathrow airport to return to Russia, and his beloved mother and father in Moscow.

He was no longer the twelve year old child he was when he left Russia for England. He was a grown man now ruggedly handsome and six feet tall, and although his mother had seen pictures of him she had not been able to hold her son in her arms for eight long years. It seemed like an eternity since she held him as tight as she could and dreaded to let go of him, at the airport in St. Petersburg Russia so long ago.

The flight from London to Moscow seemed like an eternity because Erik could not get his mind off the telegram he had received from his father, telling of his beloved mother's sickness. As the big jumbo jet touched down ever so gently on the runway at the Moscow international terminal, Erik's mind was distracted from his mother long enough for him to think of all the important changes that had taken place in this country since he left for England eight years ago.

The old guard was nearly all gone and a new and younger, more democratic form of government had taken its place under the leadership of Russia's new President. The war in Afghanistan was all but forgotten, and the war against the breakaway regime in Chechnya was under negotiations to bring about a peaceful solution. So many changes had taken place in his own life as well the most significant change was that he had become a special agent for the British intelligence service. He had been recruited by a close friend of his uncle's just a year ago when he was at Oxford.

It had been a very difficult decision to make and he knew he could not reveal it to any of his family or friends not even his beloved mama and papa.

Erik's father Ivan Roskov had held a high office in the Soviet government for fifteen years. He held intricate knowledge of the workings of the Politburo and the entire Russian government. Ivan Roskov also held the rank of a three star general in the Soviet military. He had not been active in the military since the old Soviet Union was; in effect dismantled under the leadership of former Soviet leader, Mikhail Gorbachev. If Ivan had known the political changes that were going to take place in the Soviet Union during the 1980s he may have decided differently about sending his beloved son to England to be educated. It was the result of that decision that was responsible for his son Erik being a passenger in the black sedan on this deserted mountain road.

CHAPTER 3

GRETA WAS AWAKENED ABRUPTLY by the telephone ringing by her night stand early this morning, and as she picked up the phone from its cradle and placed it to her ear she said with a very soft voice, "hello, this is Greta", "Who is this"? There was a momentary silence and then she heard a very weak stuttering voice of a man say, "Greta you don't have much time they're coming, burn all the documents and leave nothing that can be traced to the Wormwood project then do what you know you have to do", "I am so sorry but we all knew the risks", and then a click and the line went dead.

Although she did not know who the voice was on the telephone that morning she knew she had to act quickly and obey the command. Greta knew very well the risks that were involved when her and her husband Thomas, accepted a position on the Wormwood project. They both knew the possible risks along with all the other members of the project, if they were discovered before the project was ready to be executed. All of them could be imprisoned or even put to death. The old regime in Russia did not tolerate dissidents or even allow any opposition to their rule of tyranny.

"I think I burned everything, but I can't be sure; after all I didn't have much time". "I had to hurry and I could have missed something, should I have taken the cyanide pill as the man on the phone said"? "We all agreed that it should end that way for each of us if we were ever discovered before the project was executed".

"I don't know if I did the right thing by taking the files on the computer disk with me, but I felt I had to have more time to determine, if what we had agreed to do on the project was morally right". "Would it accomplish the end of wars, and bring about world peace as we all had been told it would". "If only my husband was here he would know what to do".

Greta had been grieving over her husband's disappearance, he had been missing now for six months and she was nearly out of her mind with worry. She did not have the time or the will to attend the last two project meetings, and she was beginning to think that her husband's disappearance had something to do with the project.

Her husband Thomas had raised several difficult and embarrassing questions at the last meeting they attended together in January. In answer to Thomas' questions the project leader, Colonel Boris Chechnikov said from the floor that he would answer any questions anyone had concerning the Project, in a private forum but this was not the place for that.

We heard no more until March when Thomas received a voicemail, inviting him to the project head quarters in Moscow for a meeting with Colonel Chechnikov, to answer the questions he raised at the meeting in January.

Greta had come down with a severe case of the flu, and she thought it best to stay home, so Thomas decided to attend the meeting alone. After packing an overnight bag he left the cabin in the mountains east of Moscow where they lived. It was March fifteenth, and she had not heard from him since.

The day after he left Greta received a phone call from the secretary of Colonel Chichnikov, inquiring why her husband had chosen not to attend the meeting. If he was sick she would reschedule the meeting for next week. Greta's heart leaped within her breast she immediately knew something was wrong, her husband was very diligent in letting his wife know his whereabouts at all times.

Greta picked up the phone to call the police but she hesitated and placed it back in the cradle. She decided instead that she would drive over to her and her husband's friend Otto who lived only 2 kilometers north of her cabin. Otto was always willing to help them when they needed help. He was the reason they had moved out of the apartment in the city to their cabin in the mountains. Otto had heard about this cabin being empty after an elderly man who lived there had died, he told her husband about it and Thomas made some inquiries to the elderly man's family, and was able to purchase the cabin.

Otto had said "it's so beautiful and quiet and peaceful out here, and I am only two kilometers north if you ever need anything". He had been such a good friend so Greta decided to enlist his help in locating her missing husband after he had failed to return home from the meeting. Otto was also a Colonel in the military and he knew a lot of people in government.

Greta slipped on her coat and gloves, wrapped a wool scarf around her neck (She knew that the mountain air was unusually cool even in March) then she climbed into her green Volkswagen and headed back up the mountain road. She drove about three kilometers where the road turned into a fork and made a hard left turn down the other leg of the fork towards Otto's cabin. She now had to drive three kilometers back even though his cabin was only two kilometers across the mountain ridge from her cabin. The two cabins were separated, only by a small rocky ridge that made both of their cabins impossible to be seen from the other. She arrived at Otto's to find him outside with his big Irish setter, Precious.

Greta pulled her green Volkswagen into the drive behind Otto's car, turned off the engine and got out. The big Irish setter ran to meet her with Otto right behind. "Come in Greta good to see you where's Thomas"? Greta told Otto what had happened and she began to cry, she told him she believed something terrible had happened to her husband. "There, there Greta I'll find Thomas he's probably broke down somewhere on the road to the city. You stay here with Precious and have some hot coffee, It's fresh I just made it, I'll be back with Thomas before dark".

Greta sat down on the settee to have a cup of coffee, to wait for Otto to return, he could easily run the whole route that Thomas would have taken into the city, and be back in about four hours. Otto returned home a little after Six p.m., he had been gone for six hours. When Otto entered the house Greta noticed he had a worried look on his face, and this was not like Otto he always looked happy even when things were not going well. "Did you find him"? Greta asked. "I couldn't find any trace of Thomas or his car". "But don't worry I will go into the city tomorrow and make some inquiries". "I'm sure someone must've seen him, I will check with all the hospitals as well, perhaps he had an accident and is unable to contact you don't worry we will find Thomas".

Greta drove back to her cabin to await word from Otto, and to be there in case Thomas called. That was six months ago, since then a lot had happened, Otto had checked with all the local hospitals, inquired in all the government offices in the Kremlin, where Thomas might have had business, checked all the local Garages, and towing services to see if anyone had seen his car, but he turned up nothing, it was as though Thomas Burkov had just disappeared.

CHAPTER 4

SID COULD NOW SEE a small quaint mountain cabin at the bottom of the valley, just as the sedan topped the ridge. There was a wisp of smoke curling up from the chimney and he let his mind wander; *he had often considered purchasing a small cabin somewhere in the mountains, where he could set in front of a crude stone fire place and write his memoirs after he retired. He had much he could write about, not only as a driver and companion of Erik Roskov, his boss for the past five years, but also many intriguing human interest stories that he could tell about his many experiences of eight years service in the old Soviet Union's secret police the KGB. Those were the best of times for Sid. All the undercover work and covert operations he was involved with, it was very exciting for a young man who grew up on the streets.*

That was when he first met Erik's Father. He went to work as an undercover Intelligence agent who reported directly to Ivan Roskov and then when Erik returned from England they became friends and eventually led to his becoming the personal driver for Erik.

Sid heard Erik's voice call from the rear of the sedan, which quickly brought him out of his dream state, "yes boss" "pull the car over to the side of the road and stop". Without hesitation Sid steered the black sedan to the edge of the mountain road and stopped. The back door was opened and Erik said, "It looks like were about 2 kilometers from the cabin". As he opened the door and got out of the sedan he raised a pair of binoculars to his eyes, "I want to see what I may be walking into before I am seen," said Erik in a halting voice. "Pull the car up into those trees so it can't be seen from the air Sid and you stay with the car".

Erik slipped cautiously down toward the cabin with his shoulder holster undone and his pistol at the ready, he came up to the rear of the cabin and was unable to see the green Volkswagen pull out of the driveway in the front of the cabin.

When Erik entered the cabin through the back door it was empty, but there was a computer burning in the fireplace along with a lot of paper files which he tried to retrieve but it was too late they were too far burned. He wondered who tipped her off that he was coming to arrest her.

Greta had just topped the hill out of sight in her little Volkswagen when Erik stormed through the back door with his pistol in his hand and ready to fire. As she drove away she let all kinds of thoughts race through her mind, *did I leave any trace of the project behind?*

CHAPTER 5

OTTO ZORKOV KNEW VERY well the sound of the military chopper, whirring in a low drone over his mountain cabin, he had heard it many times while he served in the prestigious Air Military Guard, of the Soviet Unions northern air command. It was an elite air attack force, but not since he was wounded in an air campaign against the rebel held bunker in the mountains of Afghanistan, and was sent home to retire, had he heard this sound of a military chopper of this class, flying this close to his cabin.

This class of military chopper usually flew in an air corridor some thirty kilometers east of his little isolated cabin. The roaring drone of the large primary props grew increasingly louder, and louder, Colonel Otto Zorkov was curious to see this military chopper so close to his cabin, he set his small glass of vodka down on the coffee table in front of the settee. He patted his large Irish setter, who was his only companion since he lost his dear wife three years ago, after a prolonged illness; and he ambled toward the back door.

As he reached for the knob to swing the door open he could not believe his ears, it was that all too familiar sound he had heard so many times during his campaign's when he was a member of the Military Guard in the air force, it was unmistakable, he heard, whoomp, whoomp, and then that shrill whistle. Otto knew two missiles had just been launched and were screaming toward his cabin. A deafening explosion and a blinding light.___ ___

Otto was lying on a small rocky ledge at the back of his cabin, where he had landed when the missiles obliterated his cabin. There was a drop-off at the rear of his cabin out from the porch about twenty feet and then there was a Rocky ledge jutting out from the side of the face of the cliff which formed a table down about six feet from the top of the cliff.

This is where Otto was now lying nearly buried with the debris from the cabin. Every bone and muscle in his body ached, but he was alive. When he had heard the missiles being launched he acted on instinct and dove off the porch to land on the ground about six feet out, in a tuck position and then rolled head over heels the remaining twelve feet or so until he dropped down onto the table rock where he was now lying.

CHAPTER 6

S OMETIME IN AUGUST, AFTER he had given up the search for Thomas Otto received a strange e-mail message that read, "stop searching and inquiring about the disappearance of T. Burkov continued inquiries will endanger the life of his wife Greta". Signed: A friend.

Otto didn't know if he should tell Greta about the e-mail message or not it could just be a crank, after all a lot of people knew Thomas was missing. He decided not to tell her, and let her get on with her life without Thomas.

Since Thomas's disappearance Greta and Otto had been spending a lot of time together, he could see a relationship was developing, but he did not want to compromise his close friendship with Thomas, whom he believed would return to Greta soon. Nothing untoward had happened between them yet, but Greta was a delightful woman and pleasant to look at and be with.

She had long auburn colored hair that cascaded like a soft stream of water falling down around her shoulders, her beautiful green eyes, and near perfect face, complimented her slight build and very well proportioned body, from her legs all the way up to her head. She was about five feet seven inches tall and strikingly beautiful.

It had been over three years since Otto had even been remotely interested in another woman, but Greta was a beautiful woman whom he enjoyed spending time with.

Otto's mind went back to the wonderful times he and his wife shared together for 14 years. He was in the military when they met and fell in love they were married shortly after they met, and lived on military bases the rest of their married life. Otto was a Colonel in the military so it was not a hard life for them they enjoyed traveling to many European countries and seeing the sights together. Otto had nearly lost his mind when his wife became suddenly sick while he was in Afghanistan and died in less than two weeks. He grieved not only because of her sudden death but that he was unable to be with her when she needed him most.

It had been three long years but this was not the time to let Greta know about his feelings toward her, Thomas was not dead he was only missing, and he was a dear friend. Otto decided he would continue to poke around quietly while he was at his office.

After he retired from the air military guard, and spent three months in a Soviet hospital due to his injuries, he was given an office in the Kremlin, and assigned to the International Space Station project, where he was responsible for reviewing procedures and government classified documents to make sure that no "Top-Secret" documents slipped through into the public arena. He was very useful in that role since he had Top-Secret clearance, from the Soviet military.

One day in September as Otto was reviewing some classified files from the space station he discovered a sealed envelope which he opened without noticing that it was stamped TOP-SECRET. It was supposed to be routed to the Department of Russian homeland security, but was placed in his mail box by mistake. Inside was a computer disk.

Otto's curiosity was aroused when he read the routing label that was attached to the envelope after he opened it. The sleeve containing the computer disk was stamped "Top Secret". He thought it seemed odd since all documents for review on the International Space Station were all stamped "Classified", and only military documents were stamped "Top-Secret".

Otto placed the disk into his computer and opened the window on his viewing screen. The file would not open without entering a password given only to the highest level of military intelligence. He was curious, and entered his "TOP-SECRET" clearance password. *That was the highest clearance in the military, why was it on a file from the Department overseeing the International Space Station*? *All of that oversight was in the pervue of the Civilian planning department, and their group of Contractors*. Otto was the more curious when he entered his high clearance password, and saw a name he was unfamiliar with, Col. Boris Chechnikov.

Otto was sure he knew all the military personnel that would have this high clearance access, so he wondered who was this Col.Chechnikov? As he scrolled down the file, he noticed it contained a lot of dates with check marks after them but then he recognized the last entry in the short list of names. It was the name of the Russian cosmonaut that was scheduled to be lifted into orbit next week, Sergeis Kerikalev. He was scheduled to take a three month tour of duty on the International Space Station, to relieve an American astronaut who had been there for three months.

Next to the name of the cosmonaut was written, "Comrade do not forget to deliver the package, the wormwood project depends on you". It was signed, Col. B. Chechnikov. Although Otto knew nothing of project wormwood he would have just closed the file and placed the envelope with the disk in the re-route mail slot to forward it to its rightful recipient but he caught a glimpse of a name as he was scrolling that got his attention Mr. and Mrs. Thomas Burkov.

CHAPTER 7

OTTO HEARD A MALE voice that seemed to be talking to someone on a two-way radio he remained very still and quiet, the man said, "there's nothing left but the foundation and kindling scattered all over the site where the cabin stood". "You won't have to worry about Mrs. Burkov anymore her remains are scattered all over the mountain valley, the chopper made a direct hit with both missiles".

"I don't see any sign of the General's son or his driver, and the sedan they were driving is no where in site, they must have taken a wrong turn and got lost and never made it to the cabin, we are returning to base now mission accomplished".

Mrs. Burkov! Otto thought as he pulled himself out from under the debris, why would anyone think Greta was here? Her cabin is 2 km. further south and who would want Greta killed? Then it dawned on him the chopper hit the wrong target.

Otto lay on the stone table for nearly two hours thinking and trying to convince his body to start working again. As he lay there thinking he remembered the computer disk that he had reviewed in his office, and the names of Thomas and Greta Burkov with others, *"could this be connected somehow"? "And what is this "Project Wormwood" that the unknown Col. Chechnikov was referring to"?*

Otto knew he had a day or two before anyone realized they had hit the wrong target. This was Monday so he would file an official report to his commander on Wednesday and act as though he was out of town since Sunday, and when he returned he found his cabin in splinters. He would then ask if some military training maneuver had gone awry and somehow destroyed his cabin with a misdirected missile. Then he would file a report to receive compensation for the damage done, and watch to see who would claim the responsibility.

Otto knew he had to contact Greta and let her know she was in great danger, but just as he was climbing up to the top of the cliff he heard a woman screaming his name, and saw Greta running toward him. Greta helped him pull himself up out of his hiding place and then she put both her arms around him and held on tight, all the time sobbing incessantly.

Otto told Greta what happened and what he over heard them saying about her. Greta became visibly shaken and for the first time she knew her life was in danger and it was somehow related to her and Thomas working on the wormwood project. Then she began to sob and said, "I believe they killed Thomas but why"?

Otto insisted that she tell him all she knew about the project. At first Greta was hesitant but then she believed she could trust him and told him all she knew. As it turned out she knew very little, the details of the project were never revealed to her or the other members, Col. Chechnikov said it was to protect us and our families. She and the other members were given assignments mostly paperwork, invoices to check, schedules and appointments to make and they were to solicit funds from people they knew by telling them that when the project was executed it would bring about world peace.

They were also told if they were discovered and the project was revealed to the old Soviet hierarchy they would be tried as Dissidents, and either be imprisoned or executed as traitors to the state.

Otto didn't know what to make of what he was hearing. He had always held the Soviet Government and their military in the highest regard.

CHAPTER 8

THE LARGE MILITARY TRANSPORT truck pulled away from the dock, and through the heavily guarded security gate at the secluded warehouse in the mountains. It was raining hard and a heavy fog had drifted in over the mountain road. The driver of the truck and his lone passenger could hardly see the road as it snaked down the mountain. They had traveled this route many times before but not in such a heavy fog. The driver knew there were steep sharp curves all along the route but he also knew he had to make it to the warehouse at the International Space Station complex near Moscow before day light.

He had been instructed by his superiors that he could not enter the complex after daylight because the guards would have already changed shifts. The day shift was unaware of the operation, and the radioactive freight they were delivering to the station on a regular basis. If they were ever discovered it would compromise the whole operation.

The driver said to his passenger," help me watch for those sharp turns we don't want to drive off of this mountain".

The man sitting next to him wearing a military uniform shook his head in acknowledgement, and all of a sudden he shouted, "look out!, there's a sharp turn dead ahead". The driver applied the brakes to the big deuce truck but it was too late he could not slow the truck down enough to make that turn. The truck turned abruptly and it was too much, the cargo shifted and the truck rolled over on its side. Neither the driver nor his passenger was injured but neither of them knew what to do now. Then the driver looked at his Bill of Lading to see if there was a phone number to call in case of an emergency.

There was a number to call, so he called the number on his cell phone. He reported to the man who answered the phone at the other end about the accident, he was told to stay with the truck and he would send a wrecker out. It was well after daylight when the wrecker arrived at the scene by then the driver had set out traffic cones to direct traffic going into the city around the accident scene.

It was just by accident that Bill Forney, a British news reporter on a local television talk show was passing by on his way into the city. He stopped and began taking a series of pictures of the truck and its cargo, he was especially interested in the crates of material scattered on the side of the road that had signs for, "Radioactive Material" painted on them. Bill began to interview the driver and took a picture of his manifest.

Just then a black sedan arrived bearing official government plates, the doors swung open and four men in military uniforms jumped out waving their hands in the air to clear the area of bystanders, and they backed up their gestures with the automatic rifles each of them were carrying.

Then a large tall man with a thick gray mustache got out of the sedan, he was wearing a Russian Officers military uniform, he walked directly over to the over turned truck and began talking to the driver and his passenger.

Bill knew it was time for him to leave the premises before his camera and his interview pad was confiscated he had enough pictures and an interview with the driver to open his morning TV show with a very interesting topic.

"Welcome to the Bill Forney morning show", the announcer said as Bill took his seat behind the desk. "Good morning friends" Bill said "we have a very interesting show today and we will go to the phones and take all your calls after we run some film that we made this morning".

"This morning as I was coming into the studio I came upon an accident on a mountain road that I drive each day, there was a large truck turned over on its side, it appeared that it failed to negotiate a sharp turn in the road due to the heavy fog last night. It was moving slow enough, so no one was injured".

"Why this is an unusual topic for discussion is, the contents of the cargo the truck was carrying". "Look at these pictures" (as the pictures Bill had taken at the scene of the accident were being displayed on the television screen), "and you tell me if there isn't something very interesting about the crates of cargo this truck was carrying". "See those Radioactive Material signs painted on the crates? What you can't see is any of the same signs anywhere on the truck, which as we know that is required by law".

"And where was this radioactive cargo being transported from"? "There are no nuclear facilities up in these mountains, and where were the military guards which are required by law to accompany any "Radioactive Material" being transported by truck"? "There was one lone military person riding inside the truck with the driver".

"If this is not odd enough listen to this, after I was there about an hour a black Government licensed, but unmarked sedan arrived on the scene, carrying four heavily armed military personnel and a Full Bird Colonel". "I have pictures of them too but you will have to tune in tomorrow morning to see them".

CHAPTER 9

O<small>TTO HAD A SMALL</small> efficiency apartment in the city where he stayed during the extreme winter months rather than trying to get to and from his office on those treacherous mountain roads when they were covered with snow and ice. He insisted that Greta stay there with him, she could sleep in the bed and he would sleep on the couch. Greta agreed to stay at least till Otto could find out who tried to kill her and why she would be a threat to anyone.

They didn't feel it was safe to return to Greta's cabin and get any clothes but she had with her, two new out fits which she had recently purchased, and had not taken them out of the car, so that would be sufficient until she felt safe to return to her cabin and get more of what she would need. She didn't know at the time how long she would have to stay with Otto. She didn't really mind, he was a charming man and she trusted him completely. She just wanted to know why and who was trying to kill her.

Otto returned to his office on Wednesday morning and went straight to his Commanders office and told him about his cabin. At first his commander thought Otto was joking but then he realized he was very serious. He instructed Otto as to the correct forms to file for compensation as he became emotionally shaken, at the thought Otto could have been inside his cabin when the missile hit. He then picked up the phone and called the chief of security operations and said "my office at once". Otto left the office as the chief of security entered.

"You incompetent fool! Your pilot did not get rid of Mrs. Burkov as you reported instead he hit the wrong target". It's no wonder that there was no sign of the General's son or the sedan they were at the right cabin and probably have Mrs. Burkov hidden away in a safe house being debriefed on the wormwood project". "Col. Chechnikov is going to be furious".

Erik was sitting in his office adjacent to his father's office on Wednesday morning when the door opened and Otto burst in all excited. "Did you hear what happened to my cabin over the weekend"? "No"! "What happened"? "The military was conducting an exercise in the mountains and one of their attack helicopters shot an armed missile and it went astray and hit my cabin and completely destroyed it". "Was anybody hurt"? Erik said, "No"! Otto exclaimed, "no one was there". "I was lucky I was out of

the city all weekend on personal business and didn't return home until Monday morning.

Erik remembered what Sid had said, as he was getting into the sedan Monday morning near the Burkov cabin about hearing an explosion and feeling the ground move it wasn't blasting as he thought it was it was a missile hitting Otto's cabin, just two kilometers north of where he and Sid were.

"Otto", Erik said, "I am so glad you're all right and I will personally have my office conduct an investigation to find out who's responsible for this". "You're a very special friend to me, you and your lovely wife before she died three years ago".

"Erik, while I'm thinking of it, I would like to ask you a question about a Colonel in the Russian military. The man's name is Boris Chechnikov, do you know him"? "I never heard the name before", Erik said, "is he someone I should know"? "I'm not sure, the name just came up in a conversation, and I thought I knew all our military officers, but I've not heard of him". (Otto wasn't comfortable enough to discuss the information he saw on the computer disk with his friend just yet).

"I'll see what I can find out about him in the course of our investigation and if I turn up anything or talk to anyone who knows him I'll let you know".

CHAPTER 10

O NLY ONE YEAR AFTER he returned to Russia from England, Erik's beloved mother had succumbed to the cancer and died. He was so glad he was able to be with her the last year she lived and during that year he hardly ever left her side.

It was difficult seeing his mother suffer with that dreadful disease, first she had to endure the chemotherapy and then the radiation treatments, but it was too late when she was diagnosed, the cancer had already spread to her vital organs and it was in the worst stages of development.

When his mother died Erik went into a deep depression his father tried to console him by taking a three-month leave from his office, and he and Erik went into the mountains in St. Petersburg where the family owned a cabin, where they could hunt and fish and just get to know each other for they had been apart for eight long years.

The days became shorter and shorter while Erik and his father spent each day either hunting bear and deer or fishing in their favorite trout streams they knew they would soon have to return to the city and his father would have to return to his office. The last week they were in the mountains Erik's father talked more and more to his son about what he wanted to pursue as his vocation.

Erik had a degree in political science that he received from Oxford University he had thought he would like to apply for some government position probably something in the military intelligence division.

Erik confided to his father that he was interested in doing military investigative work. His father was happy to hear that and offered him a position on his personal staff. He would head the Department of Military Intelligence, and report directly to him.

Since the KGB' covert intelligence agency had been dismantled the military had very few effective intelligence agent's left in the bureau. Erik accepted his father's offer knowing he would have an office adjacent to his father's and have full access to all military intelligence files. He had not told his Father that he was a British intelligence agent, and that his assignment was to uncover all the information he could on the mysterious "Project Wormwood".

Erik thought it was ironic that he was sent to England to be educated and while at Oxford University he was solicited by the British intelligence to become an MI6 agent, which he eventually accepted and now he would have free access to all the military intelligence files of the whole former Soviet Union. But he still could not reveal his identity to his beloved father that he was a spy.

The British had received an important piece of information on a back channel source a year before Erik returned to Russia, concerning a project called "Wormwood" the information they received indicated this project was being conducted by a shadow military force in Russia. It could adversely affect the whole world's economy if it was allowed to be implemented.

They didn't have any real details of what the project involved but they did have unconfirmed information from their back channel source before it ended that somehow the international space station was involved in the project.

It was because of this information that there was much anxiety in the British intelligence high command. A dozen of their field agents were given a special assignment to try and recruit a high-ranking or a very influential Russian, preferably military, that they could train and assign to investigate inside Russia and could either confirm or deny if the information was true or just a rumor being spread.

If project wormwood was proven to be true, the agent would find out all the information they could about it including the persons in the shadow military group. It took eight months of intense training and development for the British high command to be comfortable enough with Erik to reveal to him his primary assignment.

CHAPTER 11

B ILL FORNEY MET ERIK when they were at Oxford University when he was attending classes in journalism. One day his professor said they were going to have a guest lecturer who was from a prominent Soviet military family in Russia.

The professor knew this would peak Bill's interest, since he was also studying the Russian language. Bill had confided in his professor that he was interested in pursuing a journalism career in a foreign country, either Russia or the United States.

When Erik was introduced to the class Bill was surprised to see such a young man who was barely out of his teens he expected someone much older. He was captivated by this young Russian and they became very close friends.

Bill left Oxford a short time before Erik, but Erik assured his close friend that when he returned to Russia he would surely get in touch with him.

Bill flew to Moscow two weeks after he left Oxford he had applied to this new TV station that was looking for a multilingual journalist to do field investigative work and remote broadcasting. Since he applied on the Internet they summoned him to Moscow for an interview. Bill got the job and started work immediately, he loved this kind of journalism and he was given complete control of his investigations and the broadcasting of the story. The TV station manager was so pleased with his work he gave him a permanent slot on the evening broadcast. Bill Forney soon became a familiar name to all the Russian households.

After only six months of investigative reporting from the field the station manager offered Bill an anchor position on the evening news. Bill accepted it and soon after that he had his own morning TV talk show in which he was featured in exposé style of investigative reporting.

Bill was sitting in his office, going over some documents when his secretary said on her intercom "there's a gentleman here who wishes to speak with you but he won't tell me his name he just said to tell you to remember Oxford". Bill sat for a minute thinking back to Oxford and who could this be? "Erik"? Bill said as he opened his office door into the outer office "is that you"? Bill stood looking into the face of this ruggedly handsome redhead who was his old friend whom he had not seen or heard from in nearly eight months. "How long have you been back in Russia"? "Come in to the office and sit down we have a lot of catching up to do" looking at his secretary he said "hold all my calls I'm not seeing anyone or taking any calls the remainder of the day".

Erik told his old friend about his dear mother and how she was dying of cancer. Bill said, "I'm so sorry old friend is there anything I can do to help"? "No Bill it's too late she only has a short time left". Bill told Erik how he'd worked his way up the ladder at the station in such a short time, "it has been a phenomenal rise and now I have my own morning TV talk show, hey! I'll have you on some time as a guest you just tell me when you're free and I'll have my secretary book you".

It had been eight years since Erik first appeared in Bill's office at the television station and in these eight years they had become so close they were nearly inseparable, Bill was just the kind of a friend Erik needed to get over his dear mother's death. They attended nearly every social function together Erik was usually without a lady friend but Bill on the other hand was quite the ladies man, even though he was happily married.

Bill and his wife did not travel in the same circles, she was too busy raising their daughter to attend all the social functions with her husband Bill. Just about two years ago Bill and Erik were at some military social gathering that Erik's father was hosting and they met Colonel Otto Zorkov.

Otto was a pleasant man who had just recently lost his wife to a prolonged illness. Erik could empathize with him because of his mother's death, and the three of them became fast friends.

Bill was in and out of General Roskov's office complex so often that Erik's father, General Ivan Roskov jokingly said, "Erik don't let that journalist into our file cabinet he will dig out every skeleton the KGB ever buried". Then he gave a friendly laugh.

General Ivan Roskov was this jovial and friendly man who had a laugh that could be heard from a hundred yards away, and had eyes so full of affection, and set so deeply in his forehead that his face looked as if it had been sculptured out of clay by a Michael Angelo or another great artist.

This was the Father of Erik Roskov and the husband of his beloved Anna who was taken from him by a cancerous tumor that proved to be inoperable. He was a Soviet Union military hero who had led his forces through many decisive campaigns, not the least of which was the Afghanistan invasion by the old Soviet Union Government forces. It was during that campaign that General Roskov was promoted to the high rank of three star general which he continues to hold. He, Erik and Anna were an inseparable family, who were loved and respected by all the Soviet people.

When Anna died the new Russian Government insisted on a State funeral, it was as if the mother of the country had died.

It nearly broke the general's heart when he made the decision to send his twelve year old son to England to live with Anna's brother, Jerrod Stevens. Ivan believed it was the right decision because he and Anna were constantly traveling for the military, and when Erik reached the age of twelve, he wanted his son to have the finest education possible. It nearly broke Anna's heart but she knew it was the right decision also, and after all he would be living with her brother. His father could visit him often when he traveled to England on state business.

General Roskov loved Erik's friend Bill Forney like a second son and often took him and his beautiful wife and daughter with him and Erik to their family cabin in the mountains of St. Petersburg. That was where they vacationed by hunting and fishing. Bill's wife often said jokingly, "the only reason they include me is so they will have someone to clean and cook the game they catch and clean up after them".

CHAPTER 12

IT HAS BEEN A long journey for General Roskov, He began his career in the military by attending a government run school for orphans, even though the old Soviet Union did not call them orphans because they would never admit to the people that under the communist controlled state there could ever be anything but perfection in a controlled society.

His mother died when he was just an infant, he never knew her. Then his father took him and tried to raise him in his small apartment with his live in girl friend whom he never married.

He and his girlfriend drank vodka at all hours of the day and night and when they were drunk they would fight till one of them passed out in a drunken stupor. Then when they awoke the next day it would begin all over again, Mary his father's girl friend received a small allotment from the government because of her husband's death while serving in the military. His father was a mechanic but he seldom worked because he drank so much. With both of their incomes Mary and his father barely made enough to buy a little bread and beans and a little milk for Ivan to live on all the rest was used to buy vodka.

Then one day when Ivan was only six years old both his father and Mary were found dead in the apartment, they had drank so much vodka that their hearts just stopped. The Postman found them and took Ivan and turned him over to the state run school.

From the very first day at school Ivan fit in with all the other students and enjoyed being there. He excelled in everything he did and was soon a special student to all his teachers.

The first four hours of the day were devoted to academics and then for four hours, after they were served a little lunch they were required to attend the military training side of the school. Ivan excelled even more in the military training. So much that at the age of ten he was placed in a special state run military training school where he remained until he was fifteen, then he was placed in the Soviet army to serve his country.

Because of his disciplined nature he rose in rank rapidly and became a Soviet hero, who fought in many campaigns. When he was a young Lieutenant barely twenty years old he met and fell deeply in love with Anna, Erik's mother, they were married soon after they met and nine months later Erik was born. For the next eight years Ivan, Anna and young Erik traveled all over the Soviet Union and Europe.

Ivan rose to the rank of General and then two years later he was promoted to the rank of three star general. Erik was ten now and had to be left at home with a favorite aunt to attend school while his mother accompanied Ivan. He was sent off to England when he was twelve years old.

CHAPTER 13

Bill Forney was working late at the station, when he got a phone call, the man on the other end of the line, said if he would meet him down by the docks at pier thirty three tonight at 11:30 he would give him some information on the radioactive material piece he did on the show today.

This information would expose a secret shadow military project. Bill was anxious, he said, "I will be there but I will want to tape our interview", the caller said that would be okay if he didn't reveal his name, Bill agreed, it was 9:30 now, so he had two hours, he would grab a bite to eat at the diner and then head on down to the pier and wait till 11:30.

Bill arrived at the pier around 10:45, and he looked around, but stayed inside his car with it running. He was not naïve, he had been doing these kinds of meetings for a long time, and he was always prepared for any emergency. It was true Bill had a nose for news, but he also had a sixth sense for danger. It was 11:15 when the black sedan came into view, driving slowly down the docks, toward pier thirty three, with its lights out, but Bill could make out the silhouette in the moonlight. The closer the sedan got to bill's car the more uneasy Bill felt, "*something is wrong*".

Bill had purposely driven down early, so he could plan a route of escape, if it became necessary. He had his car pointed in the direction that he would escape any danger coming up behind him, and there was no way into the docks from in front of him, if he had to bolt he could cut off a car behind him, and cut through the alleys in between the dock buildings. If he kept his lights out, and just drove by moonlight, he could give the slip to any car that might be chasing him.

As the sedan moved closer to Bill's car, he became more uneasy, the sedan stopped about twenty yards behind his car, and he saw the passenger-side door on the sedan open, he couldn't see a person because they had disengaged the interior light, so it would not come on when the door was opened.

Bill sat there waiting, as the lone figure strode slowly toward his car. then it happened, both back doors of the sedan opened and two more men got out, one on either side, and Bill could clearly see by their silhouettes, both of them were carrying what looked like automatic rifles. The first man was now about ten feet from Bill's car, and he could see that he too was carrying a pistol in his hand.

Bill hit the accelerator hard, and the car bolted forward, it surprised all three men, and they began running back toward the sedan. Bill turned sharply down the first alley, drove rapidly to the next turn, and just as he made that turn he could see the sedan was pursuing him, but he was confident he could lose them, in the maze of alleyways and get back onto the road and into the mainstream of traffic without being caught.

Bill didn't return to his house in the mountains, he was afraid they would be watching for him on the narrow mountain roads. He knew they would be watching his office, so he drove around about two hours, and then called his old friend Erik. "Erik, I need somewhere to stay tonight, have you got company"? "No! I'm alone Bill, what is this all about"? "I'll explain when I get there, but right now I believe my life is in danger, someone is trying to kill me". "Come on over Bill", Erik said, "I'm up now, I will put on a pot of coffee, it sounds like this is going to be a long night".

When Bill arrived at Erik's it was well past midnight, Erik was waiting up for his old friend with a fresh pot of coffee and some sandwiches he had fixed after Bill called. "Come in and sit down Bill", Erik said "and have a cup of hot coffee, and I made some sandwiches. It looks like we have a great deal to talk about".

After Bill calmed down a little, he began to tell Erik about the incident that happened tonight, he also told him about the wreck in the mountains, the pictures and interview he took and the military Colonel at the site with his armed guards.

"It sounds like you have stumbled onto something big Bill", Erik said, "and I think whoever that Colonel is, he didn't like his picture being taken". "You say the truck driver's cargo manifest, showed the delivery of that radioactive material to be going to the international space station complex"? "That's right Erik", Bill said, "but why there? And where was he coming from"? Erik said. "The driver wouldn't tell me anything, and the passenger in the military uniform kept trying to get rid of me, he seemed embarrassed about me being there".

It was daylight when Erik finally said to his friend Bill "you look like you can use some sleep, you stay here and go to bed, don't leave here until I get back from my office, and don't contact anyone either. I'll be home around five o'clock and I will pick up some dinner for us on the way home".

Erik arrived at his office at the usual time, and said good morning to the receptionist, and went to his office, and went straight to his desk, and picked up the phone, he tapped in a number and said "good morning Otto, this is Erik, are you going to be very busy today"? "No, not really why"? Otto said, "I would like for you to stop by my office sometime today for a talk". "What's it about"? Otto said, "I'll explain when you get here, give yourself about two hours. For the meeting". "I'll be there right after lunch" Otto said, and hung up the phone.

Erik then walked across the hall, to his father's office, General Ivan Roskov, Erik's father was not in his office, so he told the receptionist he would wait in his father's office until he arrived, the receptionist smiled and acknowledged what Erik said.

CHAPTER 14

GRETA WAS SO NERVOUS, ever since she moved into Otto's apartment, she was afraid to go out in public, and because she had so much time to think about all that had happened, she found herself crying quite often. Otto was such a sweet generous man, he would bring her a hot lunch each day, and they would sit and talk,until it was time for Otto to return to his office.

She had loaded the computer discs she had brought from her cabin onto Otto's computer, and watched them over and over to try and see if there was anything on them that would be a threat to anyone. Her husband Thomas did most of the computer programming for the Project, but she did occasionally get involved herself. She saw the names of a long list of donors they had contacted, and other members of their tier group.

Then there was a list of dates of meetings that they had set up, and a short list of names which she was not familiar with, but her husband probably knew who these were. After each of these names there was a letter or a symbol, Chechnikov, she knew, there was a symbol of an eagle after his name, two other names had a "C" after them, and there were three names with stars after them, and two names had a "M" after their's.

Greta heard Otto's car drive up, *"was it lunch time already"?*, it was always the best part of the day, when she an Otto sat together and just talked at lunchtime. "Greta", Otto said as he opened the door of the apartment, "I have a nice hot lunch for you. "We're having shrimp and scallops today with a salad and that special pudding you like so well". Greta rushed toward Otto and put her arms around him and greeted him with a kiss on the cheek.

Greta and Otto had not been intimate, but she was having a difficult time suppressing her natural urges.

Greta and Otto sat down and ate their lunch together, and then Otto said he was getting worried about leaving Greta at the apartment while he was at his office all day. He knew if someone wanted her dead, and they had the military at their disposal they would surely be able to find her eventually.

Otto had been coming home late at night, because he didn't trust himself being in the apartment with Greta, until after she retired to the bedroom,

Otto was beginning to have strong feelings for her. And with the weekend coming he knew that he was going to be with her much longer than he ought to be.

Otto told Greta that he was having a meeting after lunch with a friend of his, and while he is there he would ask his friend if he could use his cabin in the mountains of St. Petersburg, to seclude her away and out of danger for a while. Just until he could find out why anyone wanted to kill her. He assured her that this friend could be trusted, and because he was in the military intelligence he could help Otto, in his investigation in trying to find out who is trying to kill her. Greta agreed to go if it could be arranged.

At 1:00 o'clock Otto was buzzed into Erik's office by his secretary. "Come in Otto and have a seat, I didn't mean to sound mysterious on the phone this morning, but I thought it best we discussed in private what I'm about to ask you to do".

"Otto", Erik said, "you review all the documents, invoices, and other paperwork for the international space station project, and I can use your help". Then Erik told Otto about their friend Bill Forney nearly being killed last night, and all the information that led up to the incident. He also told him about the wreck in the mountains, the cargo manifest, the mysterious Colonel, and the television show. "Otto", Erik said, "I would like you to see if you can find out anything that the military or the government is doing undercover, over at the International Space Station Building".

If it were exposed would it be a threat to anyone and who"? Then Otto told his friend about the computer disk he had seen, and the name of this Colonel Chechnikov, and this Wormwood Project that he didn't know anything about. And they wondered if this could be the mysterious Colonel, Bill photographed at the scene of the overturned truck in the mountains.

Then Otto confided in his friend about Greta, and the military helicopter that launched the missiles into his cabin. That was not an accident, as Otto had told his friend when it happened. "They hit the wrong target, and they were really sent to kill Greta, by blowing up her cabin".

"Greta's cabin is just two kilometers south from mine, the only thing that separates the two is a rocky ridge which apparently the helicopter pilot couldn't see over, and they hit the wrong cabin". Then Otto asked Erik if he could possibly allow Greta to stay secluded in his cabin in the mountains in St. Petersburg for a while until he was able to sort all this out to keep her safe. Erik agreed,and drew Otto a map of the location ,and how to get there.

It was like pieces of a puzzle, which was all starting to come together now. Erik could not reveal to his friend Otto, that he was a spy for the British Intelligence Agency.

Erik could not tell Otto that he was sent to take Greta into custody and send her to England for questioning, but he knew he was now involved in something that was a threat to someone high in the government or the military, or perhaps both. And he also knew it involved the International Space Station or the agency in some way, and that his investigation was leading him to the mysterious Project Wormwood, that he was assigned to find out about when he was sent from England.

Erik sent an encrypted message by e-mail to Mr. O'Donnell in England. That was the code name he was to contact inside the agency. It read, "received new and confirmed information, concerning assignment, need to know identity of source of original information". "If you can supply please do so". "Need to contact original source in Russia for help in investigation". "Assignment is becoming very dangerous".

Otto drove Greta to Erik's family cabin in the mountains of St. Petersburg, it was a pleasurable trip and Greta seemed a little more relaxed. "Otto", Greta said "I know you have done all you can to help find Thomas, or at least to find out what happened to him, and I want you to know how much I deeply appreciate it".

When they arrived at the cabin, it was dark and they would never have been able to find it, had Erik not drawn a very detailed map, it was very secluded in the mountains. Otto unloaded Greta's things from the van, along with a sufficient supply of groceries that they had stopped on the way and bought, and after everything was put away, Greta said "Otto, you're not driving back tonight". "You're going to stay here with me". Otto agreed since it was so late, and these mountain roads could be very dangerous after dark if you are unfamiliar with the area.

The cabin had one small bedroom, and there was a daybed in the main room, it also had a large stone fireplace with plenty of cut wood stacked just outside, for the chilly nights. There was no inside plumbing, and the lieu was outside in back of the cabin.

Greta busied herself making some sandwiches while Otto built up a warm fire in the fireplace, and hung an old-fashioned coffeepot over the fire full of real coffee beans that he had ground by hand on an old-fashioned coffee grinder he found at the cabin. The cabin did have electricity, but everything else was primitive, Greta would have to draw water from a nearby stream.

Greta walked over to the fireplace where Otto was sitting on the floor, on a bearskin rug, and sat down beside him. She put her arm around his neck, and drew his head toward her to kiss him, and they kissed for what seemed like a very long time to Otto. Then Greta said, "Otto you sweet man, I think I have fallen in love with you. It is still too early to allow me to express it, and I need a little more time to find out what happened to Thomas". "I feel the same for you" Otto said, "but you're right, Thomas was or is my friend, and until I know if he is dead or alive, my feelings for you cannot be adequately expressed".

Otto kissed Greta goodbye the next morning and left for Moscow. Greta had a cell phone and though the area was isolated, it had a cell phone tower just down the road and she could call and talk to Otto each day. Because all of these cabins were owned by the Russian elite the government had installed cell phone service, electricity, and satellite television in the whole area. Greta would have some of the comforts of home.

41

CHAPTER 15

O TTO HAD BEEN WATCHING in the mail room, for another mail pouch containing a computer disk, from the same source as the first one he received by mistake.

Then, after about two weeks since he took Greta to Erik's cabin, another mail pouch with a computer disk came to the mailroom. Otto took it from the mailroom and took it to his office; he excitedly opened it being very careful not to damage the pouch, so he could replace the disk in it after he ran it. This disk had similar information on it that the first one contained. After the names of Mr. and Mrs. Thomas Burkov, was, "unknown and in-flight". It also contained several lists of names that were separated into different tier groups. The Burkov's were listed in two different tiers. Thomas was in tier four, while Greta was listed in tier five, and the name of the cosmonauts that were currently on the space station, were listed in tier three. There were other unfamiliar names in tier two, alongside Col. Chechnikov, then in tier one, there were two names listed but they had been blacked out and Otto couldn't read them. Beside each tier there was a list of responsibilities or job-related duties.

Tier five's duties were, invoicing, scheduling, holding meetings with potential donors, and various other low-key duties. Beside tier four, was listed, "make personal contact with high-profile donors, computer programming, and hold public meetings to raise public awareness on issues concerning, global warming, and conflicts in the middle East.

Also the depletion of earth's energy supply, and overuse of earth's energy between have and have not nations, and the disarmament of the nuclear warheads in Russia and The United States.

Beside tier three was listed, "deliver the project packages, assembling the project wormwood, and implementing the project, at the command of members of tier one. Beside tier two was listed, "all military oversight of the space station, liaison between all tier groups below, to tier group one". That tier had no responsibilities and the two names were blacked out. Otto scrolled down through all the information on the disk, until he found a list of dates, with remarks after each one of them. It was now in the month of October, and the remarks after the dates listed in the month of June and the month of September were, "cosmonaut delivered second package, and cosmonaut delivered third package safely".

Otto knew that these dates coincided with the subsequent launches of the cosmonauts to the space station. The remarks after the December date, when the next scheduled launch was due to take place were, "send two remaining packages, and begin the assembly of the project, our schedule has been moved up, due to circumstances beyond the control of members of tier two".

Otto didn't know for sure what this information was telling him, so he copied the disk, with the intention of showing it to Erik and also to Greta. And then he repackaged the disk very carefully in the same mail pouch, and returned it to the mailroom. He could not determine who the intended recipient was, because under the words stamped "Top-Secret" there was a barcode, and he believed the barcode identified the recipient.

Erik received an e-mail message from the Agency in England; it was an encrypted code, so it had to be deciphered. It read, "Original source of the information on wormwood project, was Thomas Burkov, a field agent, he has not made contact with us, nor have we been able to contact him since the end of March last year". "Trust this information will aid in your investigation". "Good luck"! Signed: O'Donnell.

Erik told his friend Otto, he had to leave town on some business, and he would be back in his office in about three days. Bill Forney was now back at the television station doing his morning talk show, but only after he decided not to follow up on the last show, which he said he would show the photos of the mysterious Col. at the accident site. He thought that was probably why he received the unsigned e-mail message saying, "You have made an intelligent decision, you had better stick with it".

Bill was still an investigative reporter, and he knew there was an interesting story connected with that radioactive material. And he would have to get to the bottom of it, even if it meant endangering his own life.

Erik took a commercial flight to St. Petersburg, and stayed overnight in the Pravda hotel, while Sid, his driver drove down in the sedan, and met him the next morning at the hotel.

As they drove out to Erik's cabin, Erik was unusually quiet, and Sid knew he should not disturb him by asking a lot of questions. Sid knew the route to the cabin, for in the five years that he had worked for Erik; he had come here with him and his father, General Roskov to hunt and fish many times, and The General had used this cabin as a safe house a few times when Sid worked for him as well.

It seemed rather strange to Sid, when they were about one kilometer from the cabin, and Erik told him to pull off the road and park the sedan. Erik got out of the sedan, checked to make sure he had his pistol, and made sure it was loaded. Sid said, "Trouble boss", Erik said, "I want you to stay here with the car till I call you", "and make sure your cell phone is on".

Erik slipped stealthily off the road and through the trees down toward his cabin. Sid could hardly bear to stay behind, but he knew instructions from his boss, must be strictly obeyed.

Erik came out of the woods directly behind his cabin, and slipped quietly up on the back porch, where he could see in through the window, he wanted to make sure Greta was alone, before he made his presence known to her. He could see into the bedroom, and there was no one there, then he slipped quietly over to the door which had a small window, where he could see into the main room of the cabin. There she was, sitting alone on the bearskin rug in front of the burning fireplace, reading a book. He couldn't see anyone else in the cabin.

Greta looked nothing like he had pictured her in his mind, she was a beautiful woman, with long dark hair which rested on both of her shoulders, he thought, "I wonder what the relationship between her and Otto is"? As Erik stood on the porch of the cabin gazing in through the window at Greta, His mind went back to that dreadful night in England.

CHAPTER 16

ERIK WAS JUST NINETEEN years old when he met Sarah; she was also attending Oxford University. It was love at first sight for both of them; they began to date and were together at every free moment.

Sarah was from an elite, upper class English family and at first her parents did not approve of their only daughter dating a Russian military man, but Erik wormed his way into their hearts.

Just two weeks after they began dating they became engaged and were planning on getting married after both of them finished college which would have been in twelve months. They would have a spring wedding and then He would take her home to Russia to meet his beloved mother and father. They were so happy at Christmas time with all the festivities and preparing for their wedding in the spring. Erik invited Sarah to go with him during Christmas break to a beautiful Alpine resort in Switzerland. But when Sarah told her parents what they were planning, they forbid their daughter to go off for four days, and vacation with a man to whom she was not married. Erik wanted to go so bad that he invited her mom and dad to go along as chaperones. They consented and all of them went together. Sarah and Erik were on the ski slopes all day every day they were there, her mom and dad spent most of their time, sitting around the fire at the main lodge. When Erik and Sarah joined them at the end of each day they were exhausted. It was so much fun they were all sorry that it had to end, but after the four days they all boarded a plane back to England.

As they were waiting for the plane to leave the gate, the pilot spoke over the intercom and said, "A very sick man needs immediate medical care and there is no seats left on the plane". "If we can have a volunteer to deplane and wait for twelve hours until the next flight to England is scheduled, it would be greatly appreciated and may save this man's life".

Erik looked at Sarah and she knew without a word from him that he was going to give up his seat for this stranger, she kissed him goodbye and he slowly made his way to the front of the plane to tell the Captain that he would give up his seat for this man.

IT WAS EIGHTEEN HOURS later when Erik returned to his apartment in England, he was very tired but he must say good night to his love, whom he had not seen for nearly twenty four hours, Sarah's apartment was within walking distance so he decided to walk over and kiss her good night. When Erik arrived at Sarah's apartment he was met by her best friend Cindy who was also her room mate. "Erik", Cindy said have you not heard the news? Sarah's plane went down last night in a storm and there were no survivor's, Sarah and her Mother and Father are all dead".

Erik was so broken by the loss of his beloved Sarah that he never had any interest in any other woman to this day. That dreadful night would play over and over in his mind for the rest of his life.

Erik slowly turned the knob on the back door, and pushed it ever so gently, but it was fastened from the inside. Erik knew that it was fastened only with a small piece of wood, held in place with a single nail, so he drew his weapon from his holster and holding it firmly in his right hand, he threw a shoulder against the door, and it swung open with ease, Greta turned quickly to face this rugged looking red haired man, with a pistol drawn and she screamed.

"I'm not here to hurt you", Erik said "I just need to ask you some questions", Greta began to get up, half sobbing and half screaming, Erik said, "I'm Erik, Otto's friend, this is my cabin".

Greta stopped screaming, but still sobbing said, "what do you want, and why do you have a gun"? Erik put his pistol back in his holster and said, "I'm sorry, but I have to be cautious".

After nearly thirty minutes of reassuring Greta, that he meant her no harm, and he was who he said he was, Greta began to calm down and Erik began to ask her some questions. "What do you know about Project wormwood, and to what extent were you and your husband Thomas involved". Erik said he was assisting his friend Otto in trying to find her husband and how his disappearance may somehow be linked to this mysterious Project.

Without revealing to Greta that he was an agent of the British intelligence service he asked her if Thomas had any ties to the military or any special Government agency. Greta said to her knowledge he didn't have she and Thomas had only been married three years and she didn't know about his life prior to their marriage. They had met while both of them were working at the International Space Station Agency, they dated a few times and Thomas asked her to marry him and she consented. They were married five months after they met. She knew nothing of Thomas' past and he never talked about it. She remembered that Thomas had to make many trips to England and other countries, he always told her never to tell Chechnikov about his trips to England, but he never told her why.

Then Greta told Erik about receiving the telephone call that morning which instructed her to burn all the documents including the computer hard drive and suggested that she take the cyanide tablets which were given to each member when they joined the project and swore their allegiance. She told him the caller warned her, that they are coming but did not say who they were.

Erik knew that morning someone had tipped her off, that he was coming but who?. Greta also told him that she had some computer disks that pertained to the project and he could take them with him if he thought they would be useful. Erik told Greta he would take the disks with him. While Greta was getting the disks Erik used his cell phone to call Sid, who had been waiting with the car for two hours now.

"Sid, drive down to the cabin and pick me up, wait outside and I will be right out". "Okay boss is everything all right", "yes everything is fine" Erik said. Sid immediately jumped into the sedan and began the 1 Kilometer drive down the mountain road to Erik's cabin.

When Sid arrived at the cabin Erik was still inside, so Sid left the engine running but stepped outside, walked around the front of the sedan and leaned against the fender on the passenger side, and took out one of his thin cigars, placed it in his mouth lit it and began to smoke it.

Erik assured Greta, she wouldn't be out here alone much longer, He and Otto were securing a safe place for her to stay on the outskirts of the city of Moscow. They had found a small house that they had placed a lease on, but the current tenant wouldn't be out for three more days. Greta felt relieved.

Erik opened the front door of the cabin and walked out on the front porch, Greta could not be seen inside the semi dark cabin, but she could see clearly outside through the open door. She saw the sedan parked just in front of the cabin, and this slender somewhat disheveled little man smoking a cigar and leaning on the fender of the sedan. Greta nearly fainted, it seemed like all the blood rushed all at once to her head, and she gasped for air as she closed the door.

When Greta called Otto, her voice was trembling; Otto noticed there was something wrong, "what's the matter hon"?, You seem to be out of breath". "Otto, you have got to come and get me tonight, I can't stay here any longer. My life may be endangered". Otto could tell she was frantic so he didn't even ask her why, he just said, "I'll be there before daylight", and hung up the phone.

Sid drove Erik back to the airport in St. Petersburg to catch his flight. Sid had earlier asked Erik if he could take a couple weeks off to take his girlfriend on holiday to Paris. Erik had instructed Sid to leave the sedan at the airport parking garage in St. Petersburg, and catch a plane from St. Petersburg to Minsk, to pick up his girlfriend, and leave from there for Paris.

As Erik was boarding the plane, he looked at Sid and said, "enjoy yourself in Paris and you can pick up the sedan when you get back".

Otto left his office as soon as he received the call from Greta, he wanted to get to her as soon as possible, so he drove faster than he usually did, and nearly missed a sharp turn on the mountain roads, but was able to break the van quick enough to negotiate a sharp turn. He arrived at the cabin just before daylight; Greta was waiting, with all her things packed and ready to go. When she saw the headlights coming down the road toward the cabin, she slipped out through the backdoor of the cabin, and hid in the brush beside the cabin where she could see who was in the car. When the van pulled up in front of the cabin, and Greta saw it was Otto, she came out of her hiding place and ran to Otto. Otto took Greta into his arms and held her tight she was out of breath, her heart was pounding and she was sobbing uncontrollably. "Greta, what is the matter? Did a bear try to get into the cabin or what"?

"I'll tell you all about it on our way back to the city", Greta said, "I'll get my suitcase and be right out". Greta got into the van, threw her suitcase in the back, over the seat and sat very quiet, as Otto began driving back up the mountain road. "Otto Greta said after a long silence, how well do you know your friend Erik"? "I know him very well, He's the head of the Department of military intelligence, and his father is a three star general in the Russian military, why do you ask"?

"He came to the cabin yesterday and broke in on me; he wanted to ask me some questions about Project wormwood and what I knew". "He also asked me a lot of personal questions about Thomas and his disappearance, and his involvement in the project". "Erik was here"? Otto said, "yes but he assured me he was helping you trying to find out what happened to Thomas".

Greta told Otto she was now afraid for her life, and she could not stay at the cabin any longer. "Why do you think Erik is a threat to you Greta"? Because he had someone with him that I have seen at all the Project meetings, I don't know his name but he was driving the car that Erik was in". "He didn't see me but I saw him clearly". "Are you sure Greta? That it wasn't just someone who looked like Erik's driver"? "I am certain Otto, he has made speeches at the meetings and he always sits on the dais with Col.Chechnikov".

Erik arrived at the airport in Moscow late, and called a cab and went directly to his apartment; he was tired it'd been a very long day so he went right to bed.

Otto drove all night, and when he arrived at his apartment in the city he and Greta were both worn out from the long drive, and went directly to their separate beds and went right to sleep. Otto and Greta both slept all that day.

Erik still had a day before he was due back at his office, so he slept in till about 10 o'clock. When he finally got out of bed he made coffee, and put two pieces of bread in the toaster, then he took the computer disks he got from Greta at the cabin, and slipped one of them into the drive on his computer. Erik was distracted from the viewing screen when the toast popped up, he left it running while he buttered his toast and poured himself a cup of fresh coffee.

Erik sat down at his computer and began scrolling through the lists of names, none of the names were familiar to him except Thomas and Greta Burkov, he removed the first disc and inserted the second one, and it was similar to the first one. Erik was about to eject the disk from his drive, when he saw a name that was very familiar to him, Sydney Kachinski .

Otto awoke before Greta, at about four p.m. and he went out and brought back some lunch before he awakened Greta. Otto and Greta were eating lunch as they talked about Erik, and why he was with a high-profile member of the mysterious project, at the cabin, and they wondered if he knew of the involvement by his driver and confidant, in the project, or would he be as surprised as they were when Otto exposes him later this evening.

Otto called Erik at home about six p.m., and asked if he would be at home this evening, Erik assured Otto he would be home and he was glad he called because he had something he wanted to show him which he found on one of the computer disks he got from Greta. Otto said, "Erik, I'll be over about seven p.m.". Otto told Greta she should stay in the apartment, out of sight until he could get some answers about Erik.

CHAPTER 17

B ILL FORNEY HAS BEEN parking his car out of sight, from dusk to about midnight in a small lookout area on the mountain road leading to where he saw the accident, for about a week now. Hoping to see another military truck going to pick up some more of the radioactive cargo. Finally his persistence paid off, it was about 11:30 when a truck passed on the mountain roads where Bill was hiding, and it was the same type of military truck that turned over on the mountain road. It had no markings and no escort with it, as it headed in the direction, the other truck was coming from. Bill waited till it was nearly out of sight, but he could still see its tail lights, before he drove out of the lookout area and began to follow the truck, keeping his lights off.

When the truck passed the turn where the accident occurred, it drove another six kilometers or so and turned down a road Bill was not familiar with.

Bill lived about thirty kilometers east of where the truck turned off, but he was not that familiar with this area of the mountains. There were roads going in nearly every direction. Bill knew he would have to stay rather close to the truck, or he would lose him on these winding roads.

Bill tried to draw a map in his mind, as he followed the truck it must've made a dozen turns already, it was getting further and further into the mountains.

When it seemed as if the truck would never reach its destination, it began to slow down, then Bill saw a security gate just ahead, that led into a fenced in compound. The truck stopped at the gate, and the passenger got out, unlocked it and swung it open to allow the truck to pass through. Then he closed and locked it, and got back into the truck, and the truck began to move toward a large metal warehouse that Bill could see from the truck's lights.

Bill pulled his car off the road into a small clump of trees and got out, He took a pair of night vision binoculars, and slung the strap of his camera case over a shoulder, then he picked up his telephoto lens and with his video camera and his binoculars he started walking just off the road toward the fenced in compound. Bill moved down the fence line to get closer to the warehouse, he could see inside the compound but not inside the warehouse. The truck and four guards with automatic weapons were outside the building. He had to get inside the compound to see what was in the warehouse but he didn't see any way he could, the compound was fenced in completely with a twelve foot high fence, and it was electrified.

Bill walked cautiously down the fence line around the back of the warehouse, to see if there was any break in the fence. There wasn't a break but there was a tree, with a large limb hanging over the fence, Bill thought, *"if I can get up that tree and out on that limb I could drop down into the compound, it will be about a twelve foot drop but I think I can do It"*.

After dropping over the fence into the compound Bill lay on the ground for about fifteen minutes, *"that was quite a drop"* Bill said, his leg was hurting a little and he had no idea how he would get back out of the compound, but he was inside now and he was going to see what was in that warehouse.

The truck had already moved inside and the guards were nowhere to be seen, probably inside too Bill thought. Bill checked his camera and binoculars to see if they were damaged when he dropped them from the limb. Everything looked okay they were not damaged, Bill picked up his video camera, and removed it from the case, adjusted the lens and began filming his surroundings, first the entire compound, and then he focused on the warehouse, as he moved closer to the back of the building. There was a set of windows, with bars on them, in one side of the building. He was now just below the first window he stood up very carefully and looked in. Bill could now see inside the well lit building, and what he saw he could hardly believe. There was a steel beam running down through the center of the building about twelve feet off the floor, and there was a heavy five ton chain hoist located on the beam running north and south, for loading heavy equipment into the truck Bill thought. Then on one side of the building, inside a wire caged area, there were four large canisters, like nuclear waste is stored in at nuclear facilities.

Bill could see the truck and six men, the driver, his military passenger and the four armed guards. The four guards had donned radiation protection clothing and were hoisting one of the canisters into the back of the truck. The driver of the truck was sitting at a desk at the back end of the building, facing the front, he was filling out some papers, and Bill could see he was the same truck driver he interviewed at the accident site.

Bill was filming everything that was going on inside the building, but what really caught his trained eye was five crates, sitting alongside the truck, with a computer-driven electronic device in each of them, Bill knew immediately what they were because when the Soviet Union was dismantled, he was allowed to film the inside of a Soviet nuclear missile site, and was shown the nuclear triggering devices for each missile warhead, and they were the same type of devices he was filming now inside the building.

Bill continued filming till all the canisters and crates were loaded on the truck, then he began to think of how he was going to get out of the compound without being discovered.

The truck driver started the engine and one of the guards rolled open the overhead door, and the truck drove out of the building. Bill thought, *"this is my only chance when the guard closes the overhead door it will cut off the light from inside, then it will be dark behind the truck and I can run from the side of the building across the space of about twenty yards, and walk out the gate behind the truck". "For that to work the guards will have to remain inside the building till the truck is through the gate and the gate is closed and locked".*

The truck stopped at the gate, Bill had to run quietly and get behind the truck while the military guy was unlocking and opening the gate, and he had to hope the driver didn't see him in his side view mirror. As the gate opened, the truck rolled steadily through and stopped, Bill threw himself under the truck on the ground so he could not be seen when the gate was being closed and locked. As soon as the truck moved forward, Bill threw his camera case and binoculars over next to the fence, and then he rolled over and over until he was out of the drive and next to the fence. *"Good no one saw me and I have a blockbuster story and the video to back it up.*

CHAPTER 18

E RIK SHOWED OTTO THE names on the disk and pointed out his driver, Sidney's name among them, Sydney's name was listed in the list of the names on the second tier. Otto told Erik what Greta had told him about Sydney and that she thought Erik was a part of the project as well. Erik assured Otto that he was as surprised as they were.

The following day Erik returned to his office and planned how he would confront Sid with this information when he returned from Paris. Then Erik remembered something that Sid had said when they were near the cabin that morning. Erik remembered saying to Sid, "drive a little closer to the cabin and find a spot to pull off the road where the car can't be spotted from the air or seen from the road". Sid said to Erik, "I know just the place boss" "*how did he know just the place when neither he nor had ever been there*"?

"*It was Sid who tipped Greta off, he must've called her from his cell phone just after I got out of the car*".

Otto did not return to his office, Greta asked if he would drive out to her cabin and pick up some of her personal things that she would need when she moved to the safe house. Instead of Otto going directly to Greta's cabin, he drove to where his cabin used to be, and left his van there and began hiking the two kilometers across the mountain to Greta's cabin. It was a pretty rough hike, but Otto was up to it, he was in good physical condition. When he reached the top of the ridge, he thought he saw something move about twenty yards ahead of him, Otto crouched down and stayed very still for about five minutes, then he picked up a good size club off the ground and held it tightly in his hand as he began to move cautiously forward. He was now about where he thought he saw something move across his path, and he stopped again and crouched down, he began looking to the left and to the right.

All of a sudden he was knocked off his feet and pushed forward, when he fell face down onto the ground he flipped over quickly onto his back to fight off his assailant with the club he still held in his hand, he struck blindly at the huge figure that was upon him and he heard a "whelp" as the club found its mark.

"Oh my God!, Precious, I'm so sorry" Otto said as he put his arms around his old friend, and the big Irish setter began licking his face. "I thought you were killed in the blast".

Otto sat there on the side of the mountain for about an hour holding back tears and holding firmly in his arms his close companion, his big Irish setter, Precious whom he thought was lost for ever. "Come on Precious let's get down to the cabin so we can get back home, Greta will be so glad to see you".

CHAPTER 19

B ILL FORNEY WAS IN his office, working with more details of the story
he was going to air concerning the warehouse in the mountains,
and the radioactive material he had seen being loaded onto the truck.
He had decided to air this story as a Government expose piece. Bill
knew he would have to gather more information on the Space Station
Agency and on the people involved in this covert operation, and what
they were planning, before he went public. He knew there would be a lot
of fallout when he aired the story, and he did not know yet how high in
Government it would reach.

Bill's producer, Dan, knocked and entered Bill's office, "Bill"! "This
is a story that may be interesting to you". Bill was perusing the papers on
the clipboard that Dan just handed him and Dan was talking so fast that
Bill looked up and said, "Dan slowdown start over and tell me what all
the excitement is about".

Dan began slowly telling Bill about the information he was perusing
on the clipboard, as he showed him a newspaper he was holding in his
hand, "look Bill in section three there is an interesting headline that
reads, "two of this country's cosmonauts are dying in isolation from
unknown viruses, which has medical science baffled. "Dan, is this a virus
they picked up on the International Space Station"? When Bill asked he
knew that these were the two cosmonauts that had just recently returned
from the space station. "I don't know, but if it is it will make a good story

for your show". "You do some investigating on this, do you think you can get into their isolation ward and get interviews from the cosmonauts?" "I know a doctor over at the hospital that will get me in to see them and get an interview; I can also pick up some background information from the Doctor". "Go get the story then".

Dan was no more than twenty minutes into his interview with the doctor in his office, when a man wearing a gray suit walked into the office and asked Dan to step out of the office for a few minutes because he needed to speak to the doctor in private. Dan assumed that he was one of the Administration's Staff at the hospital and so he stepped out into the hallway as the man closed the door behind him. Dan heard the man speaking to the doctor in a loud and agitated voice and then a heated argument began between the doctor and the Staff member. After about fifteen minutes of shouting and arguing the man wearing the gray suit opened the door and walked out of the office and briskly disappeared down the hall without saying a word to Dan.

The doctor looked out into the hall and motioned for Dan to come back into the office, Dan could feel the tension that was left in the office that was not there when He was interviewing the doctor. The doctor said "Government censorship I have never agreed with it and I hate it". Then the doctor said "Dan I can't continue our interview at this time, I was just lectured and forbidden to allow anyone into the isolation ward to meet with the cosmonauts but you leave me your cell phone number and I will talk to you again about this matter".

Dan was at home and it was after dinner and he was having a glass of vodka, when his cell phone rang. "Dan"? The doctor said "are you busy"? "No"! Dan said, "I would like to drop by and talk to you and finish our interview in private if that's okay with you". Dan said "sure what time should I expect you"? "I'll be there about ten o'clock; I have an errand to run first". "I'll be expecting you at or around ten". The doctor then went on to say, "in case something happens and I'm unable to make it, be sure and check your mail box tomorrow morning, I have sent you a package of information, I think you'll find very interesting".

Ten o'clock came and went, Dan continued to wait for his friend the doctor until about twelve o'clock, and then he decided he wasn't coming so he went to bed.

The following morning Dan made himself a cup of coffee, sat down and turned on the television to watch the morning news. The Anchor of the morning news program said to his television audience, "This just in, a prominent doctor was found dead at the train station last night, now we're going to take you to the reporter at the scene to get a live report". The news reporter was standing with his mike in hand, waiting for a prompt from his station, and then he began his report. "A prominent medical doctor was found dead at about 1:30 this morning; here in the train station by the payphone area, it has all the appearance of a homicide, according to the medical examiner he died at about ten o'clock last night". "His name is not being revealed by the police, until his family can be notified". "Our television crew was here on the scene, just after the body was discovered this morning, and we did manage to get a still photograph of the body while the medical examiner was examining him". (The photo was flashed on the TV screen).

Dan nearly dropped his cup of coffee when he saw the photograph of his friend, the doctor on the screen. He listened for more information but that was all the information that the reporter had, and he turned it back to the Anchor on the morning news. Immediately Dan called Bill Forney, "Bill something big is developing around that cosmonauts story, I won't be in the office until this after noon, and I will tell you what I've learned, but I believe it's going to be a very big story".

Dan could hardly wait until the mail ran, he was anxious to see what the doctor had sent him, and to see what would cause someone to be so threatened that they would have to kill him for it. The mail arrived at about 12:30; Dan met the mailman at the door, and received a large manila envelope, with no return address on it. He then sat down and opened the sealed envelope; there were several sheets of paper with notes written by hand on them. "Dan", the doctor wrote, "I am fearful for my life, since they interrupted our interview yesterday". "I have raised some serious questions at the hospital, concerning the condition of the two cosmonauts in the isolation ward". "I was told by the doctor treating them that he was to tell anyone who inquired about the cosmonauts, that they had been infected with an unknown virus on the space station and were being kept in isolation until it could be determined if the virus was contagious". "And if there was an antibiotic to control it". "I went to the ward to examine the cosmonauts myself, since I am a senior staff member I was able to get in, there I discovered, it is not a virus that they suffer from but something much more sinister". "I have seen it many times before since the accident at Chernobyl, the cosmonauts are without doubt dying of a very high dosage of radiation exposure".

"From the condition of their bodies, they would have had to been exposed to a higher level, than the men closest to the core at Chernobyl at the time of the accident". "And the only place they could have been exposed was either during the trip to the space station or after their arrival". "The mystery is, there is no high-level radiation that they could be exposed to either in the space agency building or during their trip to the station or at the space station itself". "One of the cosmonauts told me, because he knows he is dying, that they were exposed to the contents of a canister that they were delivering to the space station, when it was accidentally punctured as they were offloading it onto the station". "He did not know what was in the canister but it had radioactive materials sign painted on it, and it had "Top-Secret Classified material" stenciled on the canister".

He said "My partner and I were supposed to stay at the station for a three month tour, but after we arrived we became so sick after one week, that instead of sending the other cosmonauts home who were ending their tour we had to be taken off instead, and placed here in the isolation ward". "We were both instructed by The Agency official not to talk to anyone about the canister because it was highly classified". "Dan, both of these men know that they will be dead in less than a week, and there's nothing in medical science that can save them, and I guess that's why they were willing to talk to me". "They told me that they, and the other cosmonauts have delivered at least a hundred classified packages to the space station in the last twelve months, and many of them were like the same large canisters that we were delivering". "All the cosmonauts in the program were told by the Agency, that all the packages had to be delivered via a Russian cargo run, and they must be delivered prior to the Americans being able to redeploy their space shuttles to the space station carrying their own astronauts". "They also confided in me that on the last mission to the station two of Russia's top scientists and two of our nuclear physicist engineers were sent to the station, and they remained there and are there even now".

"They told me the short time they were there the engineers and scientists were assembling several unusual devices all of which was classified, which none of the cosmonauts were allowed to be a part of".

"I do not know what covert operation is going on at the International space Station Agency, but you are in a position to investigate it and if there is anything that should be revealed to the public you are the one that can expose it".

"And if you begin an investigation, be very careful to protect yourself at all times, and trust no one in either the military intelligence or the government".

CHAPTER 20

Erik was in his office when he heard loud voices, and commotion coming from his father's office, which was just across the hall from his. He got up and walked across the hall and into his Father's outer office, and He noticed that his Father's Secretary was not in the office. He moved close to the inner door, where he could hear what was being said.

Erik heard his Father saying to someone in his office in an agitated voice, "the agency is out of control, when we agreed to be a part of Project wormwood we insisted, and you agreed that we would not use the military, nor would there be any violence". "We only agreed to speak at staged demonstrations, and take part in negotiations, so if you can't get the Agency under control, I will end the project now". "Your attack helicopters nearly killed my son, when they blew up the cabin where Mrs. Burkov was, I was never aware that the military was being used to intimidate or frighten people".

The other man spoke and said, "it was an honest mistake there was a mix-up in the coordinates of the target". "Your son was supposed to be at the cabin and have removed Mrs. Burkov for questioning, and Both he and Mrs. Burkov were supposed to be on their way back to the city before we struck the target". "I assure you, neither your son nor Mrs. Burkov was ever intended to be the target".

Erik couldn't believe what he was hearing, he slipped quietly out of the outer office and across the hall to his own office, but he stood at the window of his office to see if he could see the man whom his Father was speaking to, as he left. After about fifteen minutes the man left his Father's office, he was a large man with a full gray mustache wearing a military uniform with the markings of a full bird Colonel. Erik thought," *"Sid will be back from his vacation next week and he will have a lot of questions to answer".*

CHAPTER 21

"GENTLEMEN", GENERAL IVAN ROSKOV said as he stood at the podium in front of the Security Council of the United Nations, "it is a great honor and a grand privilege that my request was honored to address this august body, and I'm deeply humbled to be here".

"Let me say, my mission here today is not to criticize anyone of you gentlemen and or the leadership of the nation's you represent, but rather I'm here today to challenge all of you to come together and work as one world government". "It is the only way to overcome the seemingly insurmountable obstacles that are before us in this century, and must be conquered if we are to survive on our planet and live in peace with man and nature".

"Since the former Soviet Union was dismantled, and the Baltic States, and many other of the Soviet Block states have chosen to separate themselves from Mother Russia many changes have taken place in Russia, East Germany, and all the former Soviet bloc states". "Many of these changes as you know have been brought about by the introduction of democracy and the fall of communism".

"As you gentlemen are aware, there is a large quantity of enriched, weapons grade Plutonium that is missing and unaccounted for, from several nuclear facilities in the former Soviet Union". "There are also several nuclear missile sites with anti-ballistic missiles armed with nuclear warheads that are under the control and authority of unstable governments, many of them are new and have very tenuous leadership, after their break from the Soviet Union". "At any time these weapons of mass destruction could fall into the hands of terrorist extremists, if they have not already".

"Russia and the United States have stockpiles of nuclear warheads installed on anti-ballistic missiles which are capable of reaching any place on earth". "Together these two nations have more than enough weapons of mass destruction to destroy the entire earth and every living creature on it". "It is for that reason that we must work together to stop this madness and begin a serious disarmament in all nations".

General Ivan Roskov continued his speech for over two hours, as he rambled on about, how there must be a parity of the nations of the world, especially when it affects the energy supply of the whole earth. There must be world authority and world dialogue concerning the depletion of the ozone layer and other serious matters such as global warming, food distribution, and economical development.

"We must no longer allow a few western nations, to with disregard of all other nations of the world, use up as much as eighty five percent of the earth's energy supply, while all other developing nations are lacking enough natural resources to survive". "Only because these fledgling nations are not wealthy enough to purchase the needed oil and gas, building materials, food supplies and other of the earths commodities that they need, to grow and develop economically". "The few nation's who hold the power, and have access, to the largest share of the earth's natural resources, also have an insationable appetite for eighty five percent of the earth's energy as well". "The indiscriminate using of these resources has led to the pollution of earth's air and water supply, and is creating an abnormal change in the weather patterns of the earth, and the continual depletion of the Ozone layer, that surrounds the earth, and shield's us all from the deadly rays of the sun".

"Since this Agency was formed, to promote and assure peace among the nations of the world, there has been constant and chaotic hostility between nations". "The flashpoint for much of this hostility is directly related to the worst travesty of international justice that was ever initiated and approved by this Agency". "That was when the ruling nations of the world, by consent, allowed the millions of Arab populations, to be forcefully removed from their homes, and their lands in Palestine and forced to live in a hostile desert and wilderness land". "While their homes, farms, and lands, were given to another ethnic race, with not so much as compensation". That gentleman was the highest degree of genocide on the largest scale that was ever perpetrated on an ethnic race of people".

"To restore a lasting and sustainable peace on this earth the United Nations must come together and see the populations of the earth through a worldview, and you must take steps now, to right many wrongs and to give to all races and ethic groups' full parity with the rich and powerful nations of the world".

"Thank you gentlemen for allowing me to speak to you, and for your attentiveness to my words, I beg of you to act now or it may be too late".

The same day General Ivan Roskov was addressing the United Nations Security Council lower tier members of Project wormwood were arranging and organizing demonstrations in nearly every capital city and the European Union, the United States and Russia these demonstrations were on the same order as the General was proclaiming in his speech at the United Nations.

CHAPTER 22

I T WAS LATE IN the evening, Otto and Greta had just finished eating dinner, and as Greta was removing the dishes from the table and Precious was busy devouring all the table scraps the phone rang, "hello"! Otto said, "Otto this is Erik, can you stop by my office in the morning about 8:00"? "Sure", do you want to tell me what it is about"? "I'll tell you in the morning when you get here", Erik said.

Otto arrived at Erik's office early and was sitting in the outer office drinking a cup of hot coffee, and passing the time with Erik's Secretary, when Erik arrived. "Good morning hon", Erik said to his Secretary as he walked briskly toward his office door, and motioned for Otto to follow him. "Sit down Otto, and thank you for coming" Erik said, as he pushed the button on his intercom. "Hold all my calls and back up all my appointments for about two hours", Erik told his secretary.

"What is it, said Otto"? "Our friend Bill from the TV station stopped by to see me yesterday, and for four hours we went over some very interesting and disturbing information, that his producer, Dan stumbled onto by accident". Erik told Otto about the doctor who was killed, the two cosmonauts and the isolation ward at the hospital, and the contents of the envelope the doctor sent Dan before he was killed. "Otto, all of this is somehow connected to the agency over there and this Project wormwood, and somehow I feel that our national security is in jeopardy". Erik then told Otto about the conversation he overheard at his Father's office.

"As the head of the Department of military intelligence, and a close friend I am asking you to take on what may be a very dangerous assignment, I want you to check every document and every procurement invoice, and every cargo manifest, that is remotely connected with the International Space Station Agency, and see if you can find out anything about our mysterious Colonel, I think he is the one that was in my father's office".

Otto sat in his chair looking completely stunned, at what he had just learned from Erik. "Sure I can do what you ask", Otto said. "Has Sid returned from his vacation yet"? "No"! Erik said, sometime next week, and when he does, He has a lot of questions to answer.

CHAPTER 23

THE PLANE TOUCHED DOWN on the runway at St. Petersburg airport, and taxied to the gate, Sid had a great two weeks in Paris with his girlfriend but now it is back to work and the same old grind, he thought, as He made his way through the international terminal toward the baggage area. *"I believe it is time to get married and settle down, I have some money saved and with the salary Erik pays me to drive him, and the little compensation I get from Colonel Chechnikov and the project, I can make it quite well".* *"I think when I get home tonight I'll make a phone call to Minsk, and propose to my girlfriend, I think she will say yes, after all she was hinting about it all the time we were in Paris".* *"And we had a great time while we were there".* With the thought of marriage on his mind Sid retrieved his baggage and headed for the parking lot where he had parked Erik's sedan two weeks ago. As Sid left the parking lot he had an uneasy feeling, he did know what it was, and it just kind of nagged at him. He started thinking about that night in October when Colonel Chechnikov called him at home, and told him *Erik was a British agent and that he was investigating the Wormwood project and was going to shut it down. He said Erik was going in the morning to arrest Greta Burkov at her cabin and bring her in for questioning. "She will undoubtedly tell him all that he needs to know about Project wormwood, he will probably have you drive him there".*

"Take him to her cabin in the mountains, and you stay back out of the way, I will send a military helicopter with a number of soldiers and arrest him and

bring him in, and we will hold him under house arrest until the project can be executed".

"When I gave The Colonel the coordinates to the cabin, I never dreamed that he wanted to kill Erik or Mrs. Burkov. Although I felt uneasy, the same feeling I am feeling now, like something is wrong". "So I gave The Colonel the wrong coordinates, so it would take time for his pilot to find the cabin, if he found it at all". "I even told Erik we should leave an hour earlier than we had planned, so we would have time to get to the cabin, pick up Mrs. Burkov, and leave before the chopper pilot ever found the cabin". "I never dreamed they were going to fire missiles into the cabin or that there was another cabin two kilometers north, just over the ridge from the Burkov's". Erik is a good friend, British agent or not, and the Colonel may have fabricated that story, when I get back to Moscow I'm going to Erik's office first thing in the morning, and tell him all I know about Chechnikov and the project. When I signed on to work for the project there was never to be any violence, The Colonel has become a rogue leader, and the project has been taken over and changed to promote his personal agenda.

As Sid continued driving toward the city of Moscow, and home he could not shake that uneasy feeling that was gnawing at his gut. He began to let his mind wander back to the first time he had met Colonel Chechnikov.

"I was sitting in the outer office of my boss, General Ivan Roskov waiting to drive him to the airport. When this tall Soviet military Officer with a thick gray mustache walked in and sat down next to me. Since my days serving in the KGB Agency I was always leery about all Soviet military Officers, because I had investigated and informed on so many of them , I never knew when one of them or their relatives would meet up with me and take revenge. So I never spoke to the Officer until the Officer spoke to me, and then I was very cautious of what I said in response.

At first it was just small talk about the weather, if I had any family, how long had I been the General's driver, (Because I was wearing the uniform that a military driver wears when working), and then the conversation began to tilt toward politics, at first He was discussing politics of the Russian Government and then He turned his discussion to a world view.

I was becoming more comfortable talking with this gentleman, although I was still a little uneasy and kept my guard up. I kept looking at the watch on my wrist hoping that the General would step out of his office and we would be on our way to the airport. Finally after sitting and talking with the Officer for about an hour the General stepped out of his office and greeted the Officer "Good afternoon Colonel Chechnikov how long have you been here"? I didn't know you were here, my Secretary had to take the day off because of a family emergency". "I am on my way to the airport and will be out of my office for the next two weeks, why don't you ride along with me to the airport and we can talk". "My driver will bring you back into the city after my plane leaves".

On the way to the airport The General and the officer talked about a number of things but their main conversation was concerning this special Project they both seemed to be involved in called Wormwood. The Officer was giving General Roskov some dates and information about world conferences and rally's and demonstrations he would like for him to attend and speak. The General seemed to become a little agitated when the Officer insisted he attend all of these demonstrations.

I remember when we arrived at the airport and let General Roskov out of the car, before I could take off again The Colonel got out of the back seat of the car and got in the front on the passenger side, it made me a little nervous because I was always used to my passenger riding in the back, as The General always did. All the way back into the city the Colonel seemed to be interrogating me he asked how long I had worked for the General and how long I had known him and other personal questions. By then I had become more comfortable and less intimidated by the Colonel, the more we talked. Until I began to tell him more personal things about my self, and the Colonel showed more than a passing interest.

When I revealed that I had worked with Intelligence, with the KGB Agency, He began to ask more questions about the Soviet Intelligence community. He told me that He had taken over the remnants of the KGB and their Intelligence, when the Soviet Government collapsed.

Communism was replaced with a less totalitarian form of Government, and then He told me that He was looking for a good man to place in charge of the new Intelligence Agency. He then mentioned the General's son that was attending college in England as a candidate.

When we arrived at the address in the city that The Colonel had given me before getting out of the car, the Colonel wrote his telephone number on a piece of paper and gave it to me.

I was rather surprised a few weeks later when I got a call from Colonel Chechnikov, in his apartment in Moscow. "Sid" the Colonel said, "this is Colonel Chechnikov, are you going to be free tomorrow"? "I would like you to come over to my office at the Kremlin and listen to a proposal I have to make to you". "Yes I think I can do that, what time do you want me there"? "How about 10:00 a.m. is that too early"? "No that would be fine I will see you in the morning".

When I arrived at the Colonel's office I was a little surprised, I expected a large well lit office in a prime location inside the headquarters of the Kremlin after all He was a Soviet Military Officer. According to all the battle ribbons He displayed on his uniform, He was highly decorated, which I thought would make him well respected and favored in the Kremlin.

Instead of that, the Colonel's office was a very small corner room with no windows, and boxes that were packed for moving stacked on the floor and on top of a well worn table in the corner. The lighting was so dim I could hardly make out the features of the large man sitting at the desk in the center of the room." Come in and sit down" the Colonel said, " you will have to excuse the condition of my office , they are in the process of moving me over to my new headquarters at the International Space Station Agency". "I have been assigned to head that Agency, it's quite a promotion for me".

"I want to thank you, for coming on such short notice, would you like a cup of coffee"? "No, I am fine. "Lets get right to the reason for you being here", "I would like you to come and work for me and let me introduce you to some of my colleagues". "They have nothing to do with the military, but we have formed a very important organization which I think you would fit into very well, and with your KGB background you would be an essential asset to our organization".

I was curious about what this Colonel was offering me, and I said to the Colonel "I would like to hear more about this before I consider making any kind of a decision". "I understand the Colonel said, but I can't reveal too much about our organization to you until I know more about you".

I then said to the Colonel "I will have to talk to General Roscov to see if he would release me from my position that I have with him before making any decision". " The Colonel interrupted me and said it would not be necessary for me to leave my position as the General's driver in fact He would rather that I did not." I have it on the best authority that the General is about to transfer you over to his son Erik whom he is grooming to step in and take over the whole Russian intelligence community".

"It is for this very reason that I would like you to work for our organization undercover, and continue your position as driver and confidant of the General and his son Erik". "I know this must sound mysterious to you Sid and may even remind you of the old Soviet Union, KGB days when you were involved in gathering intelligence undercover". "Well Sid it's nothing like that in fact just to set your mind at ease I must tell you that General Roskov is one of the primary spokesmen for our organization".

"If you are free this weekend I would like you to accompany me to one of our organizations rallies in the city of Minsk, and then you will have a better understanding of our organization and its purpose and its goals".

Before I answered the Colonel I thought about the sweet young girl that I have been corresponding with who lives in the city of Minsk. If I went with the Colonel I would be able to meet this sweet young thing and perhaps move our relationship to a higher level.

"Yes I will be free and I would love to attend your rally to get a better understanding of what your organization and the people in it are all about". "This would help me to make my decision".

Before I left the Colonel's office the Colonel had made arrangements for me to accompany him that weekend on his flight to Minsk.

"I was excited that the Colonel was interested in him and I was looking forward to the coming weekend". Not only would it be an interesting trip and I would no doubt meet with some very interesting people". I was also looking forward to meeting face-to-face with the young girl I have been communicating with.

It was about 7 a.m. when the Colonel's car arrived and picked me up at my apartment, and the driver took me directly to the airport. When I arrived the Colonel had already boarded the plane and saved the seat next to him for me. The flight was only about an hour and the Colonel said very little during that time He kept himself busy going over a lot of papers that he carried in his briefcase. When they landed in Minsk there was a car waiting to take us downtown to the city square where the rally was going to be held.

When we arrived at the city square people had already started to gather and they were looking at all the large signs that had been erected around the city square which depicted all the environmental issues. Both in pictures and songs, which were very graphic words. I was trying to take it all in and I did not know what to make of it all. I was anxious to learn what this mysterious organization was all about.

There were no seats in the city square, and as the crowd began to enlarge it became standing room only as they pressed up toward the makeshift platform that had been erected there. It was about 10 a.m. when a man dressed in a suit approached the podium and took the microphone, and tapping it he said" is this on"? And then he addressed the crowd that gathered, first by telling them how much he appreciated their being there and then how important it was for them to be there. He introduced himself as a university professor and an eco-scientist, whose primary interest was to help preserve our planet for future generations. After he had spoken for about fifteen minutes on many ecological concerns, he then introduced Colonel Chechnikov as the primary spokesman for the organization.

I listened intensely as the Colonel spoke to the crowd for about two hours. There were bursts of applause from time to time from the audience.

What the Colonel said made a lot of sense it seemed that there had come together a large number of highly recognized eco-scientists from all over the world and joined themselves together to form this organization whose sole purpose was to do whatever was necessary to reverse the destruction of our planet, by pollution of air and water and land by the large industrial nations of the world. The Colonel said the heads of government of these environment destroying nations could not be trusted to reverse or even arrest their destructive practices and policies. We must then use whatever means we have at our disposal whether it be by force or by political persuasion we must stop the destruction of the ecology of our planet.

After the rally ended the Colonel took me and introduced me to many of the scientists of the organization. After that the Colonel said he would be tied up for about the next two hours in organizational meetings and if I would like, I could use his car and driver to take me around the city to see the sights. I accepted the Colonel's offer and this would be the perfect time for me to meet with my girlfriend. I phoned her and said I had about two hours and where could they meet for lunch. She chose a small delicatessen in the center of the city and gave me the directions, and she would meet me there in thirty minutes.

Sid was thinking about what he would say to Erik in the morning, when a large military truck came up behind him and bumped the back of the sedan, it hit so hard it jolted his passenger awake who was sleeping in the back seat. The truck hit so hard Sid almost lost control of the car. The winding mountain road was too narrow for the truck to get around him, but he knew that the mountain road turned into a four-lane highway going into Moscow, about five kilometers ahead. The truck hit the bumper again and again, but Sid was able to stay just ahead of him, and kept the sedan under control. Sid thought, *who is this and why are they trying to run me off the road? There's a sharp curve coming just at the bottom of the hill on the mountain road, just before it meets the four-lane highway, I'll have to slow the car down to negotiate that curve and it will give the truck driver the opportunity to catch me again.*

CHAPTER 24

E RIK WAS SOUND ASLEEP when the phone rang and woke him up. "Erik Roskov"? The caller said, "yes! this is Erik Roskov who's calling"? "This is Sergeant Rymer of the National Highway Police, sir; do you own a sedan with a license inscription "Government 01"? "Yes I do why? Has it been stolen from the St. Petersburg airport parking lot"? "I'm not sure the sergeant said, but it has been in a bad accident, it seems it ran off a mountain road just before you reach the highway coming from St. Petersburg". "How about the driver" Erik said, "was he injured"? "I'm afraid the driver's dead", the sergeant said, "the car is badly burned and we're trying to identify the driver now, we think we may be able to identify him from some luggage that we found inside the trunk, that is about the only thing that wasn't burned".

"We will call you at this number as soon as we get the remains of the car back up on the road and retrieve the driver's body". "Here, I'll give you my cell phone number", Erik said, "call me on it, I am leaving Moscow now and I will be there in two hours, I am the Director of military intelligence, wait till I get there, I'll identify the body of the driver".

Erik arrived at the scene about four a.m., the police were waiting for him, and they had winched the car up on the roadway. The body of the driver was lying on the side of the road covered with a tarp.

A small framed man wearing a police uniform with sergeant stripes, approached him and said, "I am Sergeant Rymer, you must be Erik

Roskov", Erik nodded, and walked over to the tarp covered body with the sergeant, another police officer pulled back the tarp to reveal a severely burned body, but there was still enough of the features on the body that was intact that Erik knew at once. "What happened"? Erik said, "it looks like the driver may have fallen asleep and missed the curve, and drove right off the mountain". "The car caught fire after it turned over several times, there's tire skid marks on the road so he probably woke up just as he reached the curve and tried to brake the car, but he was going too fast".

Erik walked around behind the car, and he noticed something peculiar, he called the sergeant over and asked him if the car had drove headlong down the mountain, and had it flipped end over end or had it rolled over and over on its side?

The Sergeant said, the car appeared to have went headfirst down the mountain, and as it dragged across the rocks it ruptured the fuel tank, and the last hundred feet or so it rolled over and over till it reached the bottom, then it burst into flames; there must have been nearly a full tank of fuel for it to burn as much as it did.

"Thanks" Erik said, and the sergeant walked away, but Erik was still wondering how the rear bumper got so severely bent, and where did the green paint come from that was on the bumper? It looked like something green had scraped the bumper of the car.

Erik and his father claimed the body and arranged for the funeral, Sid's girlfriend came down from Minsk with Sid's mother, and except for Erik, and Gen. Ivan Roskov, and a few friends of Sid's from the old KGB no one else attended the funeral.

Erik returned to his office after the funeral in the afternoon, to catch up on some paperwork, he was about to leave when Otto called, "Erik? I found something that may be of interest to your investigation, can you come over to the safe house this evening? Greta will prepare us a nice dinner and then we can talk", "okay what time would you like me to be there"? "We will have dinner about seven"; "okay I'll be there a little before seven".

After eating a well-prepared dinner, Otto and Erik retired to the living room, while Greta cleared the table in the dining room and Precious ate all the left overs. "What have you found Otto", Erik said, "well I'm not sure if it is important to your investigation or not but I thought it was interesting enough to tell you". "I was looking through some procurement files from the agency like you asked me to do, and I came across a rather interesting procurement document, look at this, they are purchasing enough dry food and bottled water to supply at least ten or fifteen people for a year or more". "The reason it seems strange to me is, I have been reviewing their procurement documents for food and water for the space station for over two years now and they have never purchased more than two or three months supply of food and water for two cosmonauts that will remain on the space station for their two or three month tour". "They are now stockpiling large quantities of supplies on the station and I'm wondering why".

Erik told Otto and Greta that he suspected Sid was murdered. And that it had something to do with his involvement in Project wormwood.

Erik then revealed to Otto and Greta that he was working undercover for The British Intelligence Agency, and his assignment was to find out what Project Wormwood was, and if it was of national security interest, and if so, who was behind it and how was the International Space station involved. And then he told Greta that her husband Thomas, was also working with the MI6 agency, and he is the person who made the first report to the agency, concerning The Project. Shortly after that he dropped out of sight, we have reason to suspect that his cover was discovered and reported to the Colonel, who probably had him killed. "I'm very sorry Greta", Erik said, "Otto, it is hard for me to accept, but somehow my own father is involved in this covert project he does not know I work for the British intelligence but I'm going to find out what his involvement in the project is, and if it is as sinister and covert as Colonel Chechnikov's seems to be, I will have to arrest him along with all the others when we finally expose this mysterious project.

Otto and Greta could hardly believe what Erik had just told them about Thomas and himself, but they both knew it must be true for Erik to expose himself as he did to them.

CHAPTER 25

D AN DROVE BACK TO the hospital to see if he could get an interview with the two cosmonauts in the isolation ward, by saying it would be a good human interest story. But when he arrived at the hospital there were military guards armed with automatic weapons at every door blocking his entrance.

He returned to the TV studio, to tell Bill what he had seen. Bill was still working on the truck story when Dan came into his office, after Dan told Bill what happened, Bill said, "Dan we need some more background on this story before I can run it". "I would like you to go back to the warehouse, where I shot the film, and see if you can get more footage for the show. "If you can get inside the warehouse that would be great, but Dan, don't put yourself in any unnecessary danger". After Bill drew Dan a map and gave him additional instructions Dan left the studio.

Otto and Greta had very recently become a couple in a serious relationship they were living together at the safe house, they were both relieved and saddened when Erik broke the news to them, that Thomas, Greta's husband was most likely dead.

Otto was still reviewing all the documents that came through his office concerning the International Space Station Agency, and reporting his findings to Erik, he was looking for any unusual procurements made by the agency.

It was December now and the agency was preparing to send two more cosmonauts to the space station. The two cosmonauts they were sending had never been on the space station, but they were the only ones that were ready, and they needed to relieve the two cosmonauts that were there now. These two had been there now five months; they were scheduled to be relieved by the two cosmonauts which had to be taken off the space station after the accident with the radioactive canister.

The two new cosmonauts were briefed about their duties and were told that all they learned in their briefing and about the cargo they were delivering to the space station was classified and Top-Secret. They were told they had three days to prepare for launch, and during this time they were instructed by Col. Chechnikov not to leave the agency's grounds and to talk to no one in the news media.

During the three days of waiting the cosmonauts watched the loading of the cargo, they saw tons of food and water being loaded onto the cargo carrier for the trip to the space station they also saw several large canisters stamped with the radioactive material sign, they were being loaded as cargo along with several crates of computerized equipment, and a dozen or so automatic rifles, and several cases of ammunition.

The day before they were scheduled for launch the two cosmonauts grew anxious of their mission and a little bit frightened by what they had seen, as cargo. They decided to slip into an office at the agency unaware to anyone, and gain access to a computer terminal.

They searched for an e-mail address for the military intelligence, when they found an address they sent this message "something strange going on at Space Station Agency, we are scheduled to depart for space station at six a.m, cargo we are delivering is classified, radioactive material, automatic weapons, tons of food and water and crates of computerized equipment". "Please investigates; do not reveal this information to Col. Chechnikov, as it would place our lives in danger."

The next day after the cosmonauts were launched, and on their way to the International Space Station, with the cargo, Erik was in his office checking his e-mail files, when he saw the message sent by the cosmonauts. He immediately called his friend Otto, and asked if it would be okay for him to stop by at the safe house to review all the information they had learned about Project Wormwood and Col. Chechnikov. Otto said they would be expecting him for dinner about seven p.m.

Otto and Greta were discussing all they had learned about the Project, and Col. Chechnikov, while they were preparing dinner for their guest.

Erik arrived at about 6:30. While Greta continued preparing dinner, Otto and Erik began exchanging information, on what each of them had learned. Erik was just about to tell Otto about the e-mail message he received from the cosmonauts, when Greta called them to the table for dinner.

By this time Greta had come to trust Erik, and they were able to speak openly about the project. After dinner Greta went with Otto and Erik to the living room to talk, she decided she could clear the table and wash the dishes after Erik left. Erik told them about the e-mail message, and said it is too late to stop the launch. "I am opening a full investigation, so we will keep what we know under wraps, until my father returns from his trip abroad", "That will be in about a week". "I will confront him and see how he is involved in the project and what he knows".

CHAPTER 26

IT HAD BEEN TWO days since the cosmonauts were launched to the Space station when an aide of Col. Chechnikov came hurriedly into the Col's office at the agency, and gave him this news. "One of the two cosmonauts has been found tied and gagged, and locked inside a maintenance closet in one of the offices at the agency". The Col. was furious, "how could this happen, and who did we send to the space station"? "The station is not scheduled to contact the control center until Saturday of this week, which will be three days from today, and we can't contact them before then".

Erik was in his office early; Wednesday morning, his father was scheduled to be back in his office next Monday and Erik wanted to put together all the files and the discs he got from Greta, and the disk he got from Otto, he wanted to make sure he had all the information he needed, including the information Bill had given him, and his suspicion that Sid had been murdered, when he questioned his father.

While Erik was assembling all this information he noticed the icon on his computer flashing, indicating he had mail, he clicked the mouse to open his e-mail and discovered a new message that was very troubling, the message read, "Erik, I am on my way to the space station, I took the place of one of the cosmonauts, I must try and stop this madman's plan to take control of, and use the International Space Station to promote his personal agenda, and perhaps become a danger to the entire world". "I have reason to believe they are assembling one or more nuclear devices on the space station, please contact Mr. O'Donnell". Signed agent Thomas Burkov.

If the message had not mentioned Mr. O'Donnell, Erik would not have believed the message was from Thomas Burkov, but he knew no one else had knowledge of O'Donnell but he and Thomas Burkov.

CHAPTER 27

D AN HAD GONE TO the warehouse as instructed by Bill but when he arrived he discovered an empty metal building with no security fence and no guards, he took some footage and returned to the studio to tell Bill what he had found.

Bill told Dan, they would open the show in the morning and run a teaser trailer concerning the exposé we will be running tomorrow morning. "We will run just enough footage to tease our audience, and run the photo of the mysterious Col., but obscure his face". "We will tell our audience to be sure and watch the show tomorrow, to learn the Col's identification and the exposé of the century". Bill left the studio about eight p.m. The following day; Bill ran the trailer Dan had put together, and informed his morning show audience, that tomorrow's show would be a feature exposé.

Upon leaving the studio Bill found lying on the roof of his car in the parking garage, a package addressed to him. He picked up the package and got into his car, he opened the package very carefully not knowing what he might find. There was a file folder in the package, and inside the folder were some photographs. Bill began looking through the photographs, and he was astonished. The first photograph in the folder was the back yard of his home in the mountains. He had a large backyard where he kept two large Doberman pincer dogs for security, his entire backyard was fenced in, and the fence line ran about 250 feet long extending from the back of his house to the edge of a sheer cliff that dropped about 1000 feet below.

Bill knew in order to take this photograph the photographer had to be inside the fence in the backyard, with the camera pointing toward the back of his house, but how could that be? The next picture Bill Saw was his sixteen year old daughter, Jenny, getting out of the Jacuzzi on their back porch, she was wearing nothing but a small bikini bathing suit. Bill's anger began to rise when he saw a photograph of Jenny, while she was undressing; it was taken through her bedroom window.

By this time Bill was shaking so hard with anger he could barely hold the photographs, there were other photographs of his daughter completely naked, and others of her and her mother leaving the driveway in their car, and others of his daughter at the school she attended.

Then Bill found a message, written on a piece of paper underneath the photographs. The message said, "if you run the exposé story, or reveal the Col's identity; you will be putting your family in grave jeopardy". "Cancel the story and destroy all the documents and camera footage as well as still photos you have, and forget any of this ever existed.

Bill was so shaken he could hardly drive his car home, how did they get past the dogs? Bill thought, and then he remembered *about a week ago his wife had called him at the studio and told him that something was wrong with the dogs, they were acting lethargic, and she wanted to know if she should call the veterinarian, and take them in for a checkup. Bill instructed his wife to call the veterinarian, and see what his instructions were. The veterinarian said, "there's no need to bring them in today, it may be just something that they ate, perhaps a toad they found in the yard, wait until tomorrow morning and if there's no change in them, then bring them in, and we'll give them a full checkup".

It was something they ate, Bill thought, someone must have baited them with some kind of tranquilizer in some meat, because they were okay the next morning, and never had to go to the vet.*

On the drive home Bill was raging inside, and he became very frightened for his wife and their daughter, *those rotten thugs, to stoop low enough to take pictures of my sixteen year old daughter undressing and completely naked, to what extremes will they go to keep this story from being exposed. Do I dare tell my wife? Bill thought, no it would worry her to death, I will cancel the story and take my wife and daughter on holiday out of Russia until I can think this through, and no story is worth the safety of my family.* He then called Dan on his cell phone. Dan I decided not to run the story, I just don't have enough factual evidence to make it a real exposé so put together another piece for tomorrows show, and I'll explain it somehow to our audience. Okay Bill, Dan said, you're the boss.

CHAPTER 28

IT WAS SATURDAY MORNING; Colonel Chechnikov was at the mission control center, with a few hand-picked operators, when the message came in from the space station. "Mission control emergency, go to encrypted code scramble mode, this message is for Colonel Chechnikov only". The Colonel looked at the operator and waved his hand, and said "leave it, I'll decide who should hear the message. The caller said, "We have a situation at the station that you should know about". "When the cargo transporter docked at the station, and the cosmonauts were unloading the cargo, one of the cosmonauts accidentally opened a hatch to the outside and was swept out into space without a tether line". "Colonel he is gone and we have no way of retrieving him".

"This is Colonel Chechnikov, code clearance CXLB". "Code number verified" said the space station caller, "go-ahead Colonel, we are in scramble mode here". "Give me the identification number of the cosmonaut that remains on the station". "Just a moment Colonel, I'll get it for you, 0811269" said the caller. The Col. looked at the identification number of the cosmonaut that was found tied and gagged at the agency, 0811268, good, thought the Colonel, *the problem has solved itself*. "There's nothing we can do about it now the Colonel said to the caller from the space station, I will notify the man's family and take care of all the arrangements here". "I will want a full report in twenty four hours".

CHAPTER 29

ERIK SENT A MESSAGE on a back channel to Mr. O'Donnell to tell him about the contact that he had from Thomas. He received a message confirming that O'Donnell knew Thomas was attempting to get on the inside of the space station, Thomas had made contact with the department five days ago O'Donnell said.

Erik arrived unannounced at the safe house the following day, and told Otto and Greta about the contact that Thomas had made with him, and that he was trying to find a way to get onto the space station. Otto and Greta turned ashen white, when they heard that Thomas was alive, they were speechless, they told Erik they did not know what they were going to do now, but they thanked him for telling them, and Erik left the safe house.

Erik was driving back to his place and thinking about all that had taken place over the last two and a half months, and how he was going to interrogate his beloved father Monday morning. What if he has to place him under arrest he thought, what would his beloved mother have thought of him?

Greta and Otto talked through the night, they both were very much in love with each other, and they both agreed that no matter what happens now even if Thomas reappears they were determined to stay together.

Monday morning Erik arrived at his office early, he wanted to make sure he had everything he needed before he talked to his father, who'd be back in his office around ten a.m., he watched from his outer office, chatting with his Secretary who came in at eight, until he saw his father enter his office across the hall at about 9:30. Erik gave his father time to settle in and get a cup of coffee, and go through his mail before he went to see him.

"Good morning son, sit down and let me tell you about my trip", General Roskov said to his son. Erik interrupted his father, and said, "Father we have some very important things to discuss, why don't you tell your Secretary to hold all your calls so we're not interrupted". "We won't be interrupted son; my Secretary won't be in the office today". "Now what is so important you couldn't tell me on the phone last night when we talked". Erik said, "I don't know where to begin, so let's begin with you telling me how you are involved with Col. Chechnikov and the project wormwood"? The general's face flushed with embarrassment, and he said, "How did you learn about Project Wormwood, that has nothing to do with the military intelligence, and why are you asking"? "Father I need to know because of information I have received".

"Well son, it is not such a secret project that you can't know, it began about eight and a half years ago, Col. Chechnikov, and your uncle Jerrod came to see me, and asked me to take part in a humanitarian project named wormwood, (I don't know why it's called that)". "Because of my high profile position in the military they thought I could be an effective spokesperson for the project". "It was to raise the awareness throughout the world, of the dangers in proliferation of nuclear weapons to other nations, world hunger, and redistribution of wealth and resources of the few wealthy nations to the third world nations, forgiving the debt of third world nations, to allow them to grow economically, and most seriously, to begin a serious nuclear disarmament of missile warheads, of the United States and Russia". "Also to raise the awareness of the injustice being suffered for so many years by the Palestinian people's in the Middle East".

"I and your uncle Jerrod have been speaking at rallies and conventions all over the world for eight years, other members of the project have been arranging peaceful demonstrations in large cities of key countries of the world. I just recently returned from America where I was invited to address the UN Security Council". "Colonel Chechnikov and Jerrod are the coordinators of the project, and I am the only military official from our government that is involved". That is all there is to the project son, now why don't you tell me what you have heard", said General Roskov.

Erik began, and told his father all the information and the suspicions he had, but he did not reveal his position with the British intelligence agency. He told him about the warehouse, the overturned truck the radioactive material, the suspicions he had about Sid's death, the missiles that struck Otto's cabin, at this point his father interrupted him with a trembling voice, and said "I don't know how that happened, that renegade Chechnikov,almost had you killed, I have reprimanded him for that and I can assure you nothing like that will ever happen again, the information you have given me helps make my decision easy, I'm going to pull the plug and shut down the project the Col.has gotten out of control". "I will call Jerrod, and tell him of my decision, I know he will remind me that he is my dear departed wife's brother, but it will not do any good, I intend to shut down the project and remove the Col. from the Department of the International Space Station agency, and reassign him to a field position outside of Moscow".

Erik was so relieved to discover that his father and his uncle Jerrod was not involved in any criminal activity, but now he had to consider how his uncle Jerrod was involved in the project. Erik left his father's office with a great deal to think about, instead of returning to his own office he drove to the television studio to talk to Bill, but Bill had not come to the studio today and no one at the studio had heard from him.

"Good morning! and welcome to the Bill Forney show" the announcer said, "Bill has taken a short leave of absence due to a family emergency, so for the next few weeks we will be running some of the best of Bill's morning show's, so just sit back and relax and watch some of the shows you may have missed the first time they aired".

Dan had hoped they could keep their viewing audience by rebroadcasting some of Bill's earlier shows, while he began searching for Bill or at least hear from him.

CHAPTER 30

A LL PASSENGERS BOARDING INTERNATIONAL flight number 586 to Holland, Rome, and final destination to England, please begin boarding your plane now at gate 201B in international concourse B, the announcer said.

"Bill you haven't told me why you decided to take a vacation trip abroad, with absolutely no notice whatsoever" Bill's wife said as they boarded the plane bound to England. "We had to take Jenny out of school, and she will have a lot of work to make up when we return home, and you haven't even told us how long we will be gone". "You just said pack enough clothes for two weeks". "When we get on the plane you're going to have to give me a full explanation". "I will" Bill said, "just as soon as we're on our way to England".

The big Airbus jet began to move back from the gate, and Bill was nervously looking out the window, when he turned to his wife sitting next to him and said, "honey, I didn't want to tell you, that you and Jenny's lives are in danger, until we were on our way to England".

Bill then told his wife about the pictures of Jenny and her, and about the threats he had received. Bill's wife and his daughter Jenny were completely stunned by what they heard, and then Jenny began crying as she was looking at the pictures. "What are we going to do" Bill's wife asked, "can't you go to the authorities and have these people arrested and put in jail"? "No"! Bill said, "that's just it, I don't know for sure who they are, and if they, are the authorities". "That's why I just had to get you and Jenny out of Russia, until I can determine who these people are and under whose authority their operating". 'When we arrive in England we can stay at my parent's house in the country, they hardly ever use it anymore since they have gotten older, and the kids have all left". "I called ahead, so the caretaker will have everything opened and ready for our arrival". "After we get settled in, I will call the studio, and tell Dan I'll be gone about two weeks, and then we'll have to sit down and decide what were going to do".

CHAPTER 31

Erik was in his office when he received a call from the police, "Erik Roskov"? The caller said, "Yes this is Erik Roskov, who's speaking"? This is the police, you'd better come over to your father's house as soon as you can get here". "Your father has been shot.

Erik hung up the phone immediately and raced over to his father's house, which was a two-hour drive from their office. When he arrived there were three police cars and an ambulance in the drive, Erik wondered why the ambulance was still here, it had been two hours since he got the call, telling him his father had been shot. Erik rushed into the house past a policeman at the front door, and was met by a Sergeant Tanner, who told him, he was the person who called, and they were awaiting his arrival before removing his father's body. Erik knew then, his father was dead.

"It looks like your father took his own life, he died of a single gunshot to the head, the bullet went through the temple area, Sgt. Tanner explained". "Erik! was he having any personal problems that you are aware of, that would cause him to take his own life", the sergeant asked? "No, not that I know of" Erik said, "he just returned from a trip abroad and he seemed in high spirits when he and I were in his office a couple of days ago".

The body was lying on a gurney covered with a sheet; Erik pulled the sheet back from his father's face and just stared in disbelief, "where was he found?" Erik asked the sergeant, "sitting at his desk; his neighbor heard a gunshot about noon and came over to see if everything was all right, when he rang the doorbell and no one answered he came in, (the door was unlocked), and found your father slumped over his desk". "When he saw what had happened, he called the police, we arrived here at about 12:45, and I called you, at one o'clock".

"There was one, thing Erik", the sergeant said, "your father scribbled something on a piece of paper he had on his desk, before he died". "What was it" Erik said? The sergeant called to one of his officers, "Carl bring that piece of paper that was on the general's desk". The officer handed the piece of paper to the sergeant, who handed it to Erik. Erik looked at the paper and there was three words scribbled on it, Revelation Wormwood Chech_____ _____", "any idea what it means Erik"? said the sergeant. "No! I don't have any idea, but I want a complete and thorough investigation of the scene". 'We will give you our complete report when we're finished" the sergeant said.

Erik had so much to think about; he wondered if his meeting and questioning of his father about the wormwood project could have had anything to do with his father taking his life.

Erik returned to his office, and called Otto to tell him the sad news. "Otto"! Erik said, "I just came from my father's house, and he has been shot, the police believe he took his own life". "Do you think it was self-inflicted Erik"? "I don't know Otto do you think he could have been murdered, and set up to look like a suicide"? "I don't know Erik, but I don't think your father was the kind of man to take his own life". "You're right Otto", Erik said, "Father had no reason to take his life, I am going to conduct my own investigation, and if it leads anywhere near the wormwood project and the Col., I'm going to shut down the whole thing, and arrest all the ranking tier members, starting with the Colonel".

Erik called his uncle Jerrod, and gave him the tragic news. Jerrod said he would fly to Russia at once.

Erik met his uncle at the airport the following day, and on the way to Erik's apartment in the city, Erik told Jerrod about the meeting he had with his father, and asked him about the Colonel, and Project Wormwood. Jerrod confirmed what the general had told Erik about their involvement with the project.

Later that night Erik told his uncle that he was working for MI6. His uncle was not surprised; he told Erik it was his idea to recruit him at Oxford. When the agency received the message from the field agent in Russia, about Project Wormwood, and the possibility it could jeopardize England's national security, they called on Jerrod, who was retired from the agency, to help recruit someone who could get inside, and see if Project Wormwood was a rogue operation, or a legitimate protest organization, as he and Ivan Roskov had been led to believe when they were recruited to be the international spokesmen for the project. Who better than the son of one of the most influential families in Russia to investigate and covertly oversee the project?

While Erik and his uncle were discussing Project wormwood, the sergeant from the investigation of his father's death called to ask Erik if he could stop in at his office sometime tomorrow, he had turned up something interesting that he would like to talk to Erik about.

Erik arrived at the police station with his uncle the following morning about 10:00, and they were shown into the office of Sergeant Tanner who was on the phone, he motioned with his hand for them to be seated. When he hung up the phone the sergeant stood up, walked around his desk and said, "Erik I'm glad you came early", and reaching out his hand to Erik, the sergeant said, "and who is this"? "This is my uncle from England, he is my father's brother-in-law, I called him as soon as I was told about my father. He and my father were very close". "I'm pleased meet you", the sergeant politely said, "I had rather it been under more pleasant circumstances". "Erik, this is what I wanted to tell you about", the sergeant was holding a file folder in his hand; "this is the report of what we uncovered at the scene, and at our police lab". "Erik we uncovered some interesting and troubling evidence during our investigation, we did a routine residual gunpowder test on your father's hand, to determine if your father fired a weapon, it is a test we always do when someone fires a weapon that opens an investigation". "We discovered to our surprise there was no residual gunpowder, not even in trace amounts on your fathers hand, and by that, there is only one conclusion, your father did not fire the weapon he was holding in his hand".

"Another interesting piece of evidence turned up in our investigation, when an autopsy was performed, a bullet was retrieved from your father's brain, if the weapon had been held against his head when the trigger was pulled, due to the caliber of the weapon, it would have sent the bullet completely through your father's head and into the wall". "We also discovered, when we ran a ballistics test on the bullet, the bullet that killed your father was not fired from the weapon he was holding, and furthermore it had to have been fired from at least six feet away from his head". "Since the bullet that we found was the same caliber as your father's weapon, I did a little investigating and found that the type, and caliber of weapon your father was holding, was only issued to Soviet military officers, and were very unique". "The end of the barrel was machine threaded so a silencer could be screwed onto it, and before each weapon was issued to an officer it was discharged, and the rifling marks of the bullet of each individual weapon, was kept in the file, of the officer to whom it was issued".

"When you came into the office I was on the phone with control files and they confirmed that, a first Lieutenant Ivan Roskov was issued one of these weapons, but by crosschecking the bullet that killed your father with all other weapons issued to officers, they found that this bullet was fired from a weapon issued to a Lieutenant Boris Chechnikov, my men went to the space station agency to arrest him but he was not at his office, we have an all points bulletin out for him". "I wanted you to know your father's death was not suicide but homicide".

"There is one thing that still troubles me" the sergeant said, "the neighbor said he only heard one shot, but your father's gun was tested and it had been fired, we are looking over the crime scene now, to see if we can find the other bullet". "I'll let you know if we turn up anything, and I will let you know as soon as we have Chechnikov in custody, the records show he is now a full bird Colonel, but we will get him".

Erik and Jerrod were still grieving over the general's death, but they were relieved to know that it was not suicide. That night Erik got a call from Sergeant Tanner, who said "Erik, we found the other bullet that was fired from your father's weapon, it was in the floor under his desk, whoever shot him fired his weapon into the floor, and covered it over with a small rug, we now believe the reason the neighbor only heard one shot fired, is because the gun that killed the general, was fitted with a silencer". "The shot heard, was the general's gun being fired into the floor to appear as though it was the weapon that killed the general". "Thank you Sergeant", Erik said, "and let me know as soon as you have the Colonel in custody".

Erik sent intelligence agents to round up all the members of the project and bring them in for questioning; he also placed two undercover agents at the International space station agency, to arrest the Colonel if he showed up there.

Erik learned upon questioning all the project members that they believed they were working for a project that was sanctioned by the Russian government, to peacefully bring about world peace.

Since General Ivan Roskov a well respected military officer and Col. Chechnikov, the military officer overseeing the International space station agency, were in the top leadership positions.

After Erik laid his dear father to rest, with a full and elaborate State funeral, Jerrod left Russia and returned home to England. The military had taken over the operations of the International space station agency and the Colonel was in hiding. Otto and Greta believed it was safe enough for them to move out of the safe house, and move into Otto's new cabin, which he had just finished rebuilding, with the compensation that he received from the military.

They had a civil wedding performed, believing Thomas was either dead, or had left Russia and gone underground.

CHAPTER 32

IT WAS NEAR THE end of December, the weather in Florida at Cape Canaveral was mild, and all the leading reporters from the leading television and newspaper and radio were there, to report the first mission of the space shuttle in two years, it had been over two years since the space shuttle Challenger had disintegrated upon re-entry into the atmosphere, and all the American astronauts were killed. The shuttle program was put on hold by NASA until a full investigation could determine the cause of the destruction of Challenger, and a consequent redesign of the shuttle.

The International space station, for the past two years had been under the control of the Russians space station agency, and inhabited by Russian cosmonauts and scientists, and completely without any oversight by the American government or NASA.

"Mission control", the flight engineer said, "all systems are go we are ready for liftoff, mark 10 9 8 7 6 5 4 3 2 1, we have ignition, the shuttle is on its way to the International space Station", all the reporters present, shielded their eyes from the sun as they pointed their cameras skyward, and watched the new redesigned space shuttle soar heavenward for the first time in over two years. America was back in the space-age which it had dominated for so many years.

"Mission control this is the commander of the space shuttle" the voice said, we have arrived at the International space Station on schedule and we are maneuvering into our docking position, will advise when docking is complete". At mission control applause broke out and there were smiles and congratulations all around.

Day five the shuttle is scheduled to leave the space station and return to earth. "Mission control we have a problem", the voice of the commander said to the flight engineer at the controls, "something is not working on the docking mechanism, we are unable to separate the shuttle from the dock at the space station, we have tried a number of maneuvers with no success please advise, standing by".

All of a sudden there was a massive hustle inside the command center, all the monitors were buzzing with information, after two full days and nights of trying to solve the problem the flight engineer radioed to the shuttle Commander, "We have instructed you to try every procedure that the computers developed and nothing has succeeded, in the undocking of the shuttle from the space station, therefore we are preparing another shuttle mission, and sending a crew of mechanics and engineers to assist you". "The shuttle launch will take place in seventy two hours, weather permitting". "If our crew of mechanics and engineers are unable to dislodge your shuttle from the space station in forty eight hours after arrival, all astronauts, engineers and American personnel on the space shuttle are to board the second shuttle and return to earth".

"The State Department and the President has been notified, and briefed of the situation". "Awaiting arrival of second shuttle" the shuttle commander said, "acknowledge your instructions".

It had been twelve hours since the second shuttle was launched, without any media present, NASA did not want the public to know the situation at the space station, everyone in Washington was preparing for Christmas which was less than a week away all the officials in government would be leaving Washington in a couple days and would not return until after the new year.

A clerk delivered the mail to the Secretary of State's office about eleven a.m., the aide at the reception's desk said, "the mail for Madame Secretary is to go to the Undersecretary of state's office for review, until she returns in January".

The clerk then took the mail, and went down the hall to the Undersecretary's office and delivered it to the aide sitting at the desk, there was a manila envelope addressed to the Secretary of State United States of America and marked personal, with bold underlined letters, and under that it was marked urgent, she immediately delivered the envelope to the Undersecretary, and returned to her desk.

The Secretary of State was arriving at the parking garage at Dulles international Airport when her cell phone rang, *only two people on earth no this number*" she thought, *the President and the Undersecretary*" " Hello! Mr. President and Merry Christmas to you and your family". "This is not the President Madame Secretary its me, I just received a message addressed to you marked urgent so I opened it and read it as you instructed me to do, Madam Secretary I think you need to cancel your flight and return to the capital. I believe you'll want to conference with the President". "If it is that urgent my Christmas plans can be changed, I will return to the Capitol at once, I should be there in about two and a half hours, meet me in my office and have the message with you".

The Under-secretary was sitting in the Secretary of State's office, when she arrived from the airport, he waited until she removed her coat, and hung it up, and sat down behind her desk, before he handed her the document, that was sent in a manila envelope, with no return address, but the postmark indicated it originated in the country of Syria.

The Secretary of State perused the document looking up at her undersecretary ever so often, and then she said "do we know anything about this Colonel Chechnikov"? "I have been making inquiries since I talked to you Madame Secretary, and I have learned through department channels that he is a Colonel in the former Soviet Union army, and that he is presently assigned to oversee the Russian space station Agency". "I've also made inquiries to the CIA but nothing has come back yet".

"Do you think it is real or some kind of terrible hoax"? the Secretary said to her subordinate. "I don't know what to think Madame Secretary, no one outside of this government, and only a few high-level Russian government officials know about the trouble at the space station with our shuttle, and our second shuttle we launched to rescue it".

"Have you contacted the president"? "No! I want to let you make that decision". "He has probably left the Oval Office for the holidays, I will call him at his ranch tonight", the Secretary said. "I want you to find out everything you can, and I will contact President Polcherko of Russia, and see what he knows, you get over to the CIA's office and instruct them to inquire through all of their back channels, to all of their field operators and see how much, if anything we can learn, before I talk to the President tonight".

Don't let anyone over there hinder you from collecting data, let them know this is a national emergency.

The response by the director of the CIA was quick and thorough, all foreign agencies were contacted through back channel resources, and all CIA foreign operations were contacted, and instructed to inquire of all their field agents, to find out anything they could or anything they had heard about Colonel Chechnikov, or the Wormwood Project.

The information started coming in about 1:00 p.m. that afternoon. There had been an interest in Colonel Chechnikov for about eight and a half years, but the chatter on the Internet was, that he was leading a group of environmental protesters, to demonstrate against a whole array of environmental issues, throughout the world. No one has been able to trace his source of income, and he has been keeping close company with a General in the Russian military as well as a wide range of eco-scientists worldwide.

In the late afternoon more information started coming in from many sources, we have learned that his father was not a Russian at all but rather he was a German. It seems that his father lived in the city of the Roel in Palestine in 1948, where he had a very successful tailoring and textile business. Prior to 1948 his father and mother lived in Germany and his father ran a large successful tailoring business. One of his largest customers was the German military during the years of the Nazi rule under the dictatorship of Adolph Hitler. His father's company had the contract to tailor all the German army officer's uniforms. When the war was over and the armies of Hitler were defeated and the allied forces poured into Berlin, his father was fearful that he would be arrested by the Russian armed forces and charged as a collaborator to the enemy. He left his tailoring business and fled, Germany as many other businessmen did, to the Middle East and settled in Palestine. There he changed his name from Chechnikoff a German name to Chechnikov a Russian name.

His father then built a successful tailoring and textile business in Palestine. Only to be driven out in 1948 as a non documented foreigner when the land of Palestine was divided and given by a decree of the United Nations and the world governments to the Jewish race as a homeland. He took his wife and his infant son Boris and fled to the former Soviet Union. He was never again able to build a successful business to provide for his family. For that he had a deep hatred for the Jews.

When Boris Chechnikov was eight years old his father placed him in a state run military school in the Soviet Union, it was there that he trained to become a soldier. Boris left the military school at the age of eighteen, and both his father and mother died before he was twenty years old. Because of what had happened to his family in Palestine in 1948 he hated the Jews with a passion. When he was twenty years old, attending a Soviet University he became very interested and involved in the eco-sciences, so much so that he left the university and joined an ecology group called Green planet.

We know that the Green planet ecology group is a radical environmental movement with an agenda to return the western nations from large industrial, environmental pollution producing nations, back into nations of agriculture as they were a hundred years ago.

They staged violent demonstrations all over the world and have in recent years linked with other environmental groups to form a formidable movement.

Boris Chechnikov was introduced a few years ago to a Professor Jerrod Stevens from England, who is an outspoken professor on the ecology of the planet and its eco-systems. After they're at introduction Boris became the radical spokesperson for Professor Jerrod's radical agenda.

It was a few years prior to the Kyoto conference on world ecology that Professor Jerrod and Boris Chechnikov began recruiting from around the world prominent eco-scientists who were of the same ilk that they were.

Boris has been traveling throughout the world to promote these radical agendas. He and Professor Jerrod recruited a three star general from the Soviet military to be a spokesman for the movement, and this general is the Brother-in-law of Professor Jerrod.

The CIA has been monitoring their movements for about eight years, Chechnikov returned to the Soviet military a few years ago and has since then rose in rank to a Colonel, He seems to have drifted away from the forefront of the movement when he was appointed by the Soviet military government to oversee the International Space station Agency in Moscow. He has recently been seen at a few of the high profile ecology conferences, and he also attended the Kyoto conference.

That's all the information that we have on Boris Chechnikov but presently His primary position inside Russia has been the military overseer of the Russian space station. The International Space station is jointly funded by the United States and Russia, and manned by the United States astronauts and Russian cosmonauts. Two and a half years ago NASA put the shuttle program on hold after the Challenger disaster.

"Mr. President", the Secretary of State said, "I hesitate to bring you this devastating news and especially to bring it to you on your holiday with your family, but something that will require your urgent attention has come up". "I believe that we need you back in Washington now". "Can we discuss it on the phone or through coded channels"?, "No Mr. President it has to be in person, and you will want some of your cabinet members and especially the Joint Chiefs of Staff back in Washington as well".

"I will be in the office at 8:00 a.m., contact the members of my Cabinet that you believe is appropriate and I will contact the Joint Chiefs and have everyone in my office, in Washington at 8:00 a.m.". "Consider it done Mr. President, and again I am so sorry".

When the president arrived at 7:30 a.m. the Secretary of State, Undersecretary, Director of CIA and several members of the White House security staff were already there waiting. The members of the Joint Chiefs of Staff arrived at about 8:00 a.m...

There were copies of the documents received the previous day at State, on the table before each person present. Realizing that the President had not yet seen the document the Secretary of State said, "Sir would you like me to begin the briefing"? "Go ahead, I'm listening". "Gentlemen", the Secretary of State said, "you have been called back to Washington, because of the documents in the file folders in front of each of you, first let me say I and the President are extremely sorry to have had to interrupt your holidays with your families".

"There are a few things you need to know before you read the document, first we do not know who sent it, and second we have not yet been able to determine if it is a hoax, third, when you read it be aware it is highly classified, and that is the reason you see no aides or stenographer's in this meeting". "All the briefing is being video taped, and is classified as Top-Secret".

"Now each of you may read the document", (a short pause) then the Secretary of State said, "this document was delivered by first-class mail to my office just before noon yesterday, it was in a plain manila envelope with no return address". "The postal markings on the envelope seemed to indicate that it was sent from someone in Syria". "Since receiving it, we have learned very little about the author". "As you can see we have only forty eight hours to carry out the instructions it contains". "Before I read the document aloud, let me remind you that not more than six of us in this room had previous knowledge of the rescue shuttle that was sent to the International Space Station".

"Most of you are learning about it from this document, each of you will remain in the loop to receive all intelligence information we receive until this is resolved". "No Members of Congress have yet been notified the President and I will do that at the appropriate time".

"Now if I can have your undivided attention, I will read the document aloud, and then I will ask for any comments you may have, beginning with you Mr. President".

"To the honorable Madame Secretary of State, of the United States of America, greetings from an avid admirer, Colonel Boris Chechnikov, officer of the Soviet people, I will keep this message to your Government brief, but you must understand it is no less urgent and sincere". "I am certain by the time you receive this message you will know that both of your space shuttles are being held hostage at our space station, along with all American crew members". "To learn why and what it will cost to release them, you must assemble all the top leaders of every nation, represented on the UN Security Council, they must be assembled within the next forty eight hours in the chambers of the UN Security Council".

"In exactly sixty hours from the time you receive this message, I will speak to all of you on a closed satellite link, at that time I will reveal to you our concerns, and also our demands". "I am assuming you are meeting at the White House today, Saturday morning, if you are you have only forty eight hours to contact and assemble all the world leaders that we spoke of".

"To give them an incentive to participate, you can tell them that we have nuclear weapons, and they have been strategically placed and aimed at many of their nations". "I will meet with you at the UN Security Council chambers in exactly forty eight hours". Signed: "Colonel Boris Chechnikov, The People's Commander of a peaceful world".

No one spoke, there was complete silence in the room, then the President said, "Gentlemen we are considering this as gravely serious, there are to be no turf wars on gathering Information, you all must use every piece of intelligence and every piece of intelligence gathering machinery and technology that you have available". "All intelligence gathered will flow into the Secretary of State's office, and that office will become our war room". "We only have forty eight hours to find out everything we can, and to assemble all the world leaders". "Thank you".

One of the Joint Chiefs said, "do we have another shuttle that we can get ready for launch, and send a contingent of armed military to the station, and forcibly take possession of the International Space Station, and bring our people and our two shuttles home"?

"No! We do not", the Secretary of State said, "and if we did we would never be allowed to dock at the space station". One of the Cabinet members said, "when will the congressional leaders be notified and how long can this be kept from the public"?

The President stood at the end of the conference table and said, "The members of Congress or the news media will not have any knowledge of this situation, until after the meeting with the UN members of the Security Council, and world leaders". "Any leaks that come out of this room, will be considered a treasonable offense, and the person or persons that leak any information that they have learned in this meeting, or that they learned through intelligence gathering will be considered a traitor to the United States government, and will be prosecuted to the full extent of the law".

"If you need to use wiretaps, to gather intelligence within the next forty eight hours, the Attorney General will authorize them, what ever resources you need, will be made available to you with no red tape". "I will sign an executive order, to protect you, and to prevent any of you or your contacts from ever being prosecuted for illegal activities concerning this intelligence gathering mission". "And you will all be protected under the homeland security act, as a national security operation".

"Now this meeting is adjourned, we have only forty eight hours".

The President sat down in the Oval Office, and picked up the red phone on his desk, he had never used it before nor had he any reason to; since the cold war between the United States and Russia had long been over. The phone rang once, and the Russian President said, "what is the urgency Mr. President"? After the president briefed the Russian President he requested that he send his Department head of military intelligence to Washington immediately, and the President agreed.

CHAPTER 33

Erik was enjoying the Christmas season at the new cabin Otto had built, with Otto and Greta when his cell phone rang, "Erik", the caller said, "this is your President, I need to know where you are at this moment, so I can send a military helicopter to pick you up and take you to a special plane that is waiting to fly you to Washington D.C. in the United States". "I will brief you of your mission, when you are in flight to United States".

Erik said, "yes Sir of course Mr. President, I will be at a clearing, at the following coordinates". And then Erik gave the President the coordinates where he could be picked up by the helicopter.

"They will be there in thirty minutes I will talk to you when you're in flight to the United States, until then goodbye".

"What is it" Otto said, "I don't know, but it sounds mysterious and urgent, I won't have time to return to my office, or my apartment". "I am being sent to Washington in the United States, on a mission for the President". "Otto" Erik said, "I may ask you to send me some personal things from my apartment when I get to Washington, so here is the key and also my office key is on there as well, in case I need any of my files to be sent to me in Washington"

Erik left Otto and Greta and met the helicopter at the rendezvous place, and was flown to the awaiting plane, and was on his way to Washington in less than an hour. It was a long flight for Erik, and the first time he had ever been to the United States. The President briefed him of his mission, in flight as he said he would. Erik told the President, that he had arranged with Otto to send him all his files he would need in Washington. He would call Otto in flight and tell him what files he would need from his office; an Otto could send them to him in Washington.

The Russian military jet was cleared for landing at Dulles International Airport; upon landing Erik boarded an awaiting Presidential helicopter, which shuttled him to the White House. When the helicopter touched down at the White House, a man wearing a pair of khaki pants and dressed very casually met Erik with his hand outstretched, Erik assumed he was one of the American Presidents aides welcoming him to Washington. "Mr. Roskov I am President Brown, your President has briefed me on your arrival, follow me and we will get right to work".

The President and Erik walked into the Oval Office, and were greeted, by two members of the Joint Chiefs of Staff and the Secretary of State. "Thank you for coming on such short notice", the Secretary of State said, as she handed Erik a file folder marked Classified, and Top Secret. "We understand that you probably know more about the person who sent this message than anyone else".

Erik opened the folder and briefly perused the file, "yes I probably do said Erik, and he is a very dangerous man, and is capable of carrying out any threat he makes". "Where would you like me to start, I can't give you specific dates until my files arrive, but I can give you some important details about this man". "We want to know everything you know Erik, President Brown said, but we want that briefing done over at the State Department in our war room".

The whole entourage then moved from the Oval Office in the White House, over to the State Department to the war room. All the rest of the members that had attended the meeting were there awaiting Erik's arrival. The President said, "Erik I want you to tell us everything that you know about Colonel Chechnikov, and his role in the International Space Station". "Don't leave out the smallest detail; because it may be important, to learn what this is all about". "I will give you as much information as I can remember, or that I know" Erik said. As he sat down at the end of a large conference table in the war room at the State Department all eyes were fixed upon this curly red haired Russian, and they gave him their undivided attention.

For two hours Erik revealed everything he knew about the Colonel and project wormwood. Beginning with Greta, and then with Otto and all they had found out, including the warehouse in the mountains, the radioactive material being sent by the truck, and all the additional food and water supplies being loaded in the cargo hold to be sent to the Russian space station. He revealed all the details that he could remember, including the death of his good friend Sid's suspicious death, and the details they uncovered about his father' death , and the words that he scribbled on the pad before his death.

Then Erik looked at the President and said, "Mr. President, will I be given clearance to attend the meeting at the UN"? "You not only will have clearance Erik, but we are counting on your briefing to assist us in assembling all the world leaders to that meeting. The President stood at the head of the table and said, "what was that again Erik that your father scribbled on the pad, before he died"? Erik said it was just three words, "Revelation Wormwood Chech___ ___"; I have no idea what it meant or what he was trying to say.

The President then thought for a moment and said, "the only thing that comes to my mind, is a book in our Christian Bibles New Testament, it's called a book of Revelation, now maybe there is something in that book that is relative to what we are experiencing now". "We'll look at it more thoroughly later".

CHAPTER 34

THE FORTY EIGHT HOUR deadline was just minutes away, all the Security Council members were present and most of the world leaders that were contacted were present in the UN council chambers when the President and the Secretary of State and all their entourage entered the chamber. Everyone was buzzing, all the world leaders that had been drawn from their holidays with their families, and had come from all over the world to this special meeting because of its urgency, and the threat of a nuclear attack upon their nation.

All eyes were fixed upon three giant screens, waiting for them to come to life. It had not been easy to convince some of the world leaders that this was not just an American problem, but when the nuclear equation entered the discussion, along with Erik's briefing, they recognized it as a world problem. The clock ticked off the minutes 10, 9, 8, 7,6,5,4, 3, 2, 1, and suddenly the giant screens lit up and came to life. Colonel Chetchnikov stood at the dais, with a large world map in the background, and several other men were seated just outside of the camera's range.

"Gentlemen I am glad you could all come to this most important meeting, let me introduce myself, and one of my colleagues that will be addressing you today". "I am Colonel Chechnikov, officer of the Soviet Union and people's supreme commander of a peaceful world". Then one of the men sitting in the shadows stood up and came forward to the dais. "This is my dear friend and faithful colleague Professor Jerrod, from

England". Erik could hardly believe his eyes, this was his uncle Jerrod, whom he had trusted and loved, but he said nothing.

"What is going to be revealed here today gentlemen, the Colonel continued, is what my colleagues and I refer to, as Project Wormwood, we chose that name because of its similarity to the Christian Bible account in the book of Revelation, which is recorded in chapter eight of that book". "We have been developing this plan, to secure a peaceful co-existence with all nations of the world". "It has taken over ten years to develop this plan". "Now we finally have everything in place that we need, to fulfill our plan, which we refer to as Project Wormwood". "I will, step out of the way and yield the floor to my dear friend and colleague, who will outline in detail, the plan that will ultimately bring lasting peace to the whole world".

Professor Jerrod stepped up to the Dias, as the Colonel took a seat behind him. The tall well dressed man gazed into the camera and gave a formal and friendly greeting. Then with a laser pointer in his hand, he began to reveal the details of Project Wormwood.

The delegates and world leaders from nearly every nation, sat quietly and attentive, they knew they were about to hear, why they had been intimidated to attend this gathering.

Professor Jerrod began to speak, in a low monotone voice, as he pointed his laser pointer toward maps, which an aide turned at his command. "My colleagues and I have been extremely concerned over the past ten years at what we have seen in every nation on this planet". "We have seen heavily armed mobs, in many nations, sanctioned by their Governments, killing and raping their fellow citizens, while looting and burning their homes, only because they were of different ethnic heritage".

"More genocide has been sanctioned by Governments, in the past twenty years, than all the atrocities that were performed by the Nazis, in World War II". "We have also witnessed industrial holocaust carried out by a handful of western and European nations". "That is bringing rapid destruction to our planet". "These few nations are raping and destroying the entire eco-system of this planet, it began with the deletion of the ozone layer, which is the only protection this planet and its life forces have against the deadly ultra-violet rays, emanating from our sun". "The destruction of the ozone layer allows the ultraviolet rays from the sun to penetrate our earth and destroy its natural habitat". "This pollution and destruction of our planet's life giving eco-system's, by a few nations, at the expense of the remaining two thirds of the population of our planet, has brought about catastrophic conditions through out the world". "We have seen global warming, in the last twenty years, (which we tried to address at the Kyoto conference, with little success), that has caused ice burgs to break off in the Antarctica, as large as the state of Maryland, of the United States". "The pollution that these nations are pumping into the atmosphere, has caused climate changes in every region of the world, the acid rain which is produced by these industrialized giants has destroyed millions of acres of forestry all over the planet". "It has destroyed what was fertile agricultural land and turned it into desert".

"Whole countries have lost their agricultural livelihood, because their crops will no longer grow, due to radical climate changes, brought about by global warming". "This wanton destruction of our planet's ecosystem has escalated the past ten years, to a degree that we can no longer tolerate". "It is for this reason that a large body of eco-scientist's from all over the world has decided that the only way this destruction can be stopped, is through the threat of nuclear destruction". "All nations of this planet will ultimately be affected". "We decided that we can no longer stand idly by, while a handful of economically wealthy nations exploit eighty five to ninety percent of this worlds natural resources, to force feed their economies at the expense of two thirds of the population of our planet". "Which make all the Third World nations, whose people are starving and killing each other enmasse, in the worst cases of genocide this world has ever known".

"These few wealthy nations control and exploit the largest share of the earth's natural resources, such as the oil, gas, timber, minerals, and even the larger share of the food sources of this planet". "Because these few nations control over ninety percent of the agricultural land on this planet they are able to use food as an intimidating weapon against the struggling poor nations and their populations who are either starving or near starvation". "While these few nations economies are running at high speed and their populations are becoming fatter and richer, two thirds of the people on this planet are falling farther and farther behind economically". "Their children are dying of starvation by the millions daily, wars, disease, and poverty are killing multiplied millions everyday. "Therefore it is time for the inequities of the peoples of poorer nations to end".

"We have not only seen all of this, and just wrung our hands in despair, but we have developed a broad world plan to change the course of the history of mankind". "To change the course of mankind on this planet, will require ultra radical changes".

"The following solutions have been thought out very carefully by all the eco-scientists that are participating in Project Wormwood". "The following requirements will be needed to change the present course of this world". "Number one, every nation must be disarmed of nuclear weapons, and the development and research of chemical and biological weapons of mass destruction, must be terminated". "Also every nation must dismantle all their armed forces, and recall all military machinery and personnel back to their country of origin, including all sea going vessels". "All chemical, biological and nuclear weapons must then be destroyed, never to be used again on any nation or any peoples".

"Every nation must collect and destroy all personal, private and government controlled weapons of any kind". "Number two, all outstanding debts owed to World Bank's and developed nations in the world, by Third World countries must be forgiven, so these Third World countries may begin to see their economies move forward, and their people begin to prosper". "Also a redistribution of all the earth's land and resources will be mandated, and equally divided among earth's populations". "Number three, the borders surrounding every nation will cease to exist". "This will allow every citizen of the earth to live and work and recreate, any place on this planet, where he or she chooses". "Number four, because of the illegal action by the world leaders in 1948 of giving the nation of Palestine to the Jews as a legitimate home-land and allowing them to drive out and disperse millions of the legal occupants of Palestine from their homes and businesses, the whole land of Palestine will be returned to It's people, to right the injustice that was done to them". "They were robbed of their homeland, and driven into the desert and wilderness areas of their region, to give these few recognized peoples a home-land in Palestine, so there will be a special allotment granted to the Palestinian people". "All documented Israelites, will be removed from the land of Palestine, and dispersed throughout the world, allowing the Palestinian people once and for all to occupy all of their rightful land of Palestine".

"Number five, there will be an equal distribution of food sources and livestock throughout the world". "Number six, due to the unjust inequities, that have been perpetrated on the rest of the known world by the United States, for over two hundred years, two thirds of the population of the United States will be exported to African nations and Third World countries, leaving all their possessions and wealth behind". "The reason for this severe measure being taken, is because the United States with its unparalleled and wealthy economy, is due in part we believe, to the slave trade of the past centuries, and we believe this economy was built on the backs of African slaves". "Therefore all living Africans should be allowed to share in this wealth".

"Thank you gentlemen for listening, and again, let me say how very sorry we all are, that we have to take these radical measures to save this planet for all future generations". "Now I will return the floor to Colonel Chechnikov, who will explain to you how these changes will be implemented, and also the consequences of Project Wormwood on the nations of the world if they are not".

"Thank you, Professor Jerrod", the Colonel said as he approached the dais, "we will pause in our presentation for thirty minutes, but we will resume our presentation in exactly thirty minutes, so do not be late, there is much more information to come".

The giant screens went dark, in the conference room. At first there was a deafening silence, in the room, and then it seemed that all the world leaders began talking at once. They were unaware that each of them was speaking in their native tongue, and none of the others could understand what they were saying. Then one of the leaders stood and said, as he motioned with his hands to put on the head phones, that were provided at each station, and then suggested that each person that wanted to speak to the rest of the body, should do so from their microphones, and the electronic equipment would automatically interpret all speech, into each ones own language. They all agreed, and put on the head phones, and each one spoke in turn, in an orderly fashion.

First, the new Russian President spoke, it was a very moving speech, it lasted for five minutes, and He humbly apologized for the lack of security, over the nuclear arsenals in the old Soviet Union, when the States were dismantled, under his predecessor. He also was sorry for not paying more attention to the oversight of the Space Station, which had He done, this may never have occurred.

Then the President of the United States spoke for fifteen minutes. After that, as many leaders that had time, before the thirty minutes was up, asked many pointed questions. And they all expressed their sorrow for the American personnel that were being held hostage at the Space Station.

After thirty minutes the satellite feed was resumed, and the screens came to life again, the Colonel was at the Diaz, beginning to speak, "many of you are probably thinking, after hearing Professor Jerrod, outline the changes that you all must make, there is no possible way, for these changes to be implemented in our respective sovereign nations". "Let me assure you, there is a way, and I'm going to tell you how".

"To help in the implementation of our plan, we have solicited the assistance of one nation, on earth, that nation is the Republic of China, their Government has agreed to put in place one million armed military soldiers, and to place them under our command".

"We have already begun to draw up plans, and set forth orders for that nation and their one million armed forces, and they are ready to be deployed and stationed throughout the earth, in every nation at our command". "They will be armed with all the strategic weapons, including nuclear, biological, and chemical laden warheads that are needed for this task".

"We have also appointed a military statesman, from a Middle Eastern country, to build, and establish a world headquarters, in the city of Jerusalem in Palestine". "We believe, since that city, more than any other city in the world, has been the flashpoint for more hostility in the whole world, than any other place, it is appropriate for that city to house the world headquarters for peace". "Shortly the construction of the world headquarters will begin construction. It will be built on the site of the Jews sacred Temple Mount, where there stands now the Islamic Holy Temple, and several other buildings, this temple and these other structures will be dismantled and moved to a new location". "There will be nothing occupying that site with the exception of the world headquarters". "This world headquarters will be the place in which the Imperial Commander of earths people, will command and control all the populations of earth".

"Since the people in all lands are either superstitious or religious we feel it is necessary to establish a new world religion". "A new temple will be erected on the holy Temple Mount in Jerusalem, and in that Temple will be placed designated priests and high priests out of every religious order, with the exception of Christianity, Christianity will be abolished forever from the face of this planet because it is through Christianity that more bloodshed and more hostility and more destruction of our planet and its peoples have occurred over the last two millenniums". "Anyone practicing or condoning Christianity will be annihilated without trial including men women and children". "All of their possessions will be confiscated by the religious leaders of the New World religion and distributed to the poor throughout the earth".

"By this time you are probably thinking, how does this madman think he is going to deploy an army on to our sovereign shores and across our borders"? "How will they occupy our nations, and have every nation lay down their arms and abdicate our authority to him"? "Well I'm going to let a colleague of ours, on the International Space Station, tell you exactly how we're going to accomplish it, without firing one-shot".

Screeeeeech, the satellite feed was disrupted for a moment and then a new face appeared on the screens.

"Gentlemen, let me introduce myself to you at this time". "My name is Dr. Haunce Weber, I am well-known as a nuclear physicist, and Doctor of science technology, and an expert on earth's eco-systems". "Many of you in this room probably will recognize me from when I spoke and warned the nations of the world at the Kyoto conference, a few years ago, that we must stop destroying our planet". "At that conference we were unable to convince the large industrialized nations, such as the United States and England, to agree to cut the pollution from their factories, which was causing world wide temperature changes". "They, along with some other nations did not believe in the global warming scenario we presented". "It was after that conference, and the blatant disregard for the earth's eco-systems, that my colleagues and I decided we must do something to save the planet, and all life forces".

"For twenty five years of my life I have studied the eco-systems of the world, and their interaction with earth's natural forces and all forms of life forces including humanity". "These forces have co-existed and worked together harmoniously for over six million years, that is until the last one hundred years, in the last one hundred years the balance of nature has been disrupted, in a most incomprehensible way by humanity".

"It is for this reason, that I have quietly recruited many of the most noted eco-scientists of the world, from every nation, to join with me to develop this plan we call Project Wormwood, and it must be implemented now, before it's too late to save this earth".

"Our project members, in the past five years have covertly located a large number of nuclear warhead missiles, in many strategic locations on this planet, thanks in part to the lack of security of the nuclear arsenals of the Soviet Union, when that great body of States was dismantled". "Every intercontinental ballistic missile we have under our control is armed with multiple warheads, which are set to target many, of the most populated and industrialized cities on this planet".

"If the requirements that we have outlined before you today, for changing this planet and its populations are rejected by any nation, we will not hesitate to deploy one or more of these nuclear missiles on to these nations and totally annihilate them from our planet". "It would be with heavy hearts that we would take this necessary action but we understand it is the only way, to sacrifice the few for the many so we can save this planet".

"Beyond that we have here on the International Space station where I am broadcasting from, two American space shuttles, which when redeployed to the earth, are capable of entering the atmosphere at any predetermined location". "These shuttles are being loaded with deadly nerve gas, biological and nuclear warheads, and other nuclear devices which will be preset to detonate at a given altitude and or at a preset atmospheric pressure, and they cannot be destroyed without destroying the earth".

"If the requirements of our project are rejected by any Pacific Rim nation, the United States or the European Union nations, we will deploy these deadly chemical, biological and nuclear loaded shuttles to target the Pacific Rim and the United States". "Upon entering the earths atmosphere these shuttles will target the largest industrialized nations, they will release deadly chemicals and biological weapons, and warheads in strategic places on the earth, and poison much of the earths fresh water supply". "Then they will enter the Pacific and Atlantic oceans at a point chosen by us and the nuclear devices within them are designed to detonate in the water, at a depth which will produce deadly earth quakes, which we calculate will be in the range of a nine or ten, on the Richter scale". "It will create tsunamis one hundred feet high, traveling at a speed across the ocean at four hundred kilometers an hour". "The water will reach temperatures in excess of six hundred degrees Fahrenheit". "They will be traveling toward the Pacific and Atlantic coasts". "When they reach the shores of these Pacific Rim nations and the Atlantic coasts, millions of people will be killed and thousands of cities will be destroyed".

"My colleagues and I are very saddened that we have to take these extreme measures to save this planet". "Thank you for your attention and you're ultimate cooperation, and now I will sign off".

Screeeeeech! The satellite feed was lost again momentarily then the Colonel reappeared on the screens.

"Gentlemen, as you've just heard we are deadly serious about implementing Project Wormwood, so now that you have learned it is not an option or choice, to participate in our plan but rather it is mandatory for all nations, let me give you the Blue print of the plan and exactly what will be required to ensure world peace".

"Once our world government is set in place with their headquarters in Jerusalem, our project teams will be sent to every major city of the world, and with the Chinese forces which will be spread throughout the world, and the restructured United Nations, we will begin to register every citizen on the earth, this will require every citizen to be brought to a registration office in the country in which they are abiding, and be implanted with an electronic coded number". "This barcode number will be placed by an electronic devise, and it can neither be altered nor removed". "If it is altered or anyone tries to remove it from their body it will self destruct and kill the person in which it is implanted instantly". "It will be implanted in his or her hand or in their forehead; so that it can be scanned each time they need to renew their supplies or they need to conduct any business, including buying or selling food". "This electronic code will be entered into an international database and when every citizen of the earth is registered, which we believe can be done in less than one year, the world government will then take control of all the worlds industry". "All commerce, all communication, energy and food supplies will be under the control of our Government".

"Every citizen of the earth will then be measured out just enough of all the world's resources, including food, shelter, and energy to live a comfortable life anywhere they choose, as long as it is approved by our committee on human affairs".

"On a predetermined basis each individual or family will be allotted just what they have need of month by month and all of these resources can only be accessed by their registration code".

"My colleagues and I know that there will be pockets of resistance to the registration code, and some citizens of earth will refuse to have the electronic chip implanted". "These renegades of resistance will be dealt with in a harsh manner, we know that they will have stockpiles of needed resources in many places, but they will be limited". "Those citizens who resist registering with the world headquarters will only be left with the alternative to flee into the mountains and wilderness areas of the world". "And these pockets of resistance will be hunted down by the armed forces that are deployed by the United Nations and destroyed, not only the men but also the women and children will be killed without any trial".

"There may indeed be some of these which will elude our armed forces for some time, but they will be unable to purchase any goods or services anywhere on earth through the world government because they will not have been registered in our database".

"Gentlemen I know the ten hours you have been here and listening to what changes must be implemented has been very tiring and now I only have one more part of our plan to share with you please be patient".

"The financial costs to implement these changes will be enormous, and it will require in the first twelve months of operation to receive a taxation from every nation, and will begin with the United States, the United States will be required to contribute to the world government one hundred billion dollars in the first twelve months, the European Union states and countries will be required to contribute an equal amount". "The amounts for the rest of the Nation's will be revealed to them in the first twelve months".

"These contributions will be needed to finance the implementation of our plan and it will be implemented through the assistance of the United Nations and the Chinese army". "After the first twelve months all the assets of every nation on earth will be placed under the control of our one world government".

"You all have set before you enormous tasks to prepare your people in your individual countries for these changes however you do so we would suggest that you do it without creating a worldwide panic". "My colleagues and I have set a timetable of twenty four months of preparation to give every nation time to prepare their people for these changes before we implement our plan". "During the first twelve months you will begin total disarmament and you will also be required to withdraw all military personnel from all foreign countries, and completely dismantle your military machinery". "You will also be required to deemphasize and destabilize your central governmental bodies and prepare your people for the shifting of your governments to one World Government".

"We are confident that all these changes can be implemented in no less than twenty four months". "If these changes are implemented in every nation according to our instructions and requirements we will never have to execute Project Wormwood".

"The world will for the first time in over two thousand years be at peace". "And although the peace throughout the world will be tenuous at first, under the leadership and the military force of the World Government and the assistance of the Chinese armed forces and the United Nations together we believe that we can bring a lasting peace to this planet". "We thank you Gentlemen for attending this conference and for your future cooperation". "You can bring lasting peace to this planet and it is in your hands". "Good day and thank you for listening".

Not a word was spoken as the giant screens went black and all the delegates at the conference center filed out of the Security chambers in an orderly fashion and drove off in their waiting vehicles.

"That meeting took place less than six months ago I do not know what each of these Government leaders are doing to prepare their people for the inevitable changes, but I, at great risk to myself have written this book to warn you of the impending challenges all of us will face in the very near future. The demands that will be required by the New World Government to implement these radical changes will affect the entire human race, and the Western world most grievously".

"Our Governments must work diligently together to stop these mad men's plans, before it is too late. Time is of the essence, we have less than two years".

CHAPTER 35

❝As ERIK AND I sat in his office in Moscow conducting our last interview for this book, he noticed the icon on his computer flashing indicating that he had an e-mail message". "He clicked on the icon and saw this message". "Erik I have very little time I am sending this message at the risk of being discovered, I am alive and well and I am in hiding on the International Space Station, I have overheard the plans that have been laid out by these mad scientist's and I am going to try with every means that I have to stop the implementation of Project Wormwood". Signed: "Agent Thomas Burkov "please inform O'Donnel".

Less than four weeks ago Erik returned to Moscow from the United States. He had been summoned by the American President to brief the World leaders on the mysterious project called Wormwood, and the head of that project, the Soviet Union' Colonel Chechnikov.

He attended a Top-Secret meeting with the U.S. President, George Brown, some of his cabinet members, the Joint Chiefs of Staff, and many world leaders. This meeting took place at the headquarters of the United Nations in New York City.

The Colonel has been an officer in the old Soviet Union military before the Soviet Union broke up, and was separated into several independent countries. Since then he has been placed in charge of the Soviet international space station program, which the United States is a partner with Russia. However it has been two years since the United States has been active in the program, ever since the last shuttle disintegrated in space with all their astronauts on board, and all of them perished. All shuttle flights to the space station were put on hold by NASA while the investigation into the cause of the accident was conducted.

During these two years the Russian Government has assumed all responsibility of supplying the space station with personnel and materials, and carrying out scientific experiments on the station. They have been sending Russian scientists and engineers on each flight to the station, with their cosmonauts. The United States Government was continuing its massive financial support for the station, but NASA or any of the Governmental departments were overseeing the operations.

Unknown to either the U.S. Government or the Russian Government the Colonel has been stockpiling all the components to build several nuclear bombs and tons of biological weapons, chemicals on the space station. He has also sent many Russian engineers and eco-scientists from around the world which he has recruited for his cause. They now have the capability to launch nuclear warheads from the space station and target any location on earth.

Prior to Erik being summoned to Washington He had assumed the position of, Director of Russian intelligence, after his father the former Director had been murdered in his home in Moscow. The murder was made to look like a suicide and the murderers were still at large. Erik believes the murderer was the Russian Colonel who was in charge of the international space station and all its operations.

The primary suspect, Colonel Boris Chechnikov left Russia soon after the general's death, and Russian intelligence sources believe that he fled to Syria in the Middle East.

Erik was still grieving over his father's death when he was sent to Washington by His President, and after the top-secret meeting that was held at the United Nations in New York in the United States Erik returned home to Moscow to continue his investigation into his Fathers death and project Wormwood.

Erik was sitting behind his desk in his office at the Department of intelligence in the Kremlin building in Russia, it was early Saturday morning and he was considering all that had happened in the last few weeks, since he had been asked by the President of the United States to search all files on the international space Station operations, to see if by chance the Colonel had left any kind of trail that could tell them where the nuclear devices were staged.

The gathering Dignitary's at the UN Headquarters were told by the Colonel's spokesman that the missiles were staged in strategic areas throughout the world, and they were positioned to strike major cities in many different countries if deployed, and the scientists would not hesitate to carry out their threat if the Leaders of World Governments refused to comply with their demands.

CHAPTER 36

E RIK THOUGHT HE HEARD a sound outside the office door, it sounded like someone walking very softly on the tile, with rubber sole shoes, he stopped shuffling papers and listened in silence, "*it must've been a sound that came from the wind blowing through the window just outside his father's office* he thought, then he returned to what he was doing. Erik removed his pistol from a drawer, and placed it on top of his desk in front of him. He had become very cautious since his father had been murdered, and the suspects had all disappeared.

Then there was that ever so familiar smell, first it tickled his nose then it irritated him, without turning to look at the open door, he said, "come on in and sit down, but leave that stinking cigar outside".

"Sorry Boss, I won't let it happen again" said the wiry little man as he entered the office and took a seat in front of Erik's desk. The little man had no hair and wore a small goatee and dark moustache, but it was unmistakably Erik's old friend and driver, Sid Kichinski.

"Been awhile since I seen you", said Erik as he held out his hand across the desk toward his old friend, Sid pushed back his chair and got up and with one fluid motion he was standing on the other side of the desk beside his old friend Erik. They stood and embraced for a long moment while both men wiped the tears from their eyes. Sid smiled, and said, "Hello! Boss it's been a long time".

"Sit down Sid and tell me all that has happened". Sid began with, when he arrived back at the St. Petersburg airport from his vacation with his girlfriend Kathy.

"When I called you from the airport I was unaware that the Colonel had your phone bugged, and when I told you I wanted to meet you in the morning at your office, and I wanted to talk to you about Project wormwood he must have been listening, and sent one of his thugs to intercept me and get rid of me before I had a chance to meet with you". "He was unaware there was a passenger in the car with me, how could he know that I offered a fellow traveler on the plane a ride in to Moscow with me". "When the truck began ramming the back of the limo I knew it was the Colonel's man and he was sent to kill me, so I unbuckled my seatbelt and got ready to bail from the limo if he tried to push us off the road down the mountain". "I was unable to warn my passenger, other than to tell him to release his seatbelt and be ready to bail out if I could not out run the truck". "When the truck forced us over the cliff at the curve my passenger was unable to open the door, and after I bailed out he apparently climbed over the seat into the front to try and steer the limo, it was unfortunate that He went over the cliff with the car and was killed".

"I was able to bail out but I broke my left leg in the fall, so I hid in the woods until I saw the police and all the emergency vehicles leave the scene". "I tried to get back up on the road to see you before you left, but I was unable to climb the hill with my broken leg". "I finally was able to pull and crawl my way up the hill onto the road, the next morning". "I stopped a car that was going by, and told the man in the car that I'd been hiking in the woods and fell from a cliff and broke my leg".

"By that time the road had been cleared of any sign of the accident". "The man took me to a Doctor he knew, that was about thirty kilometers down the road". "The Doctor set my leg and put a plaster cast on it". "The man then took me to his cabin and cared for me until my leg healed enough to remove the cast". "Then he drove me here to the city where I was able to rent a small apartment and remained out of sight till now".

"I had hoped you had seen the burned body of my passenger, and you would know it was not me". "I also knew you would somehow understand, and keep that a secret and wait for me to contact you, I thought once about putting on a disguise and showing up at my funeral, but I was afraid of being recognized by the Colonel or any of his thugs, and if they knew

I was still alive I remained a threat to exposing the true nature of their Project wormwood".

"It has been almost two months since I heard any news, you said on the phone when I called you last night that a lot has happened since my death and you would fill me in on it this morning". "Is the Colonel still a threat to me or can I come out of hiding and get on with my life"?

"I want to get in touch with my Fiancé, Kathy, and let her and my mother know I'm still alive, before she gets interested in someone else, if she hasn't already". "I am not going to call her, the shock of hearing my voice might be too much for her, I'm planning a trip to Minsk to see her, but before I do I need to be sure my life is no longer in danger".

"Old friend", Erik said, "so much has happened since the accident it is hard to know where to begin". Erik took a full pot of fresh coffee and poured Sid a cup, and offered him a stale roll (which Sid declined). Then he said, "the Colonel is no longer in Russia, I believe he has fled to Syria where he is orchestrating the unleashing of Project wormwood on the whole world".

For the next five hours Erik revealed to his old friend all that had taken place, about his father's death and him being sent to America, and the international space Station involvement and the ultimatum to the world leaders by the Colonel and his group of ecology scientists.

Sid sat silent for a long moment, then he said, "Erik, we can't let this happen we have to stop this madman before he plunges the whole world into war and mass destruction".

"You are absolutely right but we have to be very careful how we attempt to dismantle his plan, if the Colonel or any of his mad scientists discover what we're trying to do, they may release a nuclear warhead into a populated city just to show their strength, and thousands perhaps millions of people will die".

"We will have to put together a plan of action and present it to the President of the United States, he is the only one of the world leaders I can fully trust". "He told me privately before I left Washington, after the meeting at the UN headquarters, that any financing or intelligence or government employees I might need, is at my disposal". "Our plan has to remain Top-Secret and we have to work entirely off the radar screen".

"Then who can we trust"? "and how do we began this monumental operation"?. "That is where you fit in my friend, with your personal involvement with the Project wormwood and the Colonel, and you're long experience in the KGB, you have more knowledge than any one that I know, and with all of them believing you are dead, that you died in the car crash you can add much to this operation".

Sid agreed to help in any way he could, even though it meant letting his mother and fiancé continue believing he was dead.

"Sid we cannot waste any time getting started, I need you to recruit twelve men from the old KGB that you have complete trust in, don't choose anyone who is married or has children, these men have to be completely disconnected from anyone in society that might raise a question if they disappeared".

"That will be difficult Erik, but I'll do what I can, I understand the seriousness of this assignment".

"There are two additional men I have recruited, these men I would trust with my life as I do with you". "You may have met them in the course of driving for me, they are Otto Zorkov and Bill Forney".

"Otto has been working undercover for me for some time now he has been monitoring all the procurement documents and correspondence coming into the international space station agency". He is sifting through the agency's files now trying to find any lead which may identify where those nuclear missiles are located".

"Bill Forney is an old friend from Oxford, he has a television show, where he does investigative reporting and exposé journalism, he, is the one who first broke the story about the Colonel and the international space station agency".

"Bill had to move his wife and his daughter out of the country, because the Colonel's thugs threatened their lives". "He has been back in his studio doing his show for about two week's he left his wife and daughter in England somewhere in the country". "I know he will help us, I've already talked to him".

"Our operation will need to have global communication, and Bill's program can provide us with that, via satellite". "We will establish a code that can be communicated to all the members of our team, no matter where we are in a world, we will all have a portable transmitter and satellite receiver, that will receive Bill's program".

"It sounds like you've already been working on this plan, and I can't wait to get started myself".

When the meeting with Erik was over, it was late in the evening, so Sid drove back to the small apartment at the edge of the city that he had rented under the name of Vance Ullrich. Since the accident he had not made contact with anyone who knew him except Erik, and now he was wearing a black mustache and goatee beard, and he shaved all the hair from his head, he looks sinister. Even to himself but at least no one recognized who he really was.

Sid made himself a sandwich with stale bread he had in the apartment, and drank a half pint of vodka, and laid down on the daybed in the apartment and fell asleep.

It was early the following morning when Sid awoke, it was still pitch dark outside, he got out of bed, showered and change clothes, drank a cup of hot coffee and was out the door of his apartment where he got into his car that he had already started to get it warmed up, (it was extremely cold outside) then he was off on his mission.

The first man he would try to recruit for their operation was a former intelligence officer in the old Soviet Union's KGB. His name was Daniel Kirch, Daniel had never had any children and his wife died about ten years ago. Sid had not been in contact with him for at least five years, so he didn't know what his marital status was now, but he knew he could trust him with his life.

Daniel was one of those outdoor men who loved to fish and hunt, and the place Sid thought he could be found this time of the morning was a trout stream in the mountains about thirty kilometers out of the city. Sid knew he would have to be very cautious when approaching Daniel in this out-of-the-way place, because his friend always carried a side-arm and would not be hesitant to use it on a stranger approaching him. Sid thought, he must approach Daniel with extreme caution, since his old friend had only recently attended Sid's funeral.

A few of the KGB intelligence agents had a secret signal to communicate with each other when they were approaching, because they may be disguised.

They would place their right hand over their heart and extend their left hand open, and this would show the other Agent they were unarmed and friendly, all the while whistling like a warbling bird. This was a sign that only a few close knit Agents knew about.

While Sid was driving to the mountain stream he practiced his warbling whistle, and was quite surprised he still was able to do it.

CHAPTER 37

A S THE LONE FIGURE stood about knee-deep in the stream of icy cold
water, he thought he heard a sound on the path coming down to
the stream, from up on the road, it was very faint so he was unsure what
it was, so he listened for a moment to see if he could hear a squirrel
running along the ground. He turned very slowly as he reeled in his line,
and moved slowly out of the stream, to the bank. Daniel then lay down
his fishing rod on the bank, next to his camping gear lying on the bank
of the stream.

He then drew his pistol and released the safety as he walked across the
clearing and into the covering of the woods. He wanted to be out of sight
to anyone coming down the path, and He waited with his pistol ready to
fire. He was hiding behind a tree where he had a clear view of anyone on
the path and anyone who might leave the path to come down where he
was, through the woods.

Daniel's adrenaline began flowing through his bloodstream, and he
remembered the old days of the KGB and their arrest tactics, how many
times he and other agents would lie and wait to arrest someone on the
Government's list. "It takes great physical discipline, to stand dead still and not
make a sound, for long periods of time, and I can hear my own heartbeat".

"It could be another fisherman or someone hiking in the woods, or it could
be an animal, but until I know for sure that it is not someone that can harm me,
I'll keep still and silent behind this tree".

Shuuissh!, Shuuissh!, Daniel could hear on the path, now he knew it was a person, shuuissh, shuuissh, the sound was unmistakably someone coming down the snow covered path toward the stream.

The silhouette of a small framed figure suddenly appeared in the clearing, the figure stood still for a moment then walked across the clearing toward Daniel's gear.

Sid never heard his friend move swiftly up behind him until he felt the muzzle of the cold steel revolver on the back of his neck, and heard that deep Russian brogue voice say, "who are you and what is your business"?

Sid began to turn very slowly as he placed his right hand on his heart and extended his left hand to the man with the gun , and began whistling a warbling sound. Daniel kept his gun on this stranger standing before him, with the bald head and black moustache and beard, and then he asked, "What is your name"? "KGB SK" "I know he is dead and gone, I attended his funeral". Sid said "Daniel, look closely" as the early morning light shined on his face, then as his friend looked into his eyes, he dropped his gun to his side and said, "Sid"!?

Daniel thought he was looking into the face of the ghost of his dear friend, but even though he was in disguise Daniel knew somehow his dear friend was not dead as he thought, but was standing before him alive. He grabbed his old friend and embraced him, and Sid could see tears streaming down his old friend's face, and he also began to weep uncontrollably. The two old friends stood in an embrace for a long moment while they both wept unashamedly.

Daniel built a fire on the banks of the stream and put a crude looking pot of coffee on, while he and Sid talked. Sid told his old friend all about what had taken place and enlisted his participation in their operation.

As they drank strong coffee and Sid rehearsed everything Erik had revealed to him Daniel was more than enthusiastic about being a part of the operation.

Sid left Daniel at the stream and said he would be in touch with him after he completed putting together the team and had every one ready to begin the operation.

Sid then went back to the city to see if he could locate former sergeant Abram Lawrence. He would use the former sergeant to help him find and enlist ten more good reliable men for the operation.

CHAPTER 38

IT WAS MONDAY AFTERNOON when the phone rang in Bill's TV studio office, and was answered by his private secretary, "hello", "this is Erik, can I speak to Bill please"? Sandy, Bill's private secretary knew, any time Erik or Otto called she was to put them right through into Bill's office. "Oh! Hi Erik, I will put you right through to Bill it's nice to hear your voice again it has been a while". "Thank you Sandy" Erik said, then he heard the voice of his dear friend, "Erik, good to hear from you what's on your mind"?

"Bill, Otto is coming over at eight o'clock tonight and I would like you to be here I have recruited a new member to add to our planning operation and I would like you to meet him, and we can go over our plans together".

Erik, Bill and Otto had been meeting at least once every two weeks and trading the information each of them had found out about the Colonel or the wormwood project. They were all searching for information that might lead them to the locations of the nuclear missiles, which were in the hands of the Colonel and his group of ecology scientists. "Yes Erik, I can be there I may be a little late but I'll be no later than 8:30". "Good, we will see you tonight at my place Bill, and make sure you are not tailed we have to be as careful as we can be".

Bill left the studio about 6:00, that would give him time to run a couple of errands and still get to Erik's before 8:30. There was a bitter cold in the air tonight he thought, *"I'm glad we have this indoor parking garage, most people that work at the station have to park their cars outside"*, but a few executives have an inside parking garage attached to the side of the studio.

As Bill was walking down the corridor toward the parking garage he took his keypad out of his pocket, and pressed the star symbol on the front of it as he always did when it was bitter cold outside, this activated the remote starter on his car and started it, so it would start warming up before he reached the garage.

All of a sudden there was a tremendous explosion in the parking garage, the side door to the studio was blown completely out, and glass shattered all over the main floor of the studio as thick black smoke began pouring in. Bill stopped abruptly and thought, *"My God there must've been a gas pipe leaking, and was ignited when I started my car"*, he was relieved that all the station employees but a few maintenance people had already left for the day. He waited to see if there was any fire or if it was safe to exit the building.

Bill immediately called the emergency fire and police and they were already on their way to the studio because they heard the explosion.

"If you don't see any fire in the studio, and you are on the ground floor, stay where you are until we arrive and assess the damage", the dispatcher told Erik on the phone.

Bill was waiting in the exit corridor when the emergency crews arrived. "You can come out this way now", the police officer said as he motioned to Bill from the exit at the end of the corridor, where the explosion took place. "The structure is secure and the fire in the parking garage is out". Bill walked toward the policeman and out the door that had been blown off by the explosion. "What was it"? Bill said to one of the firemen who were rolling up their hoses, "a gas pipe leak"?, "no nothing like that, it appears someone set off a pipe bomb under the hood of that Mercedes", as a fireman pointed toward a parked car in the garage, "do you know who owns it"?

"My god!", Bill said, looking at his car that was blown apart "it's mine". "Bill almost collapsed as his legs begin to give way and he turned ashen white. The firemen grabbed him to keep him from falling and sat him down on the curb, while another fireman ran to the fire truck and retrieved an oxygen tank and mask. "Put your head down between your legs", the fireman said to Bill "it will help to keep you from passing out".

The fireman returned with the oxygen and mask, and placed it on Bill and said, "You must breathe deep sir, take slow and deep breaths, and you are going to be alright".

It was 9;00 o'clock, and Erik, Otto and Sid were waiting for Bill to arrive. Erik had called the studio and got no answer, and then he called Bill's cell phone and still got no answer. "He said he would be here no later than 8:30", Erik told the others, "something has happened it's 9:30, I'm not waiting any longer I'm going to look for Bill, I told Bill he would have to be careful". "I tried to make him let me put a surveillance team on him. I knew he could be in danger, after He returned from England and aired the exposé on the Colonel, and showed his picture on TV". "As long as some of the Colonel's thugs are still loose, none of us are completely safe".

Erik was walking toward the door, putting on his leather jacket over a shoulder holster, when his cell phone rang, it was Bill "where are you man? We were just leaving to find you". "I'm at the police station downtown come pick me up". "We'll be there in an hour". "Bill has been picked up by the police" Erik told Sid and Otto, he didn't say why".

As Erik was driving to the police station, Otto and Sid were quiet, giving him time to think, *"I will never forgive myself for not insisting on putting a surveillance team on Bill around the clock". "I was so happy to see my friend return from England, he was someone that I could confide in concerning the dilemma that the Colonel has placed the whole world in, I knew Sid was still alive, but he had not made contact with me, and Otto, my dear friend has been preoccupied with Greta, after they were married". "Bill and I are developing a plan to diffuse the Colonel's threats to the world and his preposterous demands. We now have a blueprint of what must be done".* Erik was still in deep thought when they arrived at the station. Otto and Sid remained in the car, Erik didn't want anyone at the station to link him with Otto, out of fear for his safety, and he didn't want anyone to recognize Sid either.

"Have a seat" the police sergeant said to Erik as he entered the office of the police Lieutenant. As Erik sat down the sergeant in the room said, "hey"! "aren't you the Director of Intelligence"? General Roskov's son"? "Yes I am", "I have seen you on television giving interviews, is this man we have here, under investigation by your department"? "No!" Erik said "he is an old friend from college".

"Just sign these papers", the sergeant said to Bill "and you're free to go with your friend, but don't leave Moscow we will want to question you some more during our investigation of the explosion". "You have my word on it and you can reach me at the television studio during business hours".

As Bill and Erik walked briskly toward Erik's car, Erik said, "explosion!, what was the sergeant talking about"? "I'll fill you in on our way to your place Erik, and by the way I would like to spend the night at your place I'm a bit shaken".

"Bill I would like you to meet my old friend and former driver", Erik said as Bill got into the front seat on the passenger side of the car, "he is the other member of the team I've been telling you about, he finally emerged from the shadows, remember what I told you about the burned body they took from my car that night in the mountains, and how Otto and I went back the next morning to search the woods for Sid". "Well this is Sid Kachinski, we believed he was injured or possibly dead, but when we couldn't find any trace of him at the accident scene we knew he was alive somewhere". "We even took Otto's dog precious to help us find him, but turned up nothing, but I knew when he felt it was safe he would get in contact with me".

"We buried the burned body and told every one it was Sid, even his fiancée and his mother doesn't know he is alive". "Sid has agreed to keep it that way and work with us, by recruiting some highly trained former Soviet agents of the KGB for the network, and help put together the teams we will need to deploy around the world to prevent the Colonel from implementing his diabolical plan".

"Don't be put off by how he looks, he is in disguise". "Hi Bill, I'm pleased to meet you I've seen some of your exposé shows on television while I was laid up with my leg crushed, I especially enjoyed the one you did on the Colonel, I can just see him fuming over that exposé".

"Well it took a lot of courage for a lot of people including Erik and Otto and his dear wife Greta to help gather all the material on that, but I can hardly wait to do the final exposé on the Colonel when he is captured and prosecuted". "I will do that one when the nuclear warheads are disarmed and the world is safe".

"Speaking of that, Sid are you having any success on your mission", asked Erik. "Yes I have two key recruiter's working on the plan to bring together the teams we will need its progressing well".

By this time they arrived back at Erik's place, Otto said "I'm going to call Greta and tell her I will be later than I had planned, so she will not be worried". Erik put on a fresh pot of coffee and all four men took a seat in the living room. "Bill" Erik said, "tell us what happened and why you were at the police station without your car, and what did the sergeant mean about the explosion"?

Bill told his friends all that had happened, and how if it had not been so cold outside he never would have used his remote starter to start his car and he would surely have been killed in the explosion.

"My God! man, they're watching you and they mean to kill you". "It doesn't matter if you like it or not", Erik said "I'm placing a full 24-hour a day surveillance team on you". "The Colonel's thugs will stop at nothing and we can't let them have another chance".

"I appreciate that Erik, I have never been so shaken in my life, I am just so thankful my wife and my daughter, are out of the country and safe from those men".

"Otto have you uncovered any files that the Colonel left behind that would give us a clue where the warheads are located"? "Nothing yet" Otto said, "but Greta is reviewing several boxes of computer disks we found in a locked storage vault at the agency warehouse". They are marked "classified documents". "If anything turns up in them I will let you know immediately".

"The coffee is ready" Erik said, as he walked into the kitchen. The other three men followed him and each poured themselves a cup, and returned to the living room.

"I'll be out of the country for two weeks" Erik said, "I have to meet with the American President, he is assigning some key intelligence staff and several agents from the CIA to work with us, then I'm going to England where I have a meeting set up with the Boss, that is my handler in MI6, I have never met him and I'm looking forward to this meeting".

"Sid you ratchet up your recruitment efforts and Bill be very careful, trust no one, we don't know how far reaching the Colonel's authority goes into the present Russian government". "Instead of going back to your place, you can stay here, and my men will take you too and from the Studio and stand guard around the clock".

"Otto you and Greta also be very careful and I'm putting a surveillance team on you guys as well", "I don't have to tell you what is at stake here, we may be the only hope the world has to prevent these madmen from carrying out their diabolical plan". "We have got to find the location of those nuclear missiles and disarm them to end the threat the Colonel has placed on the World Governments".

CHAPTER 39

ROGER WILSON WONDERED WHY he was being summoned to the State
Department to attend a meeting with the President. He was hired
by the CIA just out of college, and after three years had been asked to
join the President's national security agency, since then he was only in
one meeting where the President was even there, and then he just saw
him across the conference table and didn't really meet him. *"Why is he
wanting to meet with me at the State Department"* Roger wondered as he
parked his SUV inside the visitor's area inside the parking garage at the
State Department? As he left his vehicle he noticed there were an unusual
number of men in suits milling around in the parking lot, and four of
them were standing in front of the entrance where he was instructed to
enter, Roger knew these were undoubtedly Secret Service, so he guessed
that the President had already arrived.

Then Roger saw Karla, who had just parked her car and was walking
briskly up toward the entrance where he was standing, while the Secret
Service was checking his briefcase and his ID, Karla LaVanway, the shapely
brunette approached him, "what are you doing here at State" Roger said.
"I might ask you the same question, I was called last night at home by the
Director and asked if I could be here, he didn't say why so here I am, and
you are here for what Roger"? "I have a meeting with the man himself",
Karla said, "Is he going to do ask you to feed his dog while he is traveling"?
"Very funny" Roger said, as they both laughed.

"Well I guess I will see you back at the Department" Roger said as he entered through the metal detectors.

Karla was a new agent that was just recently assigned to Rogers Department over at the national security agency, and everyone over there was in love with her, including Roger. She was tall for a woman, about five feet, ten inches tall but very diminutive, she filled out her uniform very nicely, and her long brunette hair fell down just below her shoulders, and she was always very pleasant to everyone including all the women in the Department, but she was all business, and she let every "single" man know she was not looking for a man. On the pistol range she was top-notch she could handle and shoot a revolver as well or better than anyone in the Department.

Erik's plane arrived at Dulles international Airport at six a.m. it'd been a long night, flying from Moscow so he departed the big jet plane with a bit of jet-lag, and was met by two Secret Service agents who escorted him down to the baggage area to retrieve his baggage. Then they by-passed Customs and took him directly to an awaiting chopper bearing the U.S. seal, and flew him directly to the State Department's Heli-Port.

This is much better than having to fight the morning rush-hour traffic into the capitol" Erik thought. It took less than an hour from the time Erik's plane landed at Dulles until he was stepping out of the chopper at The State Department.

There were six men already seated around a conference table when Erik entered, the war room at the State Department. "Good morning Erik did you have a pleasant flight"? The Secretary of State asked, "I did Madame Secretary and I really appreciated the flight from Dulles".

"Let me introduce you to these gentlemen, you will all be working together", said the Secretary, as Erik took his seat at the table designated by a nameplate in front of him. The secretary said, "this is The Undersecretary whom you have met, and from left to right around the table, this is General Darryl Dole of the joint Chiefs, I believe you know him as well", and the Secretary continued around the table, "Dr. Thomas Telor, agent Billy Ray from The NSA and the Director of Homeland security Kerry Shire". After she made all the introductions she said, "Gentlemen this is Erik Roskov the Director of Russian intelligence, and the key to this whole operation". "Good morning gentlemen" Erik said with a wide smile, "I am at your service".

"Have some coffee or juice, and there are fresh rolls on the counter", and aide said, that had just stepped into the room carrying a large serving tray filled with sweet rolls. "Go ahead", the Secretary said motioning toward the counter where the coffee and juice was "we won't begin the meeting until the President arrives anyway, he is in the building somewhere, and we are awaiting the arrival of two other members of the team".

While she was yet speaking, an aide brought Roger Wilson into the room , and directed him to his designated seat at the table, when he was set down The Secretary said, "Roger Wilson an agent assigned to us from the national security agency, Roger introduce yourself to the gentlemen around the coffee bar you'll be seeing a lot of them".

All heads turned as an aide escorted the shapely brunette into the room. "Gentlemen meet the only other woman on the team, Karla LeVanway, she is also an agent assigned to us from NSA". Karla smiled as she looked around the room and to all the men in the room "good morning gentlemen it is going to be an honor to be part of this team".

As Karla took her seat at the table, Erik, who was still at the bar noticed she was directly across from his seat. He and the other men were sizing up this beautiful brunette when the President walked into the room.

"Good", said the President you're all here and I smell fresh coffee, and I'm sure State had enough in their budget to supply fresh rolls". Everyone laughed, "In truth Mr. President", the Secretary said, "they are day old rolls, but the coffee is fresh".

"We have a lot to do so let's get to it", the President said, "let's all get to the table". Everyone moved quickly to their assigned seats at the table and sat down.

Erik was seated next to the President, who was seated at the head of the conference table, and Karla was seated directly across from him, he was going to have a difficult time focusing on the business at hand. Not since he was in college, and was going to be married to his sweetheart, before that tragic accident that took her life, had he even looked at another woman like he was now looking at Karla, she was beautiful and he could see in her eyes she was looking at him the same way.

"Gentlemen and ladies you have been summoned here to undertake a task that can either lead to the destruction of much of mankind, or save all of mankind, you have been handpicked for this task, and what we are about to reveal to you, is only known by a very small number of people, including myself".

The President continued, "this, task if it is to succeed must be absolutely Top-Secret, each of you have been chosen for your expertise in your field and because you do not have wives or husbands, that would prevent you from carrying out your respective assignments".

"You may be called upon to do things that you may consider illegal or even immoral, but make no mistake, they will be necessary to succeed in this mission". It is now 10:30 a.m. I'd like to allow you about four hours to consider if you're willing to be a part of this operation, you can walk around in the city and see the sights for those of you who do not work here, or you can retire to your offices or homes while considering". "Just remember, even this meeting, though nothing has been revealed to you yet is considered Top-Secret, there will be no problem if you decide not to undertake the assignment, and the Secretary and I will fully understand, but for those of you who decide to stay with us be back in this room at 5 p.m., and be prepared for a long night".

"When you leave the room there will be an aide assigned to direct you to a car with a driver, which will be at your disposal for the next few hours, the drivers will have a government credit card that is good anywhere in the city, if you wish to have lunch or see a movie". "Good day people and thank you for coming, I'll see you at five, "enjoy the city Erik".

As the group of men and Karla left the office and were being escorted down the corridor to their waiting cars, Erik was walking alone and was in deep thought, when he felt something gently tugging at his coat. "Hey"! Erik heard a soft feminine voice say, as he turned to see who was tugging on his coat, "would you like to have lunch with me today"? Taken by surprise by the beautiful Karla's offer, without thinking Erik said, "sure I would love to but isn't it a bit early for lunch"? "That's okay we can take my car and I can show you around the city until lunchtime if that's okay with you that is". Erik said, "sure" as Karla grabbed his hand and gently pulled him out of the line and toward the elevator, "this way my car is in the visitors area".

Ding!, the elevator door opened on the ground floor and Karla still holding on to Erik's hand, said, "this way" as she walked toward the visitors entrance of the building. "That's my car over their Karla said pointing to a Jaguar, it's a birthday present from my father".

"When I was assigned to the NSA he said, in all the movies he saw the top agents always drove a cool car, He thinks the agency is a back lot for a James Bond movie".

"It is a nice car" Erik said as he slid into the passenger seat, "and it does look cool". Karla and Erik both laughed. "I know a lot about the city, where would you like to go and what would you like to see? or would you just like to go somewhere and have a cup of coffee and talk"?. "Yes! I would like that I'm not much of a sightseer anyway".

As Karla and Erik walked into the small coffee shop, the big man wearing a wide smile walked briskly toward them with his arms outstretched, "good morning darling Karla" he said as he gave her a big hug and kissed her on the cheek "who is this"? "This is my friend Erik, he is here on business from Russia". "A Ruski"? the big man said as he looked Erik over, "we could have beaten you if it had come to that you know", then he laughed as he said "I'm only kidding, I guess my daughter has told you already what a kidder I am". "Come sit down and I will get back to my business and leave you two alone, nice to meet you" the jovial man said as he headed into the back of the coffee shop.

"I should've warned you about that before we arrived, he thinks everything in life should be fun". "He seems to be a very nice person that knows how to have fun with any circumstance, what is his name"? "Dominick Shalom, it means the dominion of peace, he is Jewish as I am, my mother died when I was born and Dominick raised me by himself, he never remarried".

"When I was planning to go to college I changed my name to Karla LeVanway, because it was much easier to get a scholarship in those days in the State of Maryland if you were not Jewish".

"Now that is enough about me and my family I want to hear about you". "What do you do in Russia? And do you have a wife? or children, or both, and why are you so personal with President Brown"? "I'm sorry you don't have to answer any of those questions, sometimes I just get carried away, it's probably because my minor in college was journalism".

The waiter poured Erik and Karla a cup of coffee and handed them each menus, "that's ok Bill", she said to the waiter we will only be having coffee", with that the young boy retrieved the menus and walked away.

"First of all my mother died of cancer just after I finished college at Oxford University in England and my father died less than a year ago". "I have reason to believe that he was murdered". "I've never been married and have no children". "My position in Russia is the Director of Russian intelligence, the same as your CIA and your President has requested that I oversee this operation which you will learn much more about if you return to the war room at five".

137

Then Erik said as he held Karla's hands across the table and looked into her eyes, "I think I have fallen in love" "Oh! is it anyone I know"? "I think you might, she lives in the U.S. and she is about five feet ten inches tall, and she fills out her clothes very nicely, has a beautiful smile and long silky auburn hair, and oh yes her father owns a little coffee shop where I may be able to work in case I lose my job".

Karla smiled and squeezed Erik's hands and she said, "Erik the first time I saw you my heart began to beat so hard I thought it could be seen under my uniform, it has been a long time since a man has had that effect on me, but do you think we may be moving too fast?, I've not yet decided if I will be taking part in the operation, and you will be leaving and flying back to Russia soon".

It was now twelve o'clock and Erik said, "please, don't make any decisions now, let's go somewhere and enjoy a nice lunch". Karla agreed and said goodbye to Dominick and left the coffee shop. As they walked to her car she had butterflies in her stomach, what has this tall rugged looking red haired Russian done to her she thought. She felt like a schoolgirl on her first date.

"What do you want Erik?, red meat, chicken or seafood"? "A good fresh lobster would be nice". "I know just the place", Karla said as she swerved out of the parking area and into the heavy DC traffic.

"Two complete lobster dinners" Erik said to the waiter in a very chic restaurant in the middle of downtown, "and a bottle of nice Cabernet wine", "Now where were we"? Erik said to the beautiful tall brunette seated across the table from him who was smiling sheepishly. "I don't know what else I can say, I'm madly in love with you, I have not felt like this about a woman since I was in college". "If you don't feel the same way about me, just let me know, and I will retire to the men's room and flush myself down the toilet".

Karla laughed and said, "I do feel the same way about you Erik, but I need time to think, I'm just overwhelmed", "I understand, it is a load to place on a woman that you have only known for a few hours, so let's enjoy our lunch and cool down".

The waiter began to place the lobster dinners and a bottle of wine on the table before them and said, "Sir would you and the beautiful lady like me to pour your wine"? "Yes, thank you" Erik said as the waiter uncorked the wine bottle and moved around to the side of the table where Karla sat, and poured her glass half full, then he did the same for Erik. "Thank you" Karla said as she smiled at the waiter.

"My name is Gar`son, if you need anything I am at your service" the waiter said as he walked away from the table.

Erik picked up his wine glass along with Karla and looked deeply into her eyes as he clicked the glasses together, and said "to a beautiful and lasting relationship enjoy your lobster".

After driving around the city for the next few hours taking in some tourist sites Karla headed back toward the State Department's building, neither She or Erik said much after lunch and it was about 4:30. Karla parked her car in the visitor's area and turned off the engine, she looked over at Erik and said "it has been a wonderful day thank you very much, and she leaned over toward him and kissed him for the first time since they met. At first it was just a friendly kiss, then they embraced and it became much more than two friends kissing.

Karla's head was swimming and she said, "Erik I may see you upstairs, I need a little time to think". Erik understood, as he got out of the car and was walking toward the visitor's entrance. A lot of things were running through his mind as well. *"Will I ever see her again, did I expose my feelings for her too fast, have I lost control of my senses, after all it was I who set the criteria for being a part of this operation, no attachments I said now look at me I'm so attached to a woman I can hardly think straight".*

Erik was through security and in the war room before some of the group arrived, the President and Secretary were not there yet, it was 4:45, they still had fifteen minutes, as other members of the group began to arrive Erik couldn't help but wonder if Karla would join them.

Every man had returned and the President said, "Let's all take our seats", Erik was still thinking about Karla, when the Secretary said, "well I see we lost one member of the group", then she said to the aide standing next to the door, "please close the door on your way out and post the sign " Do not enter". Erik almost felt a relief as the aide was closing the door, then he heard a feminine voice say just outside the door as it was closing, "its alright I'm a member of the team", as Karla walked through the nearly closed door. "I'm sorry I'm late" "you are not late the Secretary said come and take your seat, we were just getting started".

The President began, "ladies and gentlemen I welcome you to this team and thank you so much for coming, I'm well aware what being a part of this operation could cost all of us and the sacrifices you are making on behalf of the entire world, which may never be revealed to anyone, but mankind will be extremely grateful if we succeed in this operation". "I'm going to give the floor to Madam Secretary at this time and she will brief you on the plan of our operation".

The Secretary of State stood up and walked over to a large easel with several sheets of maps attached, and said, "ladies and gentlemen for those who do not know my name, I am Vanessa Wright, privileged to be the Secretary of State of the greatest nation on earth, and I welcome each of you and want you to know we will all share equally in the decision-making of this undertaking". "With that said let us begin by revealing to all of you what we have learned since we witnessed, what could be the greatest threat of wanton massive destruction of mankind that the world has ever faced".

For the next three hours Vanessa Wright played video clips of the satellite feed that was witnessed by many world leaders when they were gathered at the UN Security chambers just a short time ago.

Those members who were not at the UN showing were astonished and horrified by what they were now witnessing.

The President stood and said, "we have been working with all of these World leaders to give the appearance that we have acquiesced to the demands of this insane group of scientists and military leaders".

"In truth while these World Governments are preparing their people for the inevitable, in a manner not to produce worldwide panic, we here in the United States are developing a Top-Secret plan". "This plan which all of you will take part in is designed to defuse this threat and bring all the perpetrators to justice". "This meeting today is the beginning of that operation". The meeting lasted far into the evening hours and then everyone agreed the next meeting would be hosted by Erik Roskov in the Kremlin in Moscow four weeks from today.

As the group were leaving and heading toward the parking area's Erik said to Karla, "I am so glad you came" Karla looked at Erik and smiled and said, "so am I, I am looking forward to working with you and seeing more of you". Then she said she would like to go somewhere and have a late dinner. Erik answered "I would love to but I'm afraid I can't, I have just enough time to get to Dulles and catch my flight to England". "Can I at least give you a ride to the airport"? "Yes, and we can talk on the way". On the drive to the airport, Erik learned more about Karla, she was an only child and her mother had died when she was born, her father never remarried and raised her by himself in a predominately Jewish neighborhood in Washington, DC. Her father made a living with a small sidewalk stand, selling hot coffee and home baked rolls that he would stay up most of the night baking in their small modest apartment. Karla began working with her father at the stand when she was nine or ten years old after school. She got to know a lot of the politicians in Washington. When she was fifteen and still in school her father purchased the small building he now occupies, and opened his coffee shop.

It was difficult growing up in a Jewish neighborhood and attending public school. She said she was often referred to as a Kike, and some of the kids and their parents called her father a Christ killer. Her father would tell her to "just overlook it darling they don't realize how much they are hurting you they just think they're having fun at your expense". When Karla finished high school with a 3.9 grade-point average she was chosen to speak for the graduating class at their commencement.

When Karla began planning for college, she knew as a Jewish girl in the capital city it would be very difficult to get the scholarships she would need to pay for college, so she decided to change her name from Shalom, to Karla LeVanway, and apply for scholarships under that name. She was able then to get her school records changed to her new name.

She had many offers of scholarships from several colleges and universities in the area and on the East Coast, but she settled on Harvard with a full four-year scholarship. She had every intention of becoming an Advocate Lawyer for civil rights.

Her last year at Harvard, She had several offers from prestigious law firms to join them as a paralegal, and they would pay for her postgraduate studies at a nearby university to complete her law degree, if she would commit to four years with their firms after she passed the bar exam. It all seemed like a wonderful opportunity to Karla.

Then a few weeks before she graduated from Harvard, a recruiting agent from the CIA came and spoke to the class about the opportunities in the Intelligence field of the Government, and Karla began thinking seriously about becoming a CIA agent. When she told her father he was not pleased, he wanted his daughter to become a lawyer, but he told her to follow her heart if that was what she wanted to do he would give her all of his support and love.

She joined the CIA just out of college and worked as an understudy in the field for the first year, and she was promoted to an Agent and assigned to gather information on the Governments of several Middle Eastern countries. Then after being in the field for four years she was offered a position to serve with the NSA, under the jurisdiction of the White House, and she accepted it and that is where she is currently serving.

By the time they reached the airport Erik knew a great deal about Karla, but she knew almost nothing about him and that is how they would have to leave it for now.

Erik checked his luggage and passed through security and boarded his plane bound for Heathrow airport in England. It was a long flight from the US to England, and Erik had a lot of time to think. *"I wish I knew how much Uncle Jerrod was entangled in this whole operation, I love him so much and he did so much for me when I was living with him". "He and my father were so close they were like brothers instead of brothers-in-law". "I can't believe that he had anything at all to do with my father's death, and I believe if he even had any prior knowledge of his death he would surely have prevented it".*

"When I saw him on the dais with Colonel Chechnikov my heart nearly stopped, I am so glad my mother is not alive to see what her beloved brother is involved in".

Then Erik began to think about his position in the British intelligence agency, and it was the influence of his uncle that actually caused him to decide to join the agency.

His uncle Jerrod had been in the agency before he se-mi retired, to take care of his wife, Ida who was dying of cancer. *"It was just a few months after his beloved Ida's death that he responded to my father's request to allow me to come and live with him while I attended school. It was not anything he was coerced into by my father and his sister he was more than happy to have my company in the house, even though I was just a boy". "We did many things together, and as I grew he taught me to hunt game, and when I was out of school for the summer he would take me to the intelligence agencies complex and introduce me to all his old friends at the Agency. All the agents that worked with uncle Jerrod held great respect for him and his service to the agency. It was during these visits and the many exciting stories he told me about his years of undercover operations in the agency, that peaked my interest in becoming a field agent for the British intelligence agency, but I thought I would be living in England, I had no idea my dear mother was going to get cancer and die, and I was going to return to Russia and work for my father as the Director of the former Soviet intelligence agency".*

"So much has happened in my life, and so much I can't understand" Erik thought. Then his thoughts returned to his uncle Jerrod, when Erik turned eighteen years old his uncle gave him his first pistol and trained him to use it very effectively, he still carries that pistol with him at all times. Jerrod encouraged him to enlist in the agency, and he was the one who convinced the agency to assign him to gather information on Project wormwood and the Colonel, although they did not know him

at that time. Erik wondered if the Agency knew of his uncle's or father's involvement in the project when they gave him that assignment.

The Field Agent, Thomas Burkov and Greta, how did they fit in to the puzzle? was Thomas a double agent? Would he ever hear from him again and was there anything he could do on the space station to hinder or disrupt the plan to launch the American space shuttles from the station by the scientists who are in league with the Colonel.

Then, Erik turned his thoughts to the reason he was flying to England. He had received a cryptic message through a "back channel" source while he was still in Moscow, that an agent in the Middle East had made contact with an underground double agent which said he could verify that the Soviet Colonel Chechnikov was in Syria, and under the protection of the Syrian Government even though they had vehemently denied it. He also had information concerning the Syrian Government's preparation to align itself with the nation of Iran, for the purpose of moving militarily on the nation of Israel. He would produce the undeniable evidence that Iran has nuclear warheads, that can be launched any time and they are working overtime to produce an ICBM missile, that can reach anywhere in the European Union and even the shores of the United States of America.

The director of the agency summoned Erik to England to meet with this Agent and discuss these revelations with the agency in the light of Erik's involvement with the World leaders plan to acquiesce to the Colonel's demands concerning Project wormwood. Erik thought, it would be a productive trip because he would finally, after all these years have an opportunity to meet, face to face with Mr. O'Donnell, whom he has been receiving instructions from since joining the Agency, but has never met.

When He was recruited by the British intelligence agency while at Oxford, he was trained by many agents and under the direction of his uncle Jerrod and then he was turned over to his handler who was known to him only as Mr. O'Donnell but he had never met him. That was not unusual in the intelligence community He learned later because they wanted that layer of anonymity between field agents and their handlers, in case an agent was captured he or she could not reveal the identity of their handler which may have several more agents under his supervision in the field. Erik didn't even know if O'Donnell was his real name. But at last he would get to meet him and discuss many things including Thomas Burkov and his undercover involvement with Project wormwood. He wondered if Thomas was an agent when he and Greta met and married.

Had Thomas only married Greta to better conceal his cover in the agency?, so many questions were running through Erik's mind and he couldn't get his new found love, Karla out of his mind either. He had fallen hard the first moment he saw her. He couldn't believe he could let his emotions run wild like he did.

"I am trained in both the British intelligence and Russian intelligence services I should be able to conceal my emotions, but when I am with Karla, I become like a schoolboy with a deep infatuation with the pretty girl in my class".

His mind suddenly went back to his first and only love and her tragic death, and all the years since that fateful day he has never allowed himself to become even remotely attached to another woman. *"I guess it is time, I probably should be thinking of settling down with a good woman and considering raising a family".*

Then Erik's thoughts were suddenly jolted back to reality, he had to try and stop the Colonel's plan or there may not be any place to settle down with a wife and raise a family.

As Erik was thinking of all these things he drifted off to sleep, and did not awaken until his plane touched down on the runway at Heathrow Airport in London.

"It certainly is different here In the USA I had a helicopter fly me from the airport directly to the State Department, where the U.S. President himself was waiting to welcome me". "Oh well this is the UK, and not the only superpower nation in the world", Erik thought as He was riding in a cab toward down town.

Erik arrived at the agency and went directly to the Agency Director's office on the third floor of the main building, where he was greeted by the receptionist behind a large oval desk in the outer office. "Good morning Sir, can I help you"? "I have an appointment to see the Director", "and your name is"? asked the sweet looking young receptionist as she smiled and looked over a sheet of paper with a list of names on it, "Erik Roskov" "please have a seat Mr. Roskov and I'll have someone come and escort you to the Director's office, he is expecting you".

Erik didn't much more than get sat down when a young man dressed in a dark suit came through a locked security door and walked over to where he was sitting, "Mr. Roskov?" the young man said, "yes" Erik said as he stood and reached out to shake the young man's hand, "I'm Tony if you will follow me I will show you to the Director's office". Erik was led down a lighted corridor through a set of double glass doors and into a stately office, where a well dressed, gray-haired man was sitting behind a large mahogany desk. Erik noticed there were world maps occupying one entire wall from floor to ceiling, with hundreds of multicolored pins stuck in them. "Come in" the man said as he stood and came around the desk with his hand extended to greet Erik.

The Director of the British intelligence agency was named Robert Banyan, he was a man about sixty years old with gray hair and a mustache he was a little over six feet tall, and Erik noticed he had a slight limp of his left leg as he walked.

He smiled as he greeted Erik, "good morning Sir it is a pleasure to finally meet you". "Did you have a pleasant flight from the U.S."? "Yes I did". "Have a seat" the Director said, "Erik we have a lot to discuss, and I have asked two other gentlemen to join us". "Sharon will you ask O'Donnell and General Phillips to come to my office please" the Director spoke into the intercom to his receptionist. "Sir, I believe Mr. O'Donnell has left, and General Phillips is on his way in now". "I wanted O'Donnell to take part in these discussions I didn't know he was leaving the building, but he will be in tomorrow and we can brief him then".

A short balding man in a military uniform arrayed with campaign medals appeared suddenly in the doorway of the Director's office, "come in General" the Director said as the short military man moved briskly toward Erik, who had now stood and turned facing the door, "I want you to meet Erik", "Erik I want you to meet General Mark Phillips you two will be seeing a lot of each other in the next several months". General Phillips and Erik shook hands and each said "very pleased to meet you Sir".

"Did you tell O'Donnell We wanted him in this meeting" the Director asked Phillips? "Yes Sir, as soon as I received the memo from you, I contacted O'Donnell and told him". "I don't know why he left the building, Sharon told me".

"Well he must have forgotten, but he will be in the office in the morning we'll brief him then" the Director said "it's not like O'Donnell to forget, the General said, you may need to talk to him" answered General Phillips as he closed the door to the director's office.

"Erik, "I wanted to have this meeting with you because you've been selected by my friend, President Brown as the point man for this sensitive operation. General Phillips has been working close with MI6 and their field agents to set up agency cells all over the EU countries, to be in place when the word comes that you have identified the locations of the

ICBMs". "We are ready to move and disarm the nuclear warheads at a moments notice".

Erik listened to the Director and the General and the outline of their plan, for about two hours. When the meeting was over Erik said he would stop by the office in the morning on his way to Heathrow, because he really wanted to meet Mr. O'Donnell. And see what he had learned about the Colonel.

Back in his hotel room, Erik turned his thoughts again to Karla, what was he going to do and how was he going to justify breaking his own rule to be a part of this most sensitive operation? No relationships he said the only exception being Greta and Otto but they are both a part of the operation, and Bill whose family was out of harm's way.

"Karla is already becoming a liability to me and I just met her. After reviewing all the maps, encrypted codes and locations of the Agents cells that were already set in place by the British intelligence agency, Erik placed the computer disk they were on inside his briefcase and locked it. *"If these ever fell into the hands of our enemies a lot of people and a large part of our operation would be at great risk".* He slid the case under his bed, and fell fast asleep it had been a long tiresome journey from the U.S.

Ring, ring, the telephone woke Erik from a deep sleep in his hotel room, he glanced at the lighted numbers on the clock sitting on his nightstand it was 6:05 a.m. Erik rubbed the sleep from his eyes, swung his body around and placed his feet on the floor, picked up the phone and said ," hello!" "Erik speaking, who is this"? "This is Mr. O'Donnell" the man on the line said in a low tone voice, "the Director asked me to call you, I'm sorry I missed the meeting yesterday". "The Director said you were coming by the office today and that I should call you to let you know I won't be there, I have an urgent trip out of the country". "Erik, I'll be in Russia next Friday I will come to Moscow and we can sit down to discuss all we have learned about our project and the new developments in the Middle East".

"Well I'm truly sorry to hear that Sir" Erik said, "but I will look forward to meeting you in Moscow".

CHAPTER 40

SID DROVE DOWN THE winding mountain road to the small log cabin, it was early in the morning and he had not even had a cup of coffee, he hoped the guys had some hot coffee when he got there. Sid always drew on his instincts that he had honed while serving in the KGB, he always anticipated there was a danger lurking around every corner, and it was no different now, even though you take every precaution possible when he set up this meeting at this out-of-the-way mountain cabin with the men that Daniel and Abram had recruited for the operation.

He could not take any chances of being discovered by the Colonel's thugs, and he was unsure if any of these men that the sergeant recruited may be connected in any way to any of the Colonel's inner-circle since all of these were recruited from the intelligence community.

Sid drove cautiously up to the back of the cabin even though he had to leave the road and drive through some heavy brush and rough terrain he felt it was necessary to arrive undetected by the cabin's occupants.

Sid brought his small 4X4 pickup to a stop about two hundred feet from the back of the cabin, and turned off the engine and opened the door very quietly and slipped out through the heavy brush to the back of the cabin. He couldn't see inside the main room of the cabin from the back, he would have to crawl around to the side where there was a window that would give him a view of all those inside the cabin. He noticed there were only three cars parked out front, and he recognized one of them as the sergeants.

As he rose up from below the side window he could see a number of men, some sitting on the couch and the rest standing drinking coffee. They were all talking and seemed to be at ease. He counted them, and he could see the Sergeant standing, and ten other men in the room.

It was six a.m. and still dark outside so He could see very clearly into the lighted cabin, he waited a few minutes as he watched the men.

Sid had told the sergeant he would be there at 6:30. That would give him a little time to recon the area before entering the cabin, after all he had never met any of these men, and although he trusted the sergeant and Daniel he still had to be cautious. He had instructed the sergeant to only use the name "Black Panther" when introducing and referring to him.

He told the sergeant that he would be wearing a black ski mask, any time he was with the recruits. As he started to put on his ski mask he halted for a moment, when he saw the headlights of a car coming down the road to the cabin. He waited out of sight until the car was parked in front of the cabin with the others, then he drew his revolver from inside his coat and pushed the safety off. The driver got out of the car and strolled over to the porch of the cabin, as he moved toward the door Sid wondered who could this be?

Then as the light from inside the cabin shined through the small window in the front door onto the driver's face, Sid breathed a sigh of relief, as he disengaged the safety of his revolver and slid it back into the holster under his coat.

He pulled the ski mask down over his head, as he stepped out of his hiding place and addressed the driver of the car, who was just about to open the door of the cabin. "Daniel, I wasn't sure if you were going to make it", Sid said as he walked up on the porch to join his old friend entering the cabin. "Hi! Boss or should I say Black Panther"? Daniel said, "Boss, have you met all the team that the sergeant and I have recruited"? "No I haven't, but I'm sure they're all top-notch". Sid and Daniel entered the cabin and all the men inside turned to face them, and they seemed a little startled to see Sid with a ski mask over his head completely concealing his face. "Good morning Sir" Sergeant Zolov said as he approached Sid and held out his hand.

Good morning Sergeant and Gentlemen, you will have to excuse the mask but there is a reason for my concealment as well as this secretive meeting". "Let's get right to the purpose we're all here, Sergeant", Sid said; "how much have they been told about the operation"? Very little Sir all these men are here because I asked them to come and I would trust any one of them with my life. Daniel and I have worked with everyone in this room.

"Good" Sid said as all the men sat down around a table that had been hastily constructed from several card tables. Daniel unrolled a large map out on the table, which depicted the Countries of the world laid out flat rather than a globe, and then he began telling the men what their operation was about, and the guidelines which was to be established. "We do not know yet the location of any of these nuclear arms, we will only establish the protocol that will be followed when we learn of their locations". We must also develop a plan on how we will disarm them".

"We will all probably be in different parts of the world, and will have to communicate with each other. "We have special transmission devices and receiving units which each team will have". "And all our communications will be via satellite through these units". "At this time" Daniel said as he sat down at the table "I'm going to turn the floor over to our leader, who will always be referred to as the Black Panther".

Sid stood up at the end of the table and began explaining the details of the operation, but before he did he said, "all of you gentlemen in this room may be instrumental in saving the entire world for the future of all mankind, and for that reason I must ask each of you to sign the document that sergeant Abram has passed out to each of you". "After you have read and signed this document, you will be committing to a Classified Top-Secret operation, and if there is ever a violation of the details or the protocol of this operation you will be subject to immediate Government prosecution".

For the next ten minutes there was dead silence in the cabin as each of the men perused the document that lay before them. Then all of the men one by one picked up their pen and signed their respective documents. As Sergeant Zolov collected the signed documents, Sid continued, "our communications will be through a satellite TV program aired in Moscow, called the Bill Forney television show".

"We are in the process of transmitting this show via satellite to every country on earth". "We will set up Cell groups in different parts of the world and there will be two of you in each cell group, and you will be the team leaders".

"These Cells will consist of group's of Intelligence agents that will come from the Russian intelligence community, the American CIA, the

British MI6 agency, the Israeli Mass`ad, and the French secret intelligence agency". "The team leaders will be the only persons in each team who will know the details of the operation". "The other members of the teams will learn of the operation on a need-to-know basis, to be determined by each of their team leaders". "Only the team leaders will have the cryptic codes which will allow them to transmit and receive coded information from the broadcasting service".

"These transmissions will be reviewed and approved by me through a clearing house before it is transmitted to the satellite and received by your special units". "I will have a counterpart operating in the United States".

"The communication code has been established, and is the method in which the team leaders will rely on, to validate any information from their field agents or each other". "This phrase will be, **Have you read any good book's lately**"? And the reply will be, "**No I'll wait for the movie**"". "Set that to memory, and make sure you never forget it".

Then Sid placed red X's in various places on the map that was spread out on the makeshift table, and he said, "as soon as we determine the location of each of these nuclear arms throughout the world we will send our Cell groups to those locations with their team leaders". "They will have all the arms and equipment they will need to strike quickly and precisely, the target areas and disarm the nuclear devices at each of those locations". "No strikes will be executed until all six of our Cells are in place, and then only at the signal from our Operation's Center".

"We have reason to believe there is only six locations where the nuclear devices are staged". We also believe that we will learn of their locations very soon". "Are there any questions, or do any of you need clarification on any point so far"? "None so far" one of the agents remarked, "except I do have one question" another agent said, "and that is where will the financing come from for the size of this operation"?

"All your expenses and compensation packages will be handled by your team leaders, but the source of the financing will remain secret".

"Are there any other questions"? Sid asked as he looked around the table.

"Our Worldwide network of intelligence, believes the nuclear devices are staged in the countries and the locations I have marked on the map, but we will not set up our Cells until we have absolute proof of their locations".

"When we leave this cabin none of you will have any contact or communication with each other, you will take the transmitting and receiving units with you, and wait until you are contacted by me". "I'll be using a secure "back channel" to contact each of you, by using the encrypted code that each of you will be issued privately by me before leaving this meeting". "None of your codes will be the same, and I alone will have the master code file".

As each of the men in the cabin were leaving through the front door, they were given a small piece of flash paper upon which was written a code word written by Sid, and they were instructed to memorize it immediately because it would disintegrate in one minute.

It was well into the afternoon when Sid left the cabin to return to the city and to his apartment. He could not help but wonder how long before Erik knew the locations of the nuclear devices, and if the Colonel would deploy one or more of them to show the world his strength, before they were located and disarmed.

CHAPTER 41

I T WAS ONLY THREE days before the President of Russia and Erik Roskov would host the meeting in the Kremlin with all the principles coming in from the U.S. State Department and some of the World Leaders, including the United States president and Secretary of State. And Erik could not get his mind off of Karla.

He had arranged to pick up Karla at the airport, she was flying in a day early before the meeting, to give her and Erik some time to have dinner together and talk about what they both felt concerning each other, his heart was beating faster the closer he got to the airport.

"Hi beautiful" Erik said as he greeted Karla at the gate as she disembarked from her plane, "did you have a good flight"? "It was long but very restful and it gave me a lot of time to think". "I hope your thoughts were on us and they were good thoughts, because I've been thinking good thoughts about us ever since I met you in Washington". Karla laughed and said, "that's, so sweet of you Erik, I too have been thinking about us and my thoughts have been very good also".

Erik took Karla by the hand and through her large shoulder bag on over his shoulder and said, "let's go get your luggage I have a wonderful place picked out for us to have dinner". "Great"! Karla said as she walked briskly beside Erik "I am famished they don't feed you on those planes very well".

Erik retrieved Karla's luggage from the carousel, as Karla pointed it out to him and then they went directly to where Erik's car was parked.

"Don't I have to go through customs"? Karla said as they walked out the door of the international terminal. "I am the Director of the Department of intelligence Karla if we can't trust me who can we trust"? Karla smiled affectionately and said, "How nice it is to know someone so influential".

They drove to the restaurant which Erik had chosen, without saying anything. They only exchanged demure glances at each other while smiling.

The restaurant Erik had chosen was in a very chic district of the city of Moscow, called Eurase's, it was a very chic place to dine, and when they arrived and the valet took their car and they were escorted in through the front doors, they were met by the owner, whose name was Ravien, He was a handsome man wearing a dark formal suit. He reached for Karla's hand and bowed gracefully to kiss it while saying, "Welcome to my humble establishment, it is my pleasure and honor to have you". "Erik my good friend you are also welcome" as he embraced Erik as a long-lost brother.

"It's good to see you again" Erik said as he turned to face his good friend Ravien, "this is the lovely Karla from America that I've been telling you about". "I'm so happy to see you were not making her up Erik, and she is even more beautiful than you said she was". Karla blushed with embarrassment as she said, "I am very pleased to meet you Ravien, now can we eat? I am famished". They all laughed as Ravien escorted them to their table.

They had a delightful dinner and throughout their dinner they spoke very little about their relationship, instead they each wanted to know all that the other had found out about the Colonel and the project since they departed at the airport in Washington.

After dinner Erik said good bye to his old friend, Ravien, and they left the restaurant heading for the hotel where Karla would be staying while she was in Russia. When they were in the car, before Erik started the engine, Karla slid over to him, threw her arms around his neck and drew him passionately to her and kissed him passionately. Then she said, "Erik, darling I have never felt this way about a man before, and it is delightful and at the same time confusing and scary". "I am a highly trained Agent, and I have been trained to focus on the assignment that I am involved in, because my assignments almost always put other people's lives at risk".

"I feel the same way", Erik said, "I love you so much that I spend every waking hour thinking of you, and wondering if you feel the same for me". "I wish we could turn back the clock about ten years, before either of us were involved in trying to save the world from destruction".

When they reached the hotel, and Karla got settled into her room, they sat down on the sofa and without saying a word, began kissing passionately. Karla said, "darling Erik, I have been nearly out of my mind waiting to come to Russia and be with you again, I love you so very much and I know you love me also, but I believe this assignment is too critical for both of us, for either of us to lose our focus", "and for that reason our personal relationship must be put on hold, it must be purely professional until the present danger to mankind is passed".

"I have been rehearsing what I would say to you for weeks", Karla said "and I can never conceive of not being a part of your life but I know it can never be until this assignment is completed and it is only then, I want you to embrace me and tell me you can't live without me". While Karla was still speaking Erik took her in his arms and wiped the tears with his handkerchief, that were now streaming down her face, and held her tightly against his massive chest and said, "I know darling", as tears began to form in his own eyes, "the circumstances that brought us together is also going to keep us apart and it's killing me on the inside". "I have only loved once before in my entire life and that was long ago, and is just a faint memory, and my love for you is like a raging volcano on the inside and has been ever since we met in Washington".

"Darling, Erik said ",as he looked into Karla's beautiful tear filled eyes "as soon as this assignment is finished and this world is a safer place I will come for you, and no matter where you are on this planet I will find you and take you to be Mrs. Erik Roskov, and love you for the rest of my life". " Oh Erik darling I love you with all my heart, and I cannot wait to make you happy as your loving wife".

They embraced each other for what seemed like an eternity, neither of them speaking a word then Karla said, "Boss would you like something to drink"? "I have some soft drinks the hotel left as complimentary beverages and some water". "I'll have a glass of ice water", Erik said.

Karla brought Erik a large glass of ice water and sat down on the sofa beside him and said, "Did you finally meet your mysterious Mr. O'Donnel when you were in England"? "No! I didn't and he was supposed to meet me here in Moscow when I returned but he never showed up, I am beginning to wonder if he really exists or if he is just someone that the British intelligence made up".

"I must be leaving" Erik said as he placed his glass down on the table next to the sofa, and you need to get some sleep we have a long day ahead of us tomorrow". "You're right Boss" Karla said as she embraced and kissed him, I will see you at the Kremlin". "I will come and pick you up in the morning", Erik said. "No I should drive myself just give me directions so I can find it". "Then let me send my driver to take you there if that's okay". "Okay Karla said, tell him I'll be waiting in the breakfast bar any time after 7:00".

At seven a.m. the next morning a small wiry looking man who was completely bald and wearing a small black mustache and goatee beard, approached Karla at the breakfast bar and said ", you must be Karla, Erik sent me to pick you up".

Karla turned to look at the small man wearing a chauffeur's uniform holding his hat in his hand, *he looks almost sinister if Erik had not sent him, there is no way I would get into a car with him".*

"I'm Karla and I'm ready to go" she said as she picked up her purse and briefcase, "let me take that" the driver said as he reached out for her briefcase, "thank you", she said and handed him her briefcase, and followed him out to the Government car that was parked in front of the hotel with the motor running Karla noticed the driver had a slight limp of one leg as he walked.

They were at the Kremlin building downtown in about an hour, and Karla was amazed how the driver seemed to never get stuck in the congested early morning traffic in the downtown city of Moscow, he just found an alternate road and was never at a complete standstill, he seemed to know every short-cut.

Sid drove the limo into the underground parking garage at the Kremlin as he was talking to someone on his cell phone. "We have just arrived Boss". "I will take her up from the South end in elevator no. three, as you instructed, I'll call you when she is on the elevator".

"Miss Karla", Sid said as he escorted her to the elevator, Erik will meet you at the elevator on the fifth floor and escort you to the conference room where your meeting is being held, I'll go with you and put you on the elevator, and it has been a pleasure to share your company".

Karla followed Sid to the designated elevator and while they were walking she tried to take in as much of this massive structure that she could, never in a lifetime she thought she would actually be visiting the

Kremlin in Moscow. She remembered all too well that all through her training, the Cold War between the Soviet Union and the United States, and the open hostility between the two countries.

Karla entered the elevator, and said "thank you" to Sid who she thought had been very gracious and courteous to her. "Just push the button for the fifth floor and Erik will be there to meet you", Sid said as he stepped out of the elevator.

Erik looked very handsome dressed in a dark blue business suit wearing a white shirt and dark blue tie, she had not seen him dressed in a suit before and she thought, *"He is gorgeous".* "Good morning", Erik said as he reached for her briefcase and took her by the hand, we are meeting in the main conference room down the hall don't be nervous about the armed security guards you see in the corridor we can't be too careful, after all we have the President of the two most powerful Countries on earth and all their top civilian and military leaders in one room".

Karla walked down the corridor with Erik and noticed all the armed guards in military uniforms, each of them were either holding an automatic rifle or was wearing a business suit with a clear outline of a concealed weapon under their coat. When they reached the door to the main conference room a security officer opened it and let them in, and Karla recognized some of the men and women seated around a large highly polished conference table, but some she did not. She knew the President of the United States seated next to The Secretary of State, and directly across the table from them was the New Russian President, she recognized him from the many appearances he had made on television.

Erik took his place at the end of the table after seating Karla in her seat. "I think we're all here now" Erik said, "I want to thank all of you for coming and I extend a very cordial welcome to all of you to our Country from our Government and our President".

"I think most of you know each other from our meeting in the United States, but we have some new faces as well, so I would ask each of you beginning with our honored guest, President Brown from the United States to introduce yourself and tell the other members your occupation and your position".

After President Brown greeted the members gathered around the conference table each member stood and did the same, the new President of Russia welcomed all of them and said he wished they were all there under different circumstances. Then the floor was turned back over to Erik.

Erik began by saying, "an enormous amount of preparation has occurred since we met in the United States, we have most of our teams in place and they are being trained to attack and take control of each of the ICBM locations and disarm all of the nuclear warheads at each site, before any of them can be launched". "We have not yet found the locations but we believe we are very close we are interrogating several top officers linked to the wormwood Project and the Colonel. They turned themselves into our Government within the past two weeks they were disenchanted with the Colonel and his escape to the Middle East, leaving them to be arrested for their participation in the project".

"These Officers have told us that the Colonel kept all these locations secret and that they were on a CD which was kept in his office at the ISS Agency". "We have located a box of disks which are being reviewed by two members of our team now".

"We have recruited teams in Russia, England, Israel, France, Germany and Greece as well as our friends in America, and others are being contacted". "All of these teams are being trained by our security forces, the CIA and MI6 in England". "They will all be ready to move on command from the central command center located here in the Kremlin". "All of our team members have received special transmitting and receiving devices and are being trained in their use, all Operation transmissions will be sent through Bill Forney's worldwide satellite TV program originating here in Moscow". "We owe a great deal of gratitude to all of you for your personal participation in this worldwide endeavor, and especially to President Brown and His State Department along with the Federal communications commission, who have cut through all the bureaucracy and red tape to allow us to set up the satellite links and provide all the necessary financing for this mission".

"We will be asking each of your Governments to participate in financing, the massive field operations when we give the command to move".

Many of the details of the plan and the logistics to carry them out were reviewed and discussed with all the members at the meeting which went on for about five hours, and the only point of contention among the members was the secret transmission code that only Erik and a few agents and a handful of the members would have access too. Some of the members felt they all should have the access codes, but President Brown, and the Russian President overruled that request. No date or place was set for their next meeting. Erik said they would contact each of them as soon as the disks that revealed the ICBM locations were found.

Erik drove Karla back to her apartment, where she packed her clothes and He drove her to the airport, and when they reached the airport terminal he said to her, "the hardest thing I have ever done is to let you return to the U.S., and I know I must but when this operation is over you will become Mrs. Erik Roskov, and we will never again be separated". "Erik I feel the same way" Karla said while wiping the tears from her eyes, "I can hardly wait and I know it has to be this way". Erik kissed Karla goodbye then began the long lonely walk back to his car.

Erik returned to his apartment instead of going to his office, and his mind was moving at a rapid pace all the responsibility that had been placed on him in the last few months was overwhelming, and then there was Karla.

When he entered his apartment he noticed the red light flashing on his answering machine, which alerted him he had a message, he pushed the button and heard the message from Otto, "Erik I think we have found something, as soon as you can stop by the cabin Erik it is urgent". Erik went directly to Otto's cabin, he was anxious to discover what Otto had found out. "Sit down", Otto said as he poured Erik and himself a cup of coffee "and I will show you what I am so excited about". Erik was sitting in a chair next to Otto at the computer when Otto slipped in the disk and it began to run, it was similar to the disks they had previously reviewed, a list of names and a heading titled "the wormwood file", but it also had the emblem of an eagle next to the name of the Colonel.

"This is what I want you to see" Otto said as he moved the cursor to the eagle and clicked the mouse, the screen changed and a new window opened up and the words "incorrect password access denied" flashed across the screen. Otto said "we have looked at all these disks we found at the international space station and this is the only one with that eagle symbol, we overlooked it at first, but as I was replaying it I happened to move the cursor over the eagle and it highlighted and I clicked on it and discovered this "No Access" file.

"Have you tried to access the file without using a password, through the backdoor Otto"? Erik said. "Yes, and as you know I am well trained in computer science, and have been trained to break encrypted codes of all kinds, but I've been unable to find a way into this file through a back door it has too many protective firewalls and encrypted codes like I have never seen before". "That is why I called you, to see if you can get a code breaking expert, in either your department or the CIA to see if they can break the encryptions and access the file, I believe it may contain some very important information, maybe even the location of the nuclear missiles".

"I think you may be right Otto, "I will call President Brown and see if he will send a code breaking team here from the CIA". Erik was not sure just who he could trust in their Intelligence Department, or if he could even trust the new Russian President. Too many developments had come to light in the last six months, about his Government and the new President that made him cautious about information he revealed to them.

The new President had begun to override the authority of the Politburo and began moving the Russian Government back toward a totalitarian Government and away from the state of democracy that was being developed since the fall of the Soviet empire. He had recently revealed that the Russian Government under his authority had breached the nonproliferation of nuclear missiles technology agreement, by selling the nation of Iran not only the nuclear technology but also assisting them with Russian engineers and scientists to accelerate the development, of weapons grade nuclear material, and the centrifuges to produce a nuclear bomb.

This was all done without sanctions from our own Government leaders or without regard to the rest of the European Nations national security concerns.

The only two countries that refuse to vote in the UN Security Council to implement sanctions against Iran, for refusing to stop the development of nuclear weapons grade plutonium is Russia and China. These and other developments have made Erik more cautious of what intelligence concerning the wormwood files he reveals to his new President.

Erik contacted the Secretary of State in the U.S. after not being able to reach President Brown, and requested her permission to speak directly to the Director of the CIA. Permission was granted and Erik contacted the Director and requested that he send a select group of code breakers to Russia to see if they can access the newly discovered file. The Director was more than happy to meet that request, and he would send his best team at once.

Erik sent Sid and several cars to the airport to pickup the CIA team from America, and when they arrived at his office in the Kremlin he was surprised to see Roger Wilson the agent attached to the national security agency, who was present at the first meeting in Washington where he met Karla.

"Come in gentlemen" Erik said as the team of CIA code breakers arrived outside his office door, "sit down and let's get started I am somewhat surprised to see you agent Wilson I didn't realize the Director of your CIA would send an agent from the NSA with his team of code breakers".

"I was sent by the White House", Rogers said "to oversee the operation and act as a liaison to President Brown to inform him of any breakthroughs we have, He wants to know immediately".

"We have a secure operations room set up down the hall, all the equipment you requested is there and this is Otto one of my trusted agents who will be assisting you". Otto stood to his feet and greeted everyone and said he had made accommodations for all the team members to stay right here in the Kremlin instead of separate hotel rooms. All their meals will be catered in from outside and they will work in two shifts around the clock until they have successfully accessed the file.

Everyone motioned in agreement to Otto, and Roger Wilson said "We are ready let's get the operation started".

The hours became longer as the days became shorter, as the teams of agents used every classified piece of software available, day after day and through the nights. After ten days and nights of trying to break the code for the password to access the file Erik was at his apartment and Otto was at home with Greta when the phone rang, and Otto saw it was his personal cell phone connected directly to the team in the Kremlin. "This is Otto what is it"? "We're in", said the excited voice of agent Wilson, and we need you and Erik here before we move any farther". "I'll call Erik, and we will be there in an hour, tell no one other than the other team members of the breakthrough until Erik and I get there".

Erik and Otto arrived at the Kremlin after about an hour, all the members of both teams were in the operations room drinking coffee and eating sweet rolls that had been brought in for them, and all greeted Erik and Otto as they entered the room. "We did it" they all said in unison and "we are into the files".

Otto walked over to the desk where one of the computer screens was lit up and on the screen were the words "Wormwood Top-Secret files". Otto sat down in the chair and began tapping his fingers across the key board in front of him, and then he stopped as Erik began to speak. "On behalf of the leaders of our two countries I want to say how much we appreciate the monumental task you all have accomplished, and someday you will know the great worldwide significance of it, but for now it must remain Top-Secret, and you team members do not have Top-Secret clearance with the exception of agent Wilson". "If you will pack your equipment and retrieve your personal gear and meet my driver at the north end of the corridor in the elevator in two hours, he will take you to a restaurant downtown and all of you will have a hearty breakfast, and then he will drive you to the airport where you will all board a private Government plane to take you home to America".

After the code breaking team had gathered all their equipment they had brought with them and retrieved their personal belongings from their rooms, and left the complex, Erik said to Agent Wilson, "let's see what we have found before you call President Brown".

Otto began tapping the keys again as Erik and agent Wilson looked on, at first it appeared to be just another disk that listed the name of the wormwood project participants and their rolls, but as Otto continued to scroll down through the names they saw a list of five locations in three different Countries. They were all identified with Latitude and Longitude co-ordinances, and beside each of them was the words "Wormwood ICBM armed". Then they listed the names of the commanders at each location and two officers with each of them. With almost shock Erik and agent Wilson watched as Otto scrolled down into additional information of each missal sight. There were launch codes and targeted locations for each missal to strike.

Erik said to Otto in a halting voice, "Otto burn a copy of this disk and write down the password the code breakers used to access the file and give it to agent Wilson, and He can hand deliver it to the White House, this information is much too sensitive to reveal, even through a secure encrypted transmission". "I agree" agent Wilson said "I will personally deliver it to President Brown, and I will leave within the hour".

Otto burned a copy of the Top-Secret disk and placed it in a diplomats pouch stamped with a Presidential seal and gave it to agent Wilson, who left with it immediately, in a private Russian jet which Erik arranged for, bound for America.

Sid entered the operations room after agent Wilson left and sat down next to Otto and took out of the desk a small notepad and began to write down the latitude and longitude position of each of the locations where the five ICBMs were, as shown on the computer screen. Then next to each location he copied the launch codes and the Commanders names.

CHAPTER 42

B ILL FORNEY WAS IN his office at the studio in a production meeting
with Dan his producer when the phone rang on his private line.
Dan knew the rule of Bill's office, if he is talking on his private line, it is
confidential and possibly even classified therefore since he does not have
Government security clearance, He is expected to leave the room, while
his Boss is talking.

Dan knew all about the worldwide satellite network that Bill's program
was now being broadcast over, but he was not privy to the operation that
his boss and his program are now playing, a major role in. He did not have
knowledge of the operation, or did he have Top-Secret security clearance.
When all the finances began to be available and all the necessary licenses
and broadcasting permits were obtained without any of the usual red
tape or Government bureaucracy he knew they were involved in some
Government project, but he didn't know what it was. Since they were
now broadcasting worldwide Dan had to hire more staff and reporters
and he had to re-format their entire show. They were now broadcasting
twenty four hours a day and running exposés of different Governments
in different Countries, and their leaders corruptive activities all over the
world. He and his boss rarely had time to sit and talk privately any more,
and so on this rare occasion he was upset when Bill's private phone rang
and he was expected to leave the office while Bill took the call. Dan

then left the office, and retired to his own office as soon as Bill's private phone rang.

"Good morning Bill", Erik said, "I have some great news I have located the treasure we have all been searching for". "Now it is just a matter of getting all our treasure hunting teams in place and ready to go". "That is great news Erik".

"Bill we will have a meeting at my place tonight at eight o'clock to plan our strategy". "Bill do you have complete confidence in Dan"? "Yes I do, why are you asking"? "I believe it is time to bring Dan on board and make him a part of our effort". "How do you feel about that"? "I think it is an excellent idea, Dan has been with me since the beginning of the program, and he is a very loyal and trusted friend". "Good, can you bring him with you to the meeting tonight"? "I sure will Erik, and I think he will be a great asset to the operation". "OK Bill, but have him ride in the security car with you instead of driving his own car, we can't be too careful now when we are this close to the treasure". "After tonight I will assign a driver and security team to him as well".

Bill buzzed his secretary as he hung up the phone, "send Dan back into my office" Dan returned to Bill's office and sat down he hoped that he and his boss would not be disturbed again.

"Dan I would like you to go with me to a meeting tonight are you free"? "Sure boss where at and what is it about"? "I can't tell you that" Bill said, "but it is going to place you in a role with much more responsibility". Dan wondered how much more responsibility he could take on, he ran the entire program now, he wondered if this new and increased role had anything to do with all the twenty four hour security that had recently been assigned to the station, there are guards at every door and elevator, and it is plain to see by the slight bulge in the coats that they are armed. His boss never drives his own car anymore, he is driven everywhere in a security car even to his home. Bill interrupted his thoughts and said "you will go with me in the security car, we will leave about 6:30" "Okay Boss I'll be ready".

Erik called Sid and told him the meeting would take place tonight at 8:00, and asked him to contact Daniel and the sergeant and have them there also. Then he called Otto and told him of the meeting and said he wanted Greta to attend as well as him.

Agent Roger Wilson went directly to the State Department the day after his arrival back in the United States after the meeting in Moscow, he did not reveal what he had that was urgent, on the phone to the Under

Secretary of State, but he convinced him it was urgent enough to set up a meeting with the Secretary.

All the members of the team that were contacted were present, at 8:00 and Erik began by introducing Otto and Greta to the team members they had not met, and then he introduced Bill and Dan to all the team members, and said, "Dan is the latest member to come on board with the team, he is the producer and station manager for Bill's Satellite TV program and will be the direct liaison for all our teams communications". Dan looked at Bill with a puzzled look and then said, I have not been briefed on the operation yet, but I am honored to be a part of the team".

Erik then revealed that Otto and Greta had located the disks the Colonel had left behind that gave the locations in each country the missals were staged, he then briefed all of them about the code breakers and their help. Then Erik asked if all the team leaders had been trained to operate their communicating devices. Daniel and the sergeant assured Erik that all the team leaders had been trained and are ready to go.

Erik unrolled a world map on the kitchen table and began putting the names of the teams on it, and assigning them to their respective Cell groups and the Countries they would be operating in.Ukraine, Georgia, East Pakistan, Syria' and Uzbekistan, all but one of these countries were in the old Soviet Union Block. The team leaders would be sent in pairs and each pair would command a team of fifteen to twenty five field agents. "Our plan must be flawless" Erik said "if it is to succeed". "All of our teams must be in place before the signal is given to take control of the sites and disarm the missile warheads". "In some countries yours will be a clandestine operation, and in some countries you will have the full support of that Countries Government, but in no case will anyone be recruited into the operation that we have not already trained". The logistics of each individual site will be fraught with many obstacles, getting equipment and supplies into many of the areas will be a monumental task without being discovered, and if anyone of your operations are discovered and compromised before all the teams are in place, that operation will be aborted and all other operations will be put on hold". "Ladies and Gentlemen I cannot tell you how important this operation is, it may be the preservation of life as we know it on this planet".

"Sergeant Zolov and Daniel and the Black Panther will begin staging all equipment, personnel and supplies". An agent of the NSA from the United States and I will run interference for you through the U.S.A. and in all the Countries where you will be traveling". "No part of this operation can be hindered or delayed for any reason, lack of equipment, Visa's, Passports, Finances or any Government bureaucracy, nothing can be allowed to hinder the operational forces". "All of the team leaders will have carte blanche, for anything they need, and all it takes to make it happen, is a coded contact to me or my counterpart in the United States".

Erik adjourned the meeting, and everyone left at 1 a.m., each team member understood that tremendous weight of responsibility he or she was being asked to carry.

After all the members left Erik's apartment, except Otto and Greta, Erik sat down with them and instructed them in their assignments, which was to continue reviewing all the documents that had been discovered to see if there were any other sites that were not revealed on the first disk.

Otto would preside over the space station agency and monitor all communications too and from the International space station.

Erik returned to his office early the next morning and contacted the national security agency in America and spoke to Karla and informed her that she would be his counterpart overseeing all the operations, and she would be known only as "the little lamb", and she should not respond to anyone other than those who knew her by this code name.

CHAPTER 43

E RIK TURNED ON HIS TV to the BBC World News, and discovered that
the Russian President had signed an agreement with the communist
country of China to install natural gas and oil pipelines from the
burgeoning gas and oil reserves in the Siberian Peninsula to feed that
country's rapidly growing economy. This was done without consulting
the Politburo or any of the Government Leaders in the EU countries. He
also announced a growing concern he had, of the U.S. trying to impose
their ideology and their form of Government on the Russian people, and
it was creating a fracture in the two countries relationships, and because
the U.S.A. had not been able to meet their commitments on financing
and supplying the international space station, he was discontinuing their
agreement and signing a new agreement with the Chinese Government
to jointly finance and maintain the supplies of the international space
station. This was done without consulting with the U.S.

Upon receiving word of this unilateral act president Brown said
in a news conference at the White House that "this act seems on the
surface to be a re-establishment of the old totalitarian dictatorship,
and the discarding of the Democratic Government that the people of
Russia awaited so long to see". "The new Russian Democracy has been
thriving in the country since the break-up of the old Soviet Union, and
their economy is just beginning to increase and lead them into a great
recovery". The President went on to say, "it was very disturbing to him

166

and the Government of The U.S.. A Reporter asked the President, what he thought about the agreements that Russia has made with China? "We understand", said the President "that the pipeline which is now under construction will be completed in about three years, and will supply China with approximately one million barrels of oil a day, and enough natural gas to adequately drive China's huge expanding economy". "I do not believe this is a wise and prudent move by the Russian Government, because China is a neighbor who has in recent years built up their military strength to unprecedented levels". "China is a neighbor who needs to expand her borders to accommodate her exploding population and she is bordering both with Russia and India".

While Erik was watching and listening to this disturbing news, the phone rang in his office, it was the Director of British intelligence, Robert Banyan "hello" Erik said "Sir is there something wrong"? "No Erik this is a courtesy call to let you know that agent O'Donnell will be contacting you in Moscow tomorrow morning, and he wants to set up a meeting with you". "Traveling with him is General Mark Phillips whom you met in London". "They have some interesting news to tell you". "Erik, have you discovered any information on the location of the Colonel's machines yet"? "Not yet Sir but we believe we are close". After the Director hung up the phone Erik mused, that *"The Director of MI6 was not in the loop, and he would have to wait until the British prime minister was notified through diplomatic channels by President Brown".*

The next morning Erik was waiting in his office at the Kremlin for a call from agent O'Donnell, he knew he would call on his cell phone instead of running it through the Kremlin's phone system and he would want to meet somewhere away from the Kremlin.

The British have never fully trusted the new Russian President or his Government. The call came at 10:30 a.m. "Erik this is General Phillips, can you get away from your office for a few hours to meet O'Donnell and me"? "I sure can" Erik said, "where would you like to meet"? "This is my first time in Russia so you suggest a place and we will be there". Erik had already got permission from his old friend Sid to use his rented apartment just outside the city, he is out of town on business and the apartments empty and out-of-the-way it was a perfect place to meet. Erik gave the General the directions and said he would be there at 11:30. "We will be there" the General said and hung up the phone.

Erik told his secretary he would be out of the office the rest of the day, and then drove directly to Sid's apartment, and let himself in with the key

Sid had given him. He put on a pot of coffee he found in the kitchen. He had stopped on his way to the apartment and picked up some sandwiches and sweet rolls, in case the General and O'Donnell were hungry when they arrived.

Sid's apartment was three rooms located just outside the city, he was the only tenet and he lived on the ground floor. It was a perfect place for Sid to live under his alias since he came out of hiding.

While Erik waited for his visitors to show up he wondered what O'Donnell looked like and what kind of man he was, he was relieved to know he at least existed and he would finally meet him.

As Erik watched out the window he saw a black Mercedes pull into the drive, it was about 11:30. Erik watched as two men got out, he recognized the driver, it was the General whom he had met in England, but he could not see the passengers face because he wore a wide brimmed hat that was pulled down in front and concealed his face. Both men walked toward the front door cautiously, looking around nervously. Erik opened the front door to let the men in, "good morning General Phillips", Erik said, "it is good to see you again, and welcome to Moscow".

The two men entered the apartment and Erik closed the front door after looking to see if any other cars were in sight. The other man removed his hat and turned to face Erik.

Erik nearly fainted when he saw the man that was facing him was Uncle Jerrod Stevens, who had a warrant out for his capture by Interpol, and The United States, for treason. The warrant was for his participation in the Colonel's diabolical plan to destroy the planet.

This man was now standing face to face with him, and he had not seen or heard from him since he was on the dais with the Colonel during the satellite transmission at the UN Security Council. Erik was shocked.

"Erik", Son" Jerrod said, "I have a lot of explaining to do, and that's why I'm here today". Erik said, "where is Mr. O'Donnell"? as he looked at General Phillips". "Sit down Erik" the General said and I will explain". "Your uncle Jerrod and agent O'Donnell are one in the same". Erik was dumb-founded and was and filled with disbelief as General Phillips and Jerrod Stevens began to unfold the most bizarre story he had ever heard.

"When I requested the agency to recruit you, and give you this assignment it was not without a plan". "I went undercover and infiltrated the project we are now discussing to learn first hand about it's organization and it's agenda". "The agency first learned of the project two years before you were recruited, and assigned, but we had to wait until you finished college, and we had not planned for a contingency such as your mother having cancer and dying". "I recruited your father to lecture for the organization, but he only knew it as an environmental organization that was trying to rally world governments to assist the Organization in stopping the destruction of the planet's ecology". "Our message was, the wanton release of greenhouse gases created acid rain in third world countries, destroying their soil, and preventing them from growing productive crops to feed themselves". "Because he was a three star general in the Russian military, we believed he could talk to the world leaders and bring together the people in massive rallies". "He also would have access to speak in the UN Security Council".

"Ivan began to suspect the organization was more sinister and had a clear agenda to use whatever means necessary to bring the Western Governments to their knees". "Using whatever tactics they could to stop the pollution of the planet, and that is probably why he was killed, I could not tell you any of this before now".

"A short time before your mother was stricken with cancer your father flew to England and confronted me and the agency, the agency at my behest took him into our confidence and revealed the true nature of this organization". We did not know then who the person or persons at the top of the organization were, and who was pulling the strings, or financing the operation".

"Even though I was on the inside and had some degree of knowledge, and was a spokes person I was unable to reach into the top echelon of the organization and reveal their identities". "Your father however had at his disposal the entire Soviet Intelligence service, and was able to reveal the identity of the Colonel, and his role in the organization in less than six months". "Our agency had been trying for two years just to get the Colonels name".

"Chechnikov knew that once he and his planned operation was revealed by your father it was just a matter of time that your father would have to be eliminated". "The day before your father was killed he called me in England and told me that he was going to shut down the project, because the Colonel and the organization were becoming too dangerous". "He said he had confronted Chechnikov about the incident which almost got you killed and he was going to issue orders of reassignment to him, which would remove him as the Director of the international space station agency".

"When he told him that, he went into a rage, and he must have went the next day to visit your father and see if he could get him to change his mind, but your father was already writing a new order of assignment for him, and when he told the Colonel, the Colonel shot and killed him, and arranged the scene to look like your father took his own life". "Your father had found out just how dangerous a man the Colonel was but it was too late for your father, and for that I am deeply sorry".

"I am still working undercover and the Colonel does not know my real identity in the agency, and we have to keep it that way so we can know from the inside what is taking place".

"Erik, the Colonel knows all about the codes that you discovered, which reveals the locations of the ICBMs". He also is aware of the strategic commandos you put in place to disarm them".

"Something you and President Brown do not know, and that is why we are here today and I am risking my life". "I left Syria and the Colonel two weeks ago giving the excuse I had to tie up some loose ends for the project, and when I return I am to oversee the operations from the Middle East". "The reason I really came here today was to brief you and the agency in our Government, on the discovery I made while in Syria".

"Erik you must get the information I'm going reveal to you today to President Brown and brief him as soon as possible". "Since the Colonel found out you have the ICBM locations, and he knows about the commando cells you are about to launch against the ICBMs locations, He has revealed to a select group within the Organization, that he has another plan, which is even more diabolical than what you already know". "He has no plan to try and stop your operation to take possession and disarm the missals".

"What you and President Brown are not aware of is, that when the old Soviet Union was broken up, not only did many of the top military leaders like the Colonel and top Soviet nuclear scientists leave the Country and went to Syria, but they also have in their possession an Oscar class Soviet nuclear sub that is armed with twenty nuclear missals, and multiple warheads, which are capable of striking any target on earth". "So you see how insignificant the five land-based missile launch sites are".

"Erik the Supreme Commander of the political arm of this organization who controls the Colonels military operations has decided that the U.S. is not complying with the ultimatum given it, and he is authorizing a preemptive nuclear strike on a major city in the U.S. from this sub, I do not know which city, but it will be carried out within the next thirty days". I understand that there will be a ten day warning to allow as many civilians to leave the city as possible before the missile is deployed".

"The Colonel and the Supreme Commander are aware that the U.S. can deploy its strategic Defense initiative and destroy the missile, but if they do that, then the Commander will give the order to launch ten of his ICBM's from the sub, each of them armed with multiple nuclear warheads, into ten of the most populated cities in the world, including LosAngeles, Calif., New York City and Chicago, he knows that the American Nuclear Defense shield can't stop all of them". "He plans on so many people being killed, that it will bring the American Government to their knees and force them to comply with their ultimatum".

"We have also learned that these ICBM's are armed with unique nuclear warheads, that were designed during the arms build-up in America, during the cold war between the Soviet Union and the U.S., what makes them unique is, they are detonated in the atmosphere rather than on the ground, and they kill people and leave structures nearly unscathed". "They are known as "green bombs".

"When they were first developed in the U.S., the technology was leaked to the press, and there was such a condemnation of them that, then President Reagan stopped the development of them, calling them inhumane". "The Soviet Union continued the development of them".

"Erik you must convince President Brown not to deploy the strategic Defense initiative, it will be a great sacrifice but it will only be loss of one cities population instead of a possible one third of the population of mankind, and possibly an end of life on this planet as we know it". "I wish I could go with you to Washington but that is not possible, I have to return to Syria tomorrow, but I wish you success and Godspeed".

After The General and Erik's uncle Jerrod left the meeting, Erik's mind was racing, he had so much to think about. At first he felt relieved to know his uncle was not a criminal or a traitor, and then he began to have suspicions that this may be a ploy by the Colonel. *"Could Jerrod and the General both be a part of this diabolical plan, and were they giving him this information to convince the President of The United States to disarm their nuclear Defense Shield, leaving them vulnerable to a "first strike" attack".*

As all these different thoughts were running through Erik's mind, he began to wonder if his uncle was complicit in his father's murder, and was one of the ring leaders in this Organization after all.

The next day Erik was summoned to the office of the President in the Kremlin, to discuss the overall Russian Intelligence community. He was led by armed guards into the President's office, where the President's private secretary asked him to sit and wait until the President called for him.

Erik was arranging some files he had brought with him when the door to the President's office opened and the President walked toward Erik smiling, "so glad to see you again Erik", as he reached out his hand to Erik, "come in to my office, we have a lot to talk about". Erik picked up his brief case and gathered the loose files he had been instructed to bring with him, and followed the President into his office and sat down. The President spoke to his secretary on his intercom and told her to hold all his calls, and cancel all his appointments for today.

This was the first time Erik had ever been inside The President's office, all the other meetings he had with him were conducted in conference rooms. It was a very large office and furnished in a grand style. The President's desk was placed in the center of the large room and file cabinets floor-to-ceiling lined one complete wall, the remaining walls were nicely decorated with Russian murals and hanging pictures, Erik was surprised to see a large photograph of the former American President Ronald Reagan.

"Sit down Erik, would you like to have a coffee and a roll"? No, I'm fine thank you Sir". "Erik, the reason I asked you here today is to evaluate our country's intelligence capability and to suggest a restructuring of our Department". "Since we have had to comply with the environmental ultimatum of the World Government, and been ordered to dismantle our military forces and disarm all of our nuclear warheads, it is leaving us vulnerable as a nation, to a first strike nuclear attack from the U.S. or China, the two countries that have not yet complied with the ultimatum issued at the UN last year".

"The "Council of twelve", which is The World Government's Supreme Court, has assured me that they are prepared to employ extreme measures on the U.S. that will break their will, and force them to comply very soon". "I have been instructed by the Council that I must eliminate all intelligence services of our government and grant full access to the Chinese delegates and the UN representatives". "All of our intelligence documents and files have to be made available to the Council". "I've been assured by the Council that we will be under their protection from any hostile act by any other nation".

"Your services as Operational head of our Intelligence community will no longer be required, your Government, and I as your President would like to show our gratitude for your services and your father's before you, by granting you a full Government Pension and a fully staffed office in the Kremlin, with an open Visa that will allow you to travel anywhere in the world, without restrictions". "You will also have available to you a private Military jet to be used at Government expense for your personal use".

"I have given orders that all Government Intelligence files are to be procured and handed over to the "Council of twelve's" emissary in two weeks". "Erik if there are any files you want to keep, that are personally sensitive I would remove them within the next week and place them somewhere private". "Again let me say, we wish you all the best in your retirement".

Erik was on a commercial passenger plane on his way to America it'd been two days since he had met with the President of Russia and discovered that his position in the intelligence department had been eliminated, he had left Otto in charge of removing any sensitive files from his office and from the international space station agency offices that they felt they wanted to keep for future reference. Just a week ago he had met with the general and his uncle and was still trying to determine in his own mind what he was going to say to President Brown, when he met with him in Washington.

He wanted to brief President Brown personally on the discovery of the location of the five nuclear armed ICBM missiles that were under the Colonel and the world Government's control.

The Colonel's rogue military defectors had stolen these missiles and hidden them in strategic locations after the collapse of the Soviet Union. Erik and his team of code breakers, that were sent from the United States had learned there were probably five such nuclear armed missiles and all but one of those were located in former Soviet Union states which are now independent countries. Since that discovery there had been another satellite transmission telecast to the world governments which confirmed the Colonel and his Middle Eastern partners were committed to deploying one or more of these missiles into a large major populated city of any country, and it would strike which ever country that their Governments refused to capitulate and accept their new world Government dictatorship.

CHAPTER 44

S ID AND HIS TEAMS of agents were moving men and equipment into each of these locations with an attempt to take possession of and disarm these nuclear missiles and reduce the threat the Colonel and his partners have made to the world. This mission was to be Top-Secret and a dangerous undertaking, they understood if the Colonel even suspected any of the leaders of any country was not implementing the radical instructions they were given to surrender their countries to the New World Government they would launch a nuclear strike on that country.

For this reason Erik was now traveling to the U.S. on a common carrier to meet with the U.S. President, to reduce any suspicion that he was working together with the United States to overthrow this world dictator. He could not be sure how much of his traveling was being monitored by the Colonel's agents, therefore Erik or any of his agents did not used government vehicles that could connect them to any country's government.

Now since he had learned the existence of the nuclear sub (if it was indeed real) that was under the control of the Colonel and his military agents, and the information that he had received from General Phillips and his uncle which he still did not know if it was a ploy, to stop the United States from deploying it's "nuclear defense shield", or if this diabolical plan to launch nuclear missiles in the major cities in the U.S. and other world governments was really the Dictator's plan to show the

Government's of the world his military strength, Erik was trying to sort this all out in his mind.

Even with all this going on in his mind Erik was still thinking of his beloved Karla whom he would be able to visit and spend some time with during his stay in the United States.

Erik's plane landed at Dulles Airport in Washington, and a secret service agent was there to meet him and drive him to the White House to meet with President Brown. They did not send a government helicopter but rather an unmarked vehicle with an agent from the national security agency. The agent who met him was Roger Wilson who knew how to move through the city and disappear from anyone who may be tailing them he also could get Erik into the White House without being observed. A Secret Service security agent met Erik in the private parking garage and escorted him into the "White House map room" this was the room where he would meet privately with President Brown. The map room is rarely used, and is completely off-limits for all public tours of the White House, it was used by former President Roosevelt to review all the maps of Europe daily during World War II, all the maps hanging on the walls were kept updated with different colored pins to show the locations of all American forces and their German counterparts. There were also maps showing the Pacific theater and the movement of Japanese forces.

Erik noticed, as he was led down through the halls, that there were moving boxes and shipping crates in all the hallways and most of the offices in the White House were empty. He was aware that President Brown was giving the appearance to those who may be observing his actions that he was dismantling the Government of the U.S. as was required by the World Dictator. If he did not appear to be following the instructions in the time allotted by the Dictator's regime as set forth at the UN Security Council meeting, they might make good their threat to deploy an ICBM missile carrying a nuclear warhead into a US city.

Erik was looking over all the maps hanging on the walls and was astonished at the detail in which the U.S. could identify the troop movements of the enemy during the last great world war.

"Good afternoon", spoke a familiar voice from behind Erik and he recognized it as his friend President Brown. "I'm so glad that you are here Erik" the President said, "and after you spoke to me on the phone and told me of the urgency to meet with me I cleared all my appointments and am available the entire day". "I assure you Mr. President if it were not of utmost urgency I would not have asked for this meeting.

"Sit down Erik", the President said, "and tell me what this urgency is all about". Erik began to reveal all that he had learned, including his meeting with the General and his uncle in Moscow and also the meeting with the President of Russia and all the uncertainties that he is feeling. Whether or not the information he got from his uncle was true or just another ploy of the Colonel's. President Brown was struck by what he had learned from Erik, and he was fearful that the Colonel would carry out his threat. He said he would have to have a meeting with his Joint Chiefs of Staff and his trusted intelligence operations throughout the world and see if they could determine if this plan was true or not. Then he told Erik that he thought it would be wise to initiate his operation to gain control of the missile sites and disarm them now. Erik agreed and said that he would put the operation into effect immediately and that all the teams were in place and all they had to do was recon into their strategic areas where the missiles were located.

As President Brown and Erik were sitting at the table talking and going over their plans an aide brought in a tray of sandwiches and drinks, President Brown said "Erik help yourself I think were going to be here for a while and I thought you might be hungry, and then I will tell you what we have decided that you are unaware of".

After they had finished eating and the door to the map room was securely locked President Brown began to lay out a plan that his Government had decided on.

"Erik we have decided in the Security Council and with the Joint Chiefs of Staff that we must initiate an offensive plan to disarm the missiles on the space station before they can be deployed". "If we can prevent them from being deployed we will have removed a strategic link in this World Dictator's threat to inflict massive genocide on the populations of the world". "We believe that we will then be able to move massive numbers of armed forces and armaments against the Dictator and his regime, and gain an offensive that will bring victory and restore peace in the world, and the success of your operation will allow us time to put that plan into action".

"That sounds like a good plan Sir, but how can it be achieved and how can I be of help"? "You told me that all of your Commandos cells are moving into place to disarm the ICBM's and they are ready to take control of them is this correct"? "Erik said "yes Sir but we need it least another ten days to have all the teams in place". "When we move on my command to disarm all five of these locations we are still not sure that we have all the locations of the ICBM's under the control of the Colonel identified and located". "We cannot afford to wait any longer" President Brown said, "our time is running out and now that we are aware of the nuclear submarine that is under the control of the Colonel, we have something else to deal with".

"We have already received a threat from the office of the Dictator, in Syria that we are falling behind other nations of the world, in the dismantling of our Government and moving our citizens out of the U.S., as they required".

"Chinese Agents are setting up offices all over our nation to begin the massive documentation of all our citizens". Already there is a massive infusion of third world countries populations making their way to America, and we are being told, to export at least a third of our entire population to these other Countries, and they cannot take anything with them except their clothes". "This is impossible, already our people are arming themselves and refusing to leave their homes and business's, there is going to be a blood bath like no one on earth has ever witnessed before, and we are helpless to stop it".

"Erik we can't let that happen and that's why we have decided to act now and we cannot delay". "With the information that you've given me we will have to determine by our intelligence whether it's true or not and if it is true we have less than thirty days".

"Mr. President I am at your service, and will do what ever you ask me to do". "Erik we have a space shuttle waiting on the launch pad at an undisclosed location that is equipped and ready to be launched to the international space station, until now we have kept the location and plan secret, you are the first outsider it has been revealed to". "Less than three weeks ago we received an encrypted message at the State Department from the space station, from a person who identified himself only as agent Thomas, we do not know if the message is a ploy of some kind or if it is a message we should pay attention to". "That is where you come in, because he signed off with, "contact O'Donnell and Erik Roskov".

"It is from Thomas who is an agent of the British intelligence" Erik said, "we did not know if he was alive or dead and since then have confirmed that he is on the space station incognito". May I see the massage Mr. President"? President Brown removed a folder from the briefcase he had placed on the table and handed the file folder to Erik. Erik began to read the message agent Thomas had sent.

"The two American shuttles are equipped and ready to launch, one of them is loaded with deadly viruses that is capable of poisoning the freshwater supplies of the U.S. and then crash into the ocean somewhere in the Pacific and detonate a nuclear warhead which will create a giant tsunami that will destroy over half of the Pacific rim and kill millions of people, the other one is equipped with multiple nuclear warheads and will land in the Atlantic Ocean to create the same kind of destruction and massive genocide on the East Coast". It has not been revealed to anyone on the station the exact locations or trajectory of either shuttle, they will receive orders from the Colonel very soon, every day I come closer and closer to being exposed, and when that happens they will kill me, I'm taking a great risk sending this message". "I have a plan that may help to save the world from these madmen".

"On the space station the scientists and engineers are busy with their plans and paying little attention to what I or the U.S. hostages are doing, and that is why I believe this plan can succeed".

"The space station is equipped with three docking areas, two of these are occupied with U.S. space shuttles, but unknown to all but a few people here, there is a third docking station on the far side of the space station and is never used". "It was the original docking platform for the station when it was first set in orbit but since the station has been redesigned and expanded several times the two new docking platforms were built and are exclusively used for docking the shuttles". "If you can launch a third shuttle to the space station and link up on the far side of the station at that third docking platform without being detected, I believe a small contingent of our astronauts could, with my assistance take over the space station and prevent the deployment of the shuttles".

"There are great risks involved in this plan, the greatest risk would be the docking at the station because when the new docking stations were built the old docking equipment was dismantled and removed". "To dock a shuttle at that location will have to be done manually, and all personnel will have to gain entrance to the station through a flexible tube to get to the airlock, this is very risky to perform and if I am discovered prior to the shuttle's arrival and not available to help from inside it will be an impossible task, and the Astronauts and the entire military team could be lost forever in space". "The only way this plan has a chance of succeeding is if it is carried out immediately and with great skill and a contingent of highly trained Commandos". "Signed Thomas, contact O'Donnell and Erik Roskov.

Erik looked at President Brown and said without hesitation "Sir I believe we can do that". "That is what I wanted to hear you say", let's get this plan put together and implemented". "We have the trained Astronauts standing by but we need you to supply us with highly trained agents to lead our team of Commandos, who are willing to risk their lives for world peace". "I know just the man" Erik said, "he is now overseeing the cell teams we are deploying to disarm the ICBM's". "I can make him available for this mission, and it will not affect our other mission because he has already set in place highly trained and trusted leaders over each of the cell groups.

"This man is my most trusted friend Mr. President and he will arrange for whatever you need". "I will have him here in Washington within twenty four hours, and you can brief him and take him to the launch site.

Erik left the White House and went directly to Karla's apartment, "Erik darling, it is so good to see you again" Karla said as she opened the door and let Erik in. "We have to use your communicator to contact the Black Panther" Erik said as he bolted through the door. "We will have better success if we first contact Bill Forney and have him broadcast a message to the Black Panther". "Time is of the essence darling". "Oh! forgive me darling" Erik said as he pulled Karla into his arms and kissed her passionately. "It must be important and urgent" Karla said, as she removed her communicator from her wall safe and handed it to Erik. "Bill, Erik, contact the Black Panther immediately and have him contact me via "little lamb", it's urgent".

Karla's communicator was activated at 5:30 p.m. all communication had to be delivered in code through Bill Forney's broadcasting station which was located in Russia, the code letters for the Black Panther came through into Bill's communicator at 6:00 p.m. U.S.A. time. Erik had entered the code for the "little lamb" and his cell phone number to Bill and said "call urgent".

It was 7:30 before Sid answered the call, Erik answered and Sid said, "what's up Boss, I know it's urgent or you would never have broken protocol and had me call your cell phone". "Yes it is urgent and I need you to drop everything and fly as quickly as possible to Washington, turn over your command to one of the other agents and catch a commercial flight, it is urgent".

"I can be there in about 24 hours", Sid said "as soon as I can arrange a flight from an international Airport and turn over my command". "I'll pick you up at Dulles" Erik said, "and if you have any trouble getting a flight call me at this number and I will pull some strings".

Erik ended the call, and he and Karla left her apartment and drove to her father's coffee shop for some dinner. "Hello darling" Dominic Shalom said as he greeted Karla with a big hug and a kiss on her cheek, "and I'm always glad to see you also Erik" Dominic said as he approached him with both of his massive arms extended. Erik reached out to shake the big man's hand, but Dominic grabbed him and gave him a big bear hug, and said "no hand shake this time Ruski it's time for a hug". The big jovial man reminded Erik of a big bear.

"Sit down children let me serve you a delicious dinner". Erik and Karla sat down and Dominic sat down at their table, Erik looked at Dominic and said, "Sir I would like to talk to you after dinner if you have some time". "Time that's all I do have we will talk in the back, in my living quarters". When Dominic got up and left them alone, Karla looked across the table at Erik with a puzzled look. "Erik" she said, "what was that all about"? "are you going to ask for my hand"? Erik laughed and said, "no Karla it's not that, by the way do I need to"? Erik and Karla were both giggling like high school sweethearts on the first date, so much so that Karla never realized Erik did not tell her why he wanted to talk to her father.

The dinner was delicious and Dominic took off his apron and said, "now we can talk with a good glass of wine in my quarters".

Only then did Karla remember Erik had not told her why he wanted to talk to her father. They followed Dominic into a small but well furnished modern apartment in the back of the coffee shop, "have a seat" Dominic said, "and I will get us a nice bottle of wine" "no! you won't" Karla said, "you and Erik sit down and I will get the wine", Dominic looked at Erik with a twinkle in his eye and said "she has always been bossy".

"Now Erik what is on your mind that you need to talk to Dominic about"? "Karla has told me a great deal about you and I believe I can trust you with what I'm about to say", by this time Karla was back with the wine and pouring each of them a glass and then sitting down next to Erik on the couch.

"You know your daughter works on highly classified and Top-Secret projects for the Government, and I am the Director of the Russian Department of Central intelligence, and we are currently involved in a project together which I'm not at liberty to reveal all the details but it may turn out to be the most important project either of our governments have ever been involved with".

Erik went on to tell Dominic of the importance of the satellite communication television broadcasting station that his friend Bill Forney operated in Moscow and how the government of Russia was making threats to close it down because of the criticism it has leveled at the Russian government and its leadership and other world governments. "Karla has told me you have a large empty space above your coffee shop and I'm asking if you would make that space available for a satellite transmission studio where we could relocate Bill's studio with his crew, if he has to leave Russia, where he could continue broadcasting from here". "I have not talked to Karla or anyone else about this and I don't want you to think a "no" answer will in any way affect yours or Karla's relationship with me or our governments".

"Before the two of you decide I must be very clear that there could be some danger involved with this arrangement down the road, you could be putting both your business and your life in danger". I don't want you to give me an answer now but I will need an answer before I return to Russia in one week".

The big man stood up and walked over to a desk in the room and picked up a framed picture from the desk, and turned and walked over to the sofa where Erik and his beloved daughter was sitting, Dominick said holding out a framed picture and handing it to Erik, "this is my wife she died when Karla was born but she has been in my heart always, she and darling Karla helped to fill an empty place in the heart of an old man, but I have lived long enough to raise Karla and to see her very happy for the first time in many years".

"You do love Karla don't you Erik"? Dominic said as he looked sternly into the face of Erik and retrieved the picture from him. "With all my heart Sir" Erik said, by this time Karla was wiping tears from her eyes. "Darling Karla I know you love Erik I saw it in your eyes the very first time you brought him to meet me". "Yes Daddy I do with all my heart", "then nothing else has to be discussed, I am an old man and I lived to see the joy of my life fulfilled". "So if I am now to face danger for my country which has been so good and kind to me I say I am ready to lay down my life if it will benefit my country and make this world a safer place for my grandchildren to live in". "The answer to your question Erik is yes you let me know when and I will have it ready for your friend Bill to move into and setup his broadcasting station".

"Thank you so much Erik said "the station is a vital part of this entire mission and as soon as we know it is necessary to move it out of Russia, we will contact you".

Erik said to Karla as they drove off "I want you to come with me to the White House to meet with President Brown". "Okay" Karla said "but then we have a lot to talk about before you return to Moscow".

When Erik and Karla arrived at the White House they were escorted by an agent of the Secret Service to the map room where President Brown and a handful of military and cabinet members were waiting for them. After a little small talk President Brown said, "let's get down to business", and the atmosphere in the room immediately turned from casual to very serious.

"Erik" President Brown said, were you able to find the right man for the mission we discussed"? "Yes Mr. President I have my most trusted agent arriving here, Sir he is the commander of all our military cell commandos that are moving into place across the globe to strike and disarm the nuclear missiles controlled by the Colonel, and he will choose the most suitable agent under his command for the mission".

"Have you briefed him on the nature of the mission"? "Yes and he is aware that it could be a sacrifice of the agent's life". He will arrive in Washington in twelve to eighteen hours, and he has already had an opportunity to talk to all of his commanders, so when he arrives we will know immediately whom he has chosen for the mission, then we can get him here to start training for the mission, we are aware Mr. President that time is of the essence".

After going over the plans for the mission with all the principals in the room including Karla the President said, "people the only thing we can do now is wait" then he dismissed the meeting. Erik and Karla were the last to leave because Erik asked President Brown if he might speak to him after the meeting on a private matter. The President agreed to a private meeting and even asked the Secret Service agents to wait outside the room.

"Now Erik my friend what can I do for you"? "Well Mr. President it is not for me personally but it is for a very dear friend". Then Erik revealed the concerns he had for his friend Bill Forney and his Broadcasting Program and how important it was to their entire field operation. President Brown agreed without hesitation to cut through any bureaucratic red tape necessary to get Bill and his crew visa's to enter the U.S., when Erik believed it was necessary.

Erik and Karla left the White House and returned to her apartment to wait until they heard from Sid. Karla prepared them a nice meal and after they ate and everything was cleaned up and put away Karla poured each of them a glass of wine and they sat down on the sofa. Karla sat close to Erik on the sofa and kissed him and said, "now darling we must talk about the part you asked my father to play in all this". "I know I should've talked to you first Karla, Erik said, but I had no time to do it, do you have a problem or concerns about it"? "I can see how important it is to get Bill and his crew and equipment out of Moscow and soon because the government controlled by the new President is moving his Government more and more toward a Dictatorship which will lead to censorship of all broadcasts". "Erik I am just so scared of getting my father involved I'm afraid for his life". By this time Karla was trying to hold back the tears without much success, and she laid her head on Erik's shoulder. "I understand your fears darling but if we are unable to succeed in these missions we will all be in jeopardy, and I promise you that the President and I will do everything we can to keep Bill's location a Top-Secret.

Sid was driven to the secret location of the shuttle by agent Roger Wilson and on the way there he made a cell phone call to his field commander and instructed him to send Lieutenant Karl Underwood to Washington, in America immediately.

Karl was one of the agents from the old KGB which Sergeant Zolov had recruited for the field operations and he was both loyal and trusted. He arrived in Washington the next day and was driven to the launch site by agent Roger Wilson.

Sid remained at the secret launch site with Karl for a week and helped him in the training of the three American astronauts which would fly the shuttle and the six man team of Marine commandos which would attempt to take over the space station and stop the launching of the two nuclear armed American shuttles.

Karl and all the crew members were volunteers and they knew all the risks involved in this mission, and that it may result in the loss of all or some of their lives. The Astronauts were already highly trained in the operation of the shuttle, but all the crew had to be trained to enter the space station in an unusual way through a flexible wormlike tube.

Sid and Karl had only five days to train all the crew and get them ready to launch the shuttle, the President had said the shuttle must be launched within five days, before the launch window would close, they had only twenty four hours, and if they missed it a weather pattern was moving into the area and it would delay the launching of the shuttle for at least another week.

Sid left the site after the launch decision was made and returned to Russia to oversee the field operations that would take control of and disarm the ICBM's that they had finally discovered the locations of, and all his Commando teams were in place. The shuttle was prepared for launch, all crew members and their weapons and equipment were on board and the mission control commander began the countdown, "10,9,8,7,6,5,4,3,2,1, we have ignition", the giant space ships engines suddenly burst into life as the shuttle began to move up ever so slowly away from the gantry that was holding it upright, and then began to increase in speed and lift until all that was visible from the ground was a trail of fiery white vapor.

The launch of the shuttle was flawless it was the first launch ever to be done at night, because President Brown did not want it to be detected by the Chinese agents which were now in every major city of America.

The shuttle Commander radioed to mission control that they were arriving at the space station's orbit and they were going to attempt to dock at the south end as they were instructed.

"The Eagle has landed", came the voice of the shuttle commander to mission control "it was a smooth docking and we do not think we were detected by any one inside the station". "We will now attempt to deploy the flexible worm and attach it to the old airlock and then we will send a team to cut a hole in the outside hatch to gain access to the airlock" "If we are successful in gaining access into the airlock we can begin staging all our crew and equipment inside, but we are depending on the "inside agent" to open the airlock from inside the station otherwise we will be unable to get inside the station to complete our mission".

The mission control commander said they understood, and were trying to contact the inside man now, and would let them know when contact was made.

CHAPTER 45

A GENT THOMAS BURKOV HAS remained in his quarters awaiting the predetermined signal on his receiver that the shuttle had arrived and the crews were inside the airlock. When he received the signal he would have to go unnoticed to the south end of the station. He surmised that all the engineers and scientists were busy loading the nuclear devices and the deadly chemicals onto the shuttle's to hardly notice his movements. The Colonel had sent instructions two days before the shuttle was due to arrive at the station, for the shuttles to be loaded and prepared for launching. Thomas had hoped there was still time for the Commandos to abort their launching.

Thomas reached the south end of the space station where the shuttle was docked, and he discovered that the door to the old airlock was bolted shut with a large steel bar which would have to be removed before he could make an attempt to manually open the hatch. Now he would have to return to the tool room, located in the main area of the station and get some tools. He had not considered this, and as he entered the tool room in the main compartment of the station a Russian cosmonaut came in behind him and sat down and took out a cigarette and lit it. "Have one"? he asked as he held out the pack to Thomas "No thanks", Thomas said. Thomas had assembled the tools he would need and they were in an open toolbox on the table. "What are the tools for Comrade"? The cosmonaut said "are you going to build you a rocket and fly away"? Both of the men laughed, and then Thomas said, "one of the engineers assigned me a small project and I need these tools to perform it".

The cosmonaut finished his cigarette and Thomas hoped he wouldn't light another. He got up from where he was sitting and started toward the tool room door as he looked back at Thomas and said "good luck on your project I have to get back before they miss me" and walked out the door.

Thomas hurriedly picked up the toolbox, closed the lid and walked out the door hoping everyone was too busy to notice him walking past them carrying a toolbox.

Thomas reached the airlock and began removing the bolts from the iron bar, and when he had finished removing them and had the airlock free he wondered if he would be able to turn the big iron wheel and manually open the hatch.

The call came from mission control to the shuttle commander that the "inside agent" was at the airlock standing by for it to be opened.

Creeeeek, creeeeeek the crew heard the iron wheel turning inside the airlock and the Marine Commandos had their weapons ready, then the wheel stopped turning and they could hear the sound of hammering on the hatch but it was not opening. Thomas was hammering and pushing on the hatch until it finally started to give a little, and the astronauts began pulling from the other side when suddenly they heard the sound of rushing wind and pushed the hatch closed. "There is an air leak somewhere" one of the astronauts said "if we open the hatch before we fix the leak we will be in danger of the flexible worm disengaging from the station and we can all be swept out into space.

The worm was attached to the outside of the station's airlock with ten strong magnets and a rubber seal but two of the magnets had worked loose when the crew was going back and forth to the shuttle, staging all their weapons and equipment inside the airlock. This was a dangerous situation because if it was not fixed and properly sealed when the hatch was opened a force of sudden pressure from the inside would tear the flexible tube away from the docking station and all the crew would be swept out into space and be lost. It would also prevent any of the crew from returning to the shuttle if they had too.

After the air seal was once again in place, the astronauts were able to open the hatch and gain entry to the inside of the space station, they decided to leave the hatch open in case something went wrong and they had to make a hurried exit back to the shuttle.

Thomas briefed the commandos on where they would have to overcome the Russian armed guards which were watching the shuttle's being loaded. Thomas said the authority was given to launch both shuttles and the commandos would have to act quickly to prevent their launch.

Sid returned to his field command and the same day the shuttle docked at the space station, he signaled Erik that all the teams were in place and ready to execute the operations. Erik gave Sid the command to go-ahead and begin executing the operation. All the teams were moved simultaneously onto the ICBM sites, and it was unusually quiet as the teams moved onto their respective sites and there was no movement, there were no armed guards there was no activity at all, they thought this was very strange as they moved closer to the ICBM launch pads they noticed that there was not a single person on the site every one had been evacuated.

Sid transmitted to Erik and said "there is no one at any of the sites all military personnel have abandoned all the sites our teams have the ICBM sites under our control and we are presently engaged in disarming them".

"Erik" Sid said "what do you make of all this"? "I don't know yet but it does not look good, all we can do now is to hold our breath and see if the Colonel does have a nuclear armed submarine and if he carries out his threat to deploy a nuclear missile into a city in America".

Erik called President Brown on a secure line and informed him of what they found at the ICBM sites. The President was both relieved and worried, he told Erik that the shuttle team was inside the space station and it would soon be under their control.

The armed Russian guards were well hidden as the Marine commandos from America passed them on their way toward the main compartment of the space station, then they moved out of their concealment and came up behind the commandos with weapons drawn, as a number of armed guards also stepped out in front of the Marines pointing their automatic weapons at them.

"Lay down your weapons you are completely surrounded" said a man in a Russian military officers uniform "we have been expecting you" as the Russian soldiers moved in on all sides of the Marines and took their weapons. "Agent Thomas we have been monitoring your transmissions and your receiving for some time now, we were aware of the third shuttle and its cargo". "You are in time to see the launching of the two American shuttles today, which is unfortunate for many peoples of the earth but it is completely necessary to bring all of Earth's Government leaders into submission to our plan to save the Earth for future generations".

At that moment one of the shuttles was disengaging from the dock, the Marines and the shuttle crew had no choice but to surrender their weapons to the armed Russian guards. Agent Karl Underwood was behind the Marines with two of the astronauts when they saw what was happening they turned and ran back to the airlock. As they reached the hatch that was left open, they could see the flex tube swinging violently back and forth and the astronaut's knew the air seal had come loose again and if they couldn't repair it the air pressure would pull the remaining part of the seal off and the flexible tube would swing away from the station and possibly rip a hole in the shuttle itself.

Karl and the astronauts were trying desperately to reengage the seal when a sudden swing of the flexible tube tore it loose from the dock, and a powerful suction of air pulled all of them out into space. The flexible tube continued to swing wildly until it ripped a gaping hole in the side of the shuttle, and the shuttle began to spin out of control and plummeted into the space station and burst into flames, destroying the station, and killing all those left on board.

President Brown was notified of the failed mission and the loss of the astronauts and Agent Karl. He then called his friend Erik and told him of the situation with a very sad heart. President Brown said that he would notify the families of the astronauts and tell them of their loss and their extreme bravery but he would have to keep the details of the mission from them. Erik said he would contact Sid and let him know, and he would contact his people's families if there were any, and let them know of their loss.

President Brown received a call from the new Russian President on the red phone in his office and he was informed that he had been contacted by the agents on the space station and told him that one or both American shuttles had been launched. The Russian President also told President Brown of the message he received from the Colonel. The message was, "for him to contact the American President and warn him of the impending loss of life, because he had been ordered to release a nuclear armed missile with a green warhead into a major U.S. city. This missile would be launched from their nuclear submarine somewhere in the Atlantic Ocean". "The Supreme Commander feels this is a necessary step because the United States has not shown due diligence in dismantling their military or their Government". "In twenty four hours they will be contacted and told what city is targeted and then they will have thirty days to remove as many inhabitants possible". "This launched missile will take place sometime after the nuclear armed shuttles have performed their mission". "I am so sorry President Brown" the Russian President said "I wish there was something that we could do to prevent this from happening". "Thank you Sir", President Brown said "but there is nothing either of us can do the trigger has already been pulled".

The call came within twenty four hours, the city targeted was Salt Lake City Utah President Brown sent a contingent of military personnel to help evacuate as much of the city as possible, it was nearly useless the highways were jammed, people were panicked many refused to leave their homes, but in thirty days nearly all of the residents of Salt Lake City had been evacuated safely, and when the nuclear explosion took place there were no survivors of the several hundred residents who had refused to leave, and hid out from the military. The radioactive fallout from the bomb, posed very little danger to any other American city, because of the extreme dry climate and no winds, which contained it, by the surrounding mountains. For that, President Brown and all of America was thankful.

A short time before the missal devastated the city of Salt Lake, in Utah, the first shuttle delivered it's deadly cargo into the great lakes, and poisoned nearly half of America's fresh water supply. Then it continued to the Pacific Ocean where it exploded under water and created a deadly tsunami and a series of giant earth quakes. The earth quakes completely destroyed nearly two thirds of the entire Pacific Rim, with millions of lives lost. Shortly after the first shuttle landed the Colonel carried out his diabolical threat and launched the second shuttle, which landed in the Atlantic Ocean and wiped out the whole East coast with millions more lives lost.

The mission to stop the shuttle launches was completely unsuccessful and the space station was destroyed.

The President addressed a grieving nation from the temporary office aboard Air Force one. "My dear citizens as you now know our country has been dealt a devastating and deadly cowardly blow by the leadership of the World Government which was set in place by the United Nations and its Muslim extremists in the Middle East and ratified by all the World Governments, except The United States and Israel".

"At 12:01 Eastern standard Time an ICBM missile armed with a special nuclear warhead was detonated in the atmosphere above Salt Lake City Utah, which fortunately had been evacuated, but the entire area will be un-inhabitable for more than a century". "This type of nuclear bomb was developed by our own government to be used under extreme circumstances". "When it was first developed and reviewed by our military leaders and scientists there was a unanimous decision that this technology would never be used anywhere in the world". "Somehow this technology fell into the hands of our enemies and was used on our own citizens". "The unique capability of this bomb is, that it does not destroy brick-and-mortar it is designed to only destroy human and animal life therefore Salt Lake City is nearly completely intact but over a million citizens have lost their homes and their livelihoods".

"I am speaking to you today with a grieving heart my heartfelt sympathy goes out to every living family member of those that died". "Your Government will do everything we can for those families". I am also sending a massive number of construction workers, equipment and supplies to Salt Lake City who will begin the construction of a concrete containment around the entire city to contain the radioactive debris, and fallout produced by the explosion".

"Our scientists believe it is feasible to install giant fans around the parameter of the city to blow into the city and keep the nuclear fallout from escaping the city and contaminating the surrounding areas".

"This endeavor will take months if not years, so we have given a mandatory evacuation order to all citizens and livestock within a hundred mile radius around the affected area". "Because of this mass destruction in our country and the threat of more destruction and loss of life, as your President I have decided the only way to stop the threat and the destruction of our citizens by the World Dictator in Jerusalem is to acquiesce to all their demands". "So this morning before speaking to you I telephoned the office of the Supreme Commander and spoke directly to him, and promised him a unilateral surrender of the United States to the World Government", "that was the most difficult decision I've ever had to make in all my life". "I spoke yesterday to a joint session of Congress and to our military leaders and informed them of my decision and they all agreed to abide by it".

"As you must know they were not all pleased but they accepted the inevitable". "I want all of you to know that your military, Congress and I did everything we could to overcome the threat to our country by the powers in the Middle East as soon as the ultimatum was delivered by the New World Commander". Our initial coarse of action was to feign surrender and covertly work to locate and disarm the nuclear missiles we were threatened with".

"We were successful in locating and disarming the missiles, and even sent a mission to the international space station to stop the ecology scientists and their military from sending our two space shuttles loaded with nuclear destruction and poison into our freshwater supply back to earth". "This mission arrived too late and that is why our East and West Coast have been destroyed".

"We even thought if that happened, we could rebuild and overcome that great loss without plunging the world into a nuclear holocaust". "We were unaware the Soviets had supplied the military of the World Dictator a nuclear submarine armed with twenty missiles, which can be deployed and strike anywhere in the world".

We were just unable to overcome all that they could inflict upon our nation and our people, so the only coarse of action left for us was to surrender our Military and Government to them".

"So fellow citizens of the United States it is with heavy heart I must tell you to, with all haste gather your families together and begin the mass migration to Africa and other Third World countries to begin our lives all over again under the rule and the reign of a World Dictator". "Our military will assist all of our citizens to move to the Major airports through out the country, where they will be flown to their new homes". "All commercial military and private airlines will assist in this massive migration we have been instructed that we may only take with us are clothes, we are to leave all of our wealth that we have amassed over a life time, for the taking, of the Immigrants that are pouring onto our shores from Africa, the Middle East, and other Third World countries".

"Please citizens as your President I urge you if you have weapons lay them down we have lost enough lives already with the millions that were killed on the East and West Coast and throughout the Pacific Rim. Before you leave this country if you have not already done so you must register with one of the registration offices in your state, this registration will be necessary when you arrive at your new locations to be able to buy and sell and receive needed supplies from the World Government". "We have been instructed that any of our citizens that refuse to register along with all the members of their families will be hunted down by the Premier Commander's armies and killed".

"God bless all of you, and it has been a pleasure and honor to be your President". "We have been told that we have less than six months to evacuate two thirds of our citizens".

CHAPTER 46

"HELLO DARLING" THE VOICE on the other end of the line said, "Erik, I am so glad to hear from you it seems like forever since I heard your voice". "I know darling I feel the same way but I have had to keep a low profile here in Moscow since our President removed me from my position and placed all Russian intelligence under his personal control".

"The new KGB agents follow me everywhere I go, and they have my telephone bugged it's like being under house arrest". "The agents sent here from the office of the World Government are pulling me in for questioning nearly every day, and they know that I know the whereabouts of Bill Forney since he moved his broadcasting studio out of Moscow". "They know he is my friend and believe they can get to him through me, they have a worldwide warrant for his arrest since he was tried in abstention for high treason, for his world wide television broadcast exposing the real agenda of this World Government".

"I was able to shake the tail they have on me and make this call to you darling, I have longed to be with you for such a long time I should never have left you in the United States and returned to Russia, but I knew it was the only way to get Bill and his crew out of Russia I am so grateful for your President's help through the State Department by issuing visas for Bill and all of his crew to relocate and settle in America".

"I also want to thank you and your father for allowing him to set up his broadcasting studio where he is now, as you know his satellite broadcasts are the only link of communications to our field agents". "I'm calling from my friend Ravien's, you know the one you met when we had dinner at his place". "He is the only true friend I have here in Moscow that I can completely trust".

"I have an appointment at the Kremlin tomorrow morning at ten a.m., General Siki has sent one of his Council of twelve to Moscow to interrogate me, and I believe they are going to arrest me". "I do not intend to make the appointment and when I don't show they will put out a worldwide arrest warrant on me charging me with high treason as well". "I have made arrangements to leave Moscow for St. Petersburg tonight, Otto and Greta are taking me to my cabin in the mountains, I'm going to stay there with them until Monday night, then Otto is going to drive me to the airport where I will board a plane and fly to England". "Darling I'm not going to be in touch with you for a little while I am on the run but I gave you Otto's cell phone number and you can keep in touch with him and Greta they're going to stay at my cabin, they will be safe there".

"The next time you hear from me I will be at an undisclosed location somewhere in England". "I love you darling and I can hardly wait until we can be together forever, I know it will be a whole new world under this World Dictator but we will find a way to make a happy life for ourselves".

"I haven't heard from Sid since we met him in Washington, other than the brief call that he made to me after the failed shuttle mission". "All of our agents have been disbursed through out the world and even though they were unable to stop the Colonel's military from deploying the missile into America and we were unable to stop the two shuttles that has devastated that country, we are still going to be a force that must be reckoned with by the World Government leaders and we are going to do everything that we can to disrupt them and all the UN and Chinese agents in every corner of the world that we can".

"When I briefly talked to Sid he told me that his top commander Daniel Kershi has been assigned to a special mission, but he would not say what it was". "When I asked him what it was he said just keep watching Bill Forney's newsflash".

"Well darling I have to go now, I want you to stay safe and tell your father once again how much we appreciate him". "The next communication from me will be an encrypted code on your communicator, and then you will go directly to Bill's studio and give all our field agents the signal that

I gave you to activate our operations, which will begin our guerrilla war of resistance against the New World Government".

"I love you darling Erik and I miss you so much please keep yourself safe, and I'll be waiting for the signal". "Tell Otto and Greta that I love them both, goodbye my darling".

CHAPTER 47

IT LOOKED LIKE JUST another group of homeless refugees streaming over the Syrian border from neighboring lands.

Since the world commander had ordered the destruction of the city of Utah in America, and the President and his Government has acquiesced their power and authority to him he has driven all the Jews out of their homeland in Jerusalem, Tel Aviv, and all other cities of Israel and forced the occupation of that nation by Palestinians. The entire Middle East is a dangerous place for anyone traveling there. The Dictator has kept his promise and removed the Muslim temple and all other buildings from the Temple Square in Jerusalem and built a world headquarters on the Temple Mount.

With his legions of Chinese and UN soldiers spread out in all major cities of the world he is able to control all commerce and communication, with the exception of Bill Forney's twenty four hour broadcast from the satellite, which until now, they have been unable to stop.

There is chaos and anarchy in nearly every country of the world, and the Chinese soldiers and the legions of UN soldiers have thus far been unable to contain it, even though the Imperial Commander and his Council of twelve is in control of all World Governments.

There are many pockets of resistance to their regime throughout the world, mainly from the Christian right wing extremists, who have refused to be registered in the national database. These Christians have united themselves together, and are being led by a strong Christian group that was forced out of America into Africa, but even in exile they have made alliances with other Christian groups all over the world, and through their resistance and guerrilla warfare they have become a real threat to the New World Government.

All of these rebel groups are able to communicate and plan their strategy's, in all parts of the world through Bill Forney's world telecasts, and that is why the Council of twelve has offered a reward to anyone who helps them locate this broadcasting facility.

Daniel knew that he was placing his life in jeopardy by traveling in the Middle East and even though he was in disguise, he knew if he was caught he would be killed immediately, with no trial.

No one noticed the tall woman dressed in a Burkah with her head and face completely covered with the traditional Muslim headdress and it would have been inappropriate to ask her or any of the other Muslim women to submit to a physical body search, the World Governments border guards had to just let them all into Syria, after all had not the New World Government declared that there would no longer be any sovereign borders of any country.

All the refugees continued on into Damascus where they would be required to register. Just inside the city the tall woman slipped out of the procession unnoticed by anyone.

Daniel Kershi slipped into an abandoned street front building carrying a small suitcase and removed the Muslim headdress and Burkah. He then opened the suitcase which he had laid on a desk in the room, and inside the suitcase there was an automatic pistol, a silencer and several clips of ammunition. Underneath the Muslim Burkah Sgt. Daniel Kershi was wearing a Russian military uniform arrayed with several rows of campaign medals and ribbons from the old Soviet Union. He carefully checked the weapon and slid a clip of ammunition into it and engaged a round to the magazine. He then picked up the remaining clips of ammunition and strapped them to his body underneath his clothing. Then he carefully screwed the silencer on to the barrel of his gun and slipped the weapon into a leather holster which was tucked under his rib cage and concealed by his coat.

Sergeant Kershi then lifted a cover in the bottom of the suitcase to reveal several small packets of C-4 explosives wrapped together in a wide leather belt. These explosives were all tied together to a single detonating trigger. He picked up the device and very gently strapped the belt around his waist, and put his military coat on which he had removed and laid on the desk, he wished he had a mirror to see if everything was concealed but he did not. He then ran the wire which was attached to the explosives up under his coat and slit a hole in the bottom of his coat pocket so he could pull the detonating trigger up into his pocket and it would still be concealed from view.

Sgt. Daniel Kershi was quick to volunteer for this dangerous mission, when his longtime friend and now his Commander asked if anyone would risk their life to assassinate Colonel Chechnikov inside Syria. Daniel knew it may turn out to be a suicide mission but he was willing anyhow. All of Erik's field agents and their cells were now dispersed in all areas of the world and were striking at the World Governments military with guerrilla warfare force.

Sid had gathered them all together at a secret meeting in Afghanistan to go over the details of their field operations and give them final instructions. Their communications link would be through Bill Forney's world wide satellite TV program, and they were also combining with all the Christian groups that have allied themselves against this Dictator Government. Sid told all of his commanders that what they were doing was for the future of mankind and thanked them for their loyal service, and then he offered this very dangerous mission to any volunteer, and Daniel accepted it.

Sid said he may never see any of them again and they were all very saddened but they knew it was for a great cause that they had all been brought together and none of them regretted anything that had happened thus far, they had successfully disarmed the five ICBM sites that the Colonel had set up and they were no longer a threat.

Even though the rogue submarine still had missiles that could be deployed anywhere in the world, the mission for Sid and his commanders were to do everything they could to destroy communications and the ability for the World Government leaders to continue their reign. All of these commanders had grown to love Sid and when they left the meeting in Afghanistan there was not a dry eye among them.

Sergeant Kershi rehearsed his plan in his mind before he stepped out of the building and began walking toward the Government building where their intelligence had reported the Colonel's office to be. "It was easy getting this far" he thought coming into Iraq dressed as a Muslim woman and then into Syria with a group of refugees, they had been picked up just across the border by a caravan of military trucks and given a ride into Damascus.

It was not too difficult to move around in the Middle East now since the United States and the EU had withdrawn all their military. General Siki's New World Government has eliminated all sovereign borders, however if you are Caucasian, it is more difficult because the Chinese armies working in conjunction with the Council of twelve, to establish world peace and enforce environmental laws are much more likely to arrest and detain anyone that is Caucasian until they can determine through the universal registration data bank if they are American.

There have been several attempts by former CIA agents and other clandestine agents to assassinate members of the new Governments leadership especially targeted has been Colonel Chechnikov, since he gave the order to deploy a missile from a nuclear sub armed with one of the green bombs onto an American city and create havoc for millions of its citizens.

As Sergeant Dan Kershi walked cautiously down the street in Damascus toward the General's Government's building which was long ago vacated by General Siki and his New World Government which are now installed in the world headquarters in Israel in the city of Jerusalem, awaiting the final completion of the new headquarters building on the Temple Mount.

The Colonel and his Military arm of the New World Government and Chinese Government officials now occupy this building.

It is daylight in Damascus and the streets of the capital are filled with Chinese and UN soldiers in various kinds of military uniforms, so it is easy for Sergeant Kershi to walk undisturbed up to the Capitol building. There are military convoys and government vehicles going in every direction. As Daniel nears the building he sees a large black Mercedes with a flag flying from each front fender emblazoned with the New World Government symbol, he instinctively knew this was the Colonel's staff car it was parked near a side entrance to the building which he knew would be locked.

There were a contingent of heavily armed guards at the front entrance and he did not dare take a chance of being caught, not because he was afraid of being arrested but his mission must at all costs succeed. Then he walked toward the unguarded limousine and stood beside it while looking around to see if he was being observed.

He didn't see any cameras or surveillance equipment so he slid himself underneath the limousine. Then he unbuttoned his coat and with much effort removed it to gain access to the plastic explosives he had around his waist, He began very gently placing the plastic explosives under the frame of the Colonel's limousine and carefully wiring each of them together, there was enough explosive to destroy the limousine and blow up half the Government building. Now all he had to do was set the remote timing device, and crawl out from under the limousine and conceal himself about two blocks away from the limousine and wait till the Colonel and his staff were in the car.

Before Dan could extricate himself from under the car, the side entry door opened and three men in military uniforms stepped out of the building and walked toward the limousine. Daniel remained motionless underneath the limousine as the three men approached and opened the doors. Then he began to sweat profusely as each man got into the car and closed the doors, he had to make a quick decision since he could not be sure one of these men was the Colonel, he could only see them from their waist down, as he lay under the car. He wasn't afraid to die himself if he could be sure his mission was accomplished. The engine turned over in the car, and Daniel made a split second decision, he clicked the trigger on the timing device and there was a giant explosion.

The following day the communications satellite of the World Government carried this story. "Yesterday an attempt was made to assassinate one of our great leaders, Colonel Boris Chechnikov, we are pleased to announce that the Colonel was not injured and that the enemies of your World Government have failed in their mission". "We are putting out a call to all the citizens of the World Government, if you know the whereabouts of any of these Christian cells we urge you to contact your local offices and expose them".

"These terrorist groups of Christians are causing delay in the efforts of your Government to establish a lasting world peace". "The loyal citizens of the World Government that will expose these radical Christian cells will be rewarded by given a one-year exemption of rationing, for them and all the members of their family, they will have complete and free access to all the resources under the control of the World Government for one year".

Sid heard the broadcast and wondered if his good friend and companion, Dan Kershi had given his life for the cause of freedom. He contacted Erik and told him of the failed attempt to assassinate the

Colonel, who was responsible for his father's death. Erik was saddened by the news, not only that the assassination attempt had failed but for the loss of Daniel Kershi.

CHAPTER 48

I T WAS TO BE a day of celebration, the World Government had completed its headquarters building in Jerusalem and all their staff and equipment had been moved in, and all the former Governments of the world including the United States had acquiesced to the authority of the new World Government. The Middle Eastern Countries, which were led by Syria, has appointed a world leader, who was recognized and ratified by the UN Security Council that had been reformed. The New World leader was going to be introduced and inaugurated on this day.

As the Council of twelve prominent men who had been appointed as a special Cabinet in the World Government was about to reveal their leader to the whole world including the remnants of humanity in all four corners of the earth, something completely unexpected happened.

It was to be a worldwide satellite TV transmission to reveal the New World Government as the People's Republic of Earth and introduce and inaugurate the first Premiere of all the earth's people.

First there would be an introduction of His Majesty, Premiere Mustaf Siki Assahdam, who was a young, strongman military leader and statesmen from Damascus. He had been chosen by the world Council of twelve to lead this New World Government. He has been given authority by the leaders of all nations to use any and all means necessary to bring full compliance to the environmental constitution which was drawn up and presented to the UN Security Council and ratified by all member nations.

A few days before the inauguration was to take place, a strange phenomena occurred, which was un-explainable.

Many people in every nation on earth reported seeing what they described as a blinding light in the sky, it was so bright it blotted out the sun and only lasted for an instant. The Council of twelve immediately began researching all satellite photos believing that someone had detonated a nuclear explosion, and they were determined to bring whoever had violated the environmental treaty to justice in the World Court. Their suspicions, were toward the Country of the former United States, since they were the very last Country to sign the treaty, and turn control of their military and nuclear arsenals over to the World Government. They only acquiesced after much negotiating and coercion by the United Nations and then only after Colonel Chechnikov's military group launched an ICBM missal, armed with a nuclear warhead into one of their major cities, and the captured American shuttles were launched from the international space station with their loads of deadly cargo which devastated the East and West Coasts of that nation.

If they were found to be the ones responsible for the nuclear explosion, and they have other hidden nuclear missiles under their control we will launch an unprovoked nuclear attack on two more of their major cities the Council of twelve determined.

During the next few days the scientists poured over all the satellite transmission data and all the satellite photos from around the world, and their conclusion was that this ultra bright light which was reported in many countries did not originate from anywhere on earth and that the light registered brighter than any known light emanating from a nuclear explosion, it was brighter than even the solar sun.

The scientists report was on Premiere Siki's desk and he was discussing it with members of the Council when his secretary spoke into the intercom in his office and said "Sir there is a gentleman in your outer office who is demanding to see you he says it is extremely urgent". "Tell him if he interrupts this meeting and does not have information which we consider urgent he will suffer severe consequences, and if he is willing to take a chance then send him in".

The door to the Premiere's office opened and a well-dressed European man stood in the entry with a leather briefcase held at his side. "Come in" Siki said in his Harvard trained American accent "what is so urgent to interrupt such an important meeting"? The man stepped forward while looking around at the men in the room and nodded politely. He then sat his briefcase on the desk and opened it. "My name is Jason Traughber, and I am an investigative reporter for the BBC World News, we've been following up on the story of the bright light phenomena, when some very interesting and unexplained news began coming into the newsroom from all over the world". "And this news is" Siki asked "get on with it one of the Council members said scolding, you're wasting precious time". "Yes forgive me" the reporter said, "the news is gentlemen that from every nation on earth, from every state, every village, and every family people have strangely vanished". "What do you mean vanished, how many people are we talking about"? "Sir we don't know for sure but the reports seem to indicate several million and reports are still coming in". "Millions vanished into thin air"? "What do you take me for a fool"? "I have a good mind to have you executed along with all the others that put you up to this". "No sir it is not a joke it is real I have here in my briefcase, (as he began nervously laying out reams of computer print outs on the desk,) all the reports, and they seem to be tied to the same time every one witnessed that ultra bright flash of light". "We have sent reporters and investigators to every country to verify our reports and try to determine if the light and the disappearances are somehow connected".

The Premiere and the members of the Council who had now gathered around the desk began reviewing information on the computer print out sheets. There was complete silence in the room for the next ten minutes, and then Siki said, "we have got to get to the bottom of this quickly before world wide panic spreads out of control". "Thank you Jason for bringing this to our attention and not going public with it, you are to go back to your superiors and tell them the Council has determined this information to be classified as Top-Secret". "We'll keep these print outs for further review, you may leave the office now and again thank you for coming".

As the reporter left the office and closed the door the Premiere looked around at the council members and said, in a nervous voice "what do you make of all this"? "I don't know", one of the council members said "but we had better postpone the inauguration of the New Government until we can make sense and explain this". "I agree" Siki said "we have got to keep this information from leaking out, send a memo to all the news agencies which are linked to our Satellite Communication's Grid let them know they are to classify any information related to the light or the disappearances and it is to be Top-Secret.

One of the council members said "we control all world news agencies but one, and that is that Bill Forney's International Satellite broadcast, and we have been unable to discover where he broadcasts from, since he moved his transmission equipment out of Moscow and relocated somewhere else, we believe it is located in the United States but we have been unsuccessful in blocking his satellite feeds". We believe he is working covertly with the United States Government but we have so far been unable to prove it. If he gets this information there'll be no stopping him from broadcasting it around the world".

Premiere Siki interrupted and said, "call for a meeting of your scientific colleagues and see if they have any ideas, and include those United States scientists also, I regret saying it but they usually have an answer for everything". "The word was sent out to all the scientists from every part of the earth, they were summoned to Brussels by the Council of twelve, and their participation was mandatory. They were instructed to drop everything they were working on and in ten days arrive in Brussels for a world planning session.

They arrived from all over the world and the meeting was convened. The Premiere and his Council of twelve chaired the meeting, there were over 5000 scientists present, and the council had arranged for all of the great meeting rooms in the city to be available for the delegates, as well as the best hotels. They had linked all the meeting places together via satellite with large viewing screens in each location. And all the delegates were linked with communications to allow each of them to participate in the dialog.

The Premiere opened the meeting by welcoming all the delegates and explaining to them that the nature of the information in this meeting is extremely sensitive and therefore should be classified as Top-Secret. "Any information gleaned from this meeting that is leaked to the public by any delegate will be deemed an act of treason by the World Government and they will be executed".

The meeting began with the chairman of the Council revealing the reason for the meeting and submitting copies of the BBC information. After all the delegates had ample opportunity to review the information, the floor was opened for discussion. A prominent scientist in the field of biophysics, the delegate from South Africa stood and said "I am pleased to be here and take part in this great symposium", and then he said; "not only am I pleased to be here and have the opportunity to participate in this great symposium with so many of my colleagues, but more than that I am pleased to learn that this phenomena did not just take place in South Africa, we were all afraid it did and we did not report it to anyone". "When the reports began coming into my office as well as all my colleagues throughout South Africa, we did not report it to any other nation, believing it had only occurred in our country". "My colleagues and I have been studying this phenomena since it first occurred, and we have no scientific explanation for the disappearance of hundreds of thousands of our citizens". "We believe that somehow these mass disappearances are in some way connected to the super bright light which was seen all over South Africa just before the reports began coming in". All the delegates in unison shouted "here, here".

Then a delegate from the United States stood and addressed the members and said, "my colleagues and I in America have been discussing this phenomena and have concluded that perhaps it was the catching away of a great multitude of people by someone the Christians call Jesus Christ, and transported them to another planet called Heaven as alluded to in the Christian Bible, and believed by their churches, that it would actually take place".

"No, No, No", all the delegates cried in unison. A delegate from Rome stood and said, "many of our people in many of our churches also believe in the so-called rapture, even our Pope". The Holy Father of Rome believes it, so when the sudden disappearance of thousands of people from all over Italy became apparent we sent a delegation to Rome to consult with the Holy Father and inquire if this is possibly what has happened". "He assured us it was not, and then to offer proof he said, look at all the Catholic Church's that are still well attended and look at me I am your living proof".

Then all the delegates began shouting, "many of our churches have had no one vanish from them, so let's put aside that hypothesis and begin exploring a more logical explanation for this phenomena".

The time had slipped away and it was time to break for lunch, the chairman of the council stood and said we will break for one hour we will reconvene in one hour don't be late.

The meeting rooms filled up again after lunch and the Chairman opened the floor for discussion. At first there was not much new information, it ranged from extraterrestrial abductions to religious belief in a catching away of all Christians. Then late in the afternoon a well-dressed gentleman stood and asked if he may speak to the delegates from the dais. "My name is Professor Ian Stone, "I am from the United

Kingdom and my specialty study is in evolutionary processes, I have been studying and performing research on the evolution scale for thirty five years, most of that time I have concentrated my research on the evolution leap". "The evolution leap can be explained in the following way, there are well known and defining gaps in the evolutionary scale, we have been unable to determine when our ancestors came out of the dark forest of Homo erectus and leaped into the present age of Homo sapiens".

"We have thus far, though try as we may, been unable to find any scientific or credible evidence of that missing link". "During my years of research I have discovered there have been many unexplainable missing links in the evolutionary scale, or what we call species leaps". The professor continued his lecture to an attentive audience of delegates far into the night, and after he finished his lecture and the delegates were dismissed for the night the professor was asked to stay and meet with the council.

"Professor Stone is it"? the chairman of the council said "yes Sir that is correct" "while you were lecturing before the delegates the council members and The Premiere were greatly impressed with your supposition, so much so, that we are requesting that you submit your supposition in writing in a clear and understandable way that can be presented by the Premiere on a worldwide telecast to all the citizens of the earth, to relieve their fears". "I will be more than happy to do that and I will try to have it available to you within one week". "Thank you sir, and the Council and the Premiere cannot express our gratitude enough".

After a good nights sleep the delegates were in the coffee shops and breakfast bars and roaming through the city trying to locate colleagues that they had not seen for years. Since the next session would not convene until 2:00 p.m., they had free time. It soon became apparent by scrolling through the attendance records which was made available to each of the delegates that a great number of renown scientists which were well known by their colleagues were missing.

The attendance records revealed, that most of the scientists that were missing were known in the community as either "intelligent design" or "creationist" theorists. The assumption was made by the attending delegates that these colleagues had not been invited to the symposium. Many of the delegates from the United States were hoping that one of their prominent "Creation" Theorists, a Mrs. Stacy Czuba, would attend. They wished Stacy was here, not because they embraced her theory but because she was such an eloquent speaker and had been known to debate her theories so forcefully in a public forum that her opponent, after hour upon hour just simply refused to continue and left the platform, but she was probably not invited either.

The meeting of the delegates reconvened at 2:00 p.m. and the chairman opened the meeting in absence of the Premiere, "Gentleman and Ladies" he said; "we wish to thank all of you for coming to Brussels to what was planned as a week's symposium, however due to the supposition of Professor Ian Stone; that clearly explained the massive disappearance of a great number of our citizens from all over our planet, we can adjourn this meeting today". "The Premiere and the council will submit, in a public worldwide telecast in two weeks from today a final summation and clear explanation of this phenomenon, which will be in part from the Professor's research and supposition".

"So with that let me remind all of you once more before we are adjourned that everything you have heard is to remain classified as Top-Secret until after it is made public". "This meeting is now adjourned".

Two weeks after the meeting in Brussels the Council took control of all satellite transmissions and informed the whole of humanity of the speech that would be telecast live to every part of the world, which would give a full and clear understanding of the vanishing phenomena.

The Premiere and the Council members had reviewed the Professor's supposition and rewrote it several times for clarity. At 1:00 p.m. Middle Eastern time everyone in every place on earth was sitting anxiously waiting the explanation. In some countries it was the middle of the night but the network of workers in this new World Government had installed satellite dishes in every village and in every city and hamlet in every part of the world, where there was human life. They had set up satellite feed transmission towers and placed millions of television receivers and large screens throughout the entire habitable planet, because the new rulers demanded to have personal contact with all of their subjects. They had been working on this project for over six months it'd been a monumental undertaking and a huge financial cost but great sums of money and all of earths resources were at their disposal and the task was finally completed.

"Good morning citizens of the new World Government, I am coming to you today because many of you have had great losses and are grieving for your loved ones, I am also grieving with you, until a week ago I was as fearful and perplexed as you are concerning this massive vanishing phenomena". "I have good news for you today that will explain this to you, and bring comfort to your souls".

"First I would like to say how pleased we are to be able to make this telecast to every world citizen in every country in the world, due to the amazing advances in technology which we are using to communicate with all of our citizens and keep all of you informed, to the changes taking place in your World Government".

"We assured all of you at the time of your registration and the implantation of your personal identity chip, that you were all an important part of this process and we will continue to inform you of all important events and changes that you need to be aware of". "We also wish to assure you that the armed soldiers of the New World Armed Forces that are occupying your homeland are for your own protection and the safety of all the world citizens".

"Our government has been receiving reports from throughout the world that millions of humanity have vanished from our planet". "Many of them have vanished from homes or offices and in the agricultural fields in rural areas without causing any incidents to others, however there have been other reports from all parts of the world that both men and women operating machinery such as in the field of transportation i.e. planes trains buses and other types of transportation equipment have also vanished leaving their passengers helpless and involved in terrible and catastrophic events". "We are sending aid in massive amounts to every corner of the earth to help your leaders defray the enormous costs and loss of life to our citizens that these catastrophic events have caused".

"We want to assure all the citizens of the New World Government, that your leaders have been working diligently to determine the cause of this massive vanishing phenomena". "Two weeks ago we convened a special symposium with scientists from all over the world, to seek an explanation from the greatest minds in the world, 5000 of them". "From that meeting we have a clear understanding of what we, and the citizens of our new world have witnessed, and today you will hear the summation of what has happened".

"This supposition is the result of thirty five years of intensive study and research by Professor Ian Stone of the former United Kingdom, and we wish to thank him for this answer we have all been searching for".

"From the Professor's intensive study, along with many other great scientific minds we have learned that humanity as a unique species is a result of millions of years of evolution". "We are continuing to learn more and more about the evolutionary scale". "There are yet many unanswered questions, we do not know definitively, when the species Homo erectus moved out of the jungles of Africa and evolved into Homo sapiens". "There have been several gaps in the evolutionary process which are unexplainable, Professor Darwin called them evolutionary leaps". "The science of evolution has taught us that Mother Nature in the natural order of things governs the evolutionary process, and it is that natural order that culls out the weakest of the species, to allow the strongest to exist and multiply". "Our planet is capable of sustaining only a certain number of people with the natural resources that it has available".

"Throughout the millions of years of life on our planet, Mother Nature has been able, through attrition (death and life cycle) maintain that number". "From time to time she needed some help from humanity itself". "Therefore we have fought numerous wars and eliminated much of humanity, sometimes nature raises up certain individuals to eliminate large populations and entire races to protect the overpopulation of our planet i.e. Nero, Hitler, Stalin and other great men, these men were used to cull out millions of humanity of weaker nature in order to assure the stronger would survive, to continue the evolutionary process", they were pawns of nature".

"However all the wars that were fought and all the attrition through natural catastrophic events carried out by nature herself was not enough to prevent the overpopulation of the planet, and that is why the evolution of the species had to take giant leaps". "Some of these leaps are well known to us, for example the complete elimination of any trace of the continent and peoples of Atlantis of which the Greek writer Homer described in vivid detail as a great civilization". "Or closer to our own time the citizens of the Myan and Aztec nations which have vanished without a trace, from Central and South America".

"We have witnessed the largest population explosion in our planet's history during the last 200 years and we have used up more of the planet's natural resources than any time in the history of mankind, it is for this reason that your Government leadership has taken control of all earth's natural resources and allocated them to each citizen in a just and equitable way according to your needs".

"The summation of our finding is, that humanity has reached a place on the evolutionary scale where it has become necessary for nature to take another giant leap to assure the continual preservation of our planet for the strongest and fittest of humanity". "Therefore she had to remove millions of the weaker inhabitants of our species and take another step forward to allow the evolutionary process to continue". "Therefore fellow citizens of your New World we urge you to continue grieving for your losses but take heart in knowing you have been thrust ahead into a new dimension of evolution, and we are all standing on the threshold of new and challenging discoveries where no other man has ever stood". "You and I have been chosen to usher in a new and exciting world of peace and harmony". "I welcome you fellow citizens to the making of a New World, good night, good day and thank you so much for listening"

Then the head of the Council of twelve took the dais and said, "Citizens of a New World, in one week from today we will have an inauguration of our World Premiere, and all of you will be able to view it". This official inauguration of your Premiere will be held in the city of Jerusalem, and there will be seven days of continual celebrations in every part of the earth". "All of you can participate in your own place of residence".

CHAPTER 49

IT WAS UNUSUALLY DARK in the English countryside tonight, there were no stars and only a sliver of light shone from the moon, it looked as if a black tapestry had been pulled over the entire sky.

Eva Forney and her daughter Jennifer were clearing the dishes from the table and feeding their two Doberman's leftover scraps, when Jennifer told her mother that there was a car coming down the lane toward the house, she could see the headlights.

"I wonder who that could be this time of night"? They rarely had any visitors out here in the country at Bill's parents country estate where they had taken up a permanent residents, and moved some of their furnishings and their two dogs there, from Russia.

It was also a safe and secluded place for them since her husband Bill had returned to the United States to continue his television program. Bill said he felt it necessary to get her and her daughter out of Russia and hidden from the Colonel's thugs since he was threatened by them in Moscow for broadcasting the exposés on the Colonel and his covert shadow Government.

They felt safe here in England and Bill would visit often. The car drove up to the house and turned off its lights and the engine was turned off, and Eva heard a car door shut and she walked toward the front door to see who was there. As she turned on the outside lights to see who was there, she saw two well-dressed men standing on the front porch, she opened the door and was about to speak to one of them when both of the Doberman's began charging across the room toward the door, they were barking and extremely agitated, Eva said to the man closest to the door "wait one moment let me put the dogs in the backyard and she closed the door".

"Jenny" she called "get these dogs outside so I can see what these men want. When the dogs were outside Eva opened the door again and apologized for the behavior of the dogs. The one man close to the door said they had a message from her husband which they had to deliver in person because it was too sensitive to discuss on the telephone. Eva opened the door and invited them in and closed the door behind them. "I don't see Bill as often as I would like, since he moved his entire broadcasting studio out of Moscow", she said. "Would you gentlemen care for some coffee" Eva said as the two men sat down on the couch.

"That would be nice" one of the men said "but don't go to any trouble" "it's no trouble at all" Eva said, "Jenny would you get these gentlemen a cup of coffee; they have come with a message from your father".

As Jenny brought the two men a cup of coffee she said, "and how is my father back there in Los Angeles"? "I'll bet it is hot there this time of year". Before Eva could correct her daughter, one of the men said; "yes it is warm and your father is having a difficult time adjusting to the desert heat".

Eva looked at her daughter making eye contact with her and said to the men "what is the message you bring from Bill"? The man who had done most of the speaking said, "We were sent to England to pick up a package for Bill and then we are flying to Moscow on urgent business for the studio". "There is a classified transcript inside the package that must be in Bill's hands no later than ten days from now to be broadcast to the world". "We need you to address the package and we will drop it off at the air freight office in the morning".

"Mom can I see you in the kitchen? Jenny called, Eva said to the men "excuse me I need to see what Jenny wants". Eva walked into the kitchen where Jenny was and said in a whispered voice, "Jenny get out the back door and get the car running I will meet you in the car as soon as I can get away without making them suspicious".

"It's too late for that" the man said standing in the doorway of the kitchen with a gun in his hand, "I had hoped we could resolve this without any violence but that is not going to happen now, now both of you get back in the living room and take a seat on the couch".

By this time Jenny was so frightened she could not hold back the tears, the other man was standing and also holding a gun and he said, "all we want is the location of your husband's satellite broadcasting station; we know it is somewhere in the United States and you're going to tell us where".

"It is somewhere in Los Angeles, California, but we do not know the exact location we have never been there" Jenny said, as one of the men was already dialing a number on his cell phone. "The studio is in LA can we triangulate the location"? A strange look came over the face of the man on the phone and he said, "oh I see okay we will take it from here and he ended the conversation".

The man then walked over to Eva and slapped her across the face with his open hand as he said, "we are just getting started". He looked at his partner who was standing in front of Jenny and said, "they lied our people have already determined that the studio is in Washington, DC not LA, now all we need to know is where in Washington". "Take the girl into the bedroom and see if you can convince her to tell us where her father's studio is located in Washington".

By this time Jenny was sobbing uncontrollably. "Please" Eva said; "don't harm my daughter I'll tell you anything you want to know just please don't hurt her". "Do you have the address of the studio in Washington"? "Yes I have letters Bill has sent me with the address on them". "Get the letters your father sent Jenny, they are in the top right hand drawer of my dresser" Jenny got up and started toward her mother's bedroom when the man standing near her grabbed her arm and said, "hold on little girl you're not going anywhere without me". Then he followed her into the bedroom. The man standing next to Eva said, "Your husband is wanted for treason by the New World government and we have been sent to find him and bring him to the World Court to be tried and sentenced". "We know He has been helping, and supporting the rebels with his satellite broadcasts, who have banded together worldwide in an attempt to overthrow the New World government".

The other man and Jenny came back into the room, Jenny's dress was torn almost completely off, she was holding it up in front to conceal her naked body, and the man was holding his gun in one hand and several envelopes in the other, "they were in there just like she said but as you can see it took a little time to find them, we have the location of the studio". "Now just go and leave us alone" Eva said, "You have what you came for".

"We would like to do that but I'm afraid we can't, we have orders not to leave you alive". "Oh my god"! Eva said to Jenny "they're going to kill us".

Four shots were fired two in the head of each of the women as they slumped to the floor the Dobermans began barking and jumping up against the back door as the two men left the house and drove off into the night.

CHAPTER 50

B ILL FORNEY AND DAN, his producer began their broadcast with this announcement, "the following broadcast will reveal in detail the personal profile of this New World leader". "His name is Mustaf Siki Assahdam, he is a General in the Syrian Military and a world renown statesman". "He was appointed by the United Nations Security Council, to the position of Premiere and Supreme Commander of the New World Government, following his appointment it was ratified by the World Governments".

"The General is a man with a physical stature of approximately six feet four inches tall, much taller than the average Arab descendent, he is a handsome man with Middle Eastern dark complexion and jet black wavy hair which is always covered in public with the traditional Muslim headdress". "He is forty two years old, rather young for the position he holds". "He was born in Syria to a poor peasant family, and he has no siblings, which is very unusual for an Arab family, his father sent him to a military school in Egypt when he was eight years old and he did not return home to Syria until he was four teen years old". "Then he cared for his aging parents until they died when he was only seventeen years old".

"After the death of his parents Siki, as he was known was taken in by a benevolent and very wealthy Sheik who had lost his wife to cancer and had no children of his own, this wealthy Arab Sheik whose name was, Assahdam wanted the very best for his young charge, so he arranged through a prominent diplomat in the Syrian government to send Siki to the United States to attend Harvard University". Siki attended Harvard for four years and obtained a degree in both law and science". "He graduated with high honors at the top of this class".

While he attended Harvard he was an unusually quiet and even tempered student, and because of his Muslim faith he did not party with the students where alcohol and drugs were present". "He made very few friends because of his Muslim faith and he did not date any girls for the four years he attended Harvard". "His debating skills in his law class were brilliant, many of the old alumni compared him to that great orator, William Jennings Brian".

"After receiving his law degree he was offered a prestigious position in several different Fortune 500 companies in America, but rejected them all to return to his home in Syria".

"Upon his arrival back in Syria he was welcomed by the President and offered a prominent position in His Government, which Siki accepted, and he became known throughout the Middle East and all the European Union Nations and all the Asian Peoples as a great statesman and peace negotiator".

"Through his diplomatic skills and his personal charm he has succeeded where all others have failed, to bring the Arab nations together in a united cohesive kingdom which are all sharing the wealth of the giant oil deposits throughout the Arab kingdom of the Middle East". "He has established a foundation in the name of his benefactor, and is fully funded by the oil revenues flowing into the kingdom from the United States and the European Union, which guarantees any Muslim Boy a University education any where in the world".

"This foundation also makes available funds in scholarships to any Muslim girl student that applies herself academically to attend the college or university of their choice anywhere in the world". "The foundation also has built and is continuing to build state-of-the-art educational facilities and premier hospitals and health-care facilities all over the Middle East".

"He has brokered and brought the three superpowers, India, Russia, and China together in peace negotiations".

"His achievements have been lauded and welcomed all over the world, the Queen of England has bestowed upon him the highest order of knighthood".

"His rapid rise in political popularity and his methods of bringing world governments into compliance with these edicts by use of extreme force have some, very uncomfortable, especially the United States, the Government and the people in that country have never accepted justification for the "green bomb" released on one of its cities. Or the capture and use of their space shuttles, that were released from the international space station, which carried their deadly cargo and devastated the East and West coasts of the United States".

"Since unleashing "Wormwood" and plunging the United States and Japan into economic chaos the General has promised that his World Government would not have to take that kind of action again, because all the world governments are now moving to comply with his necessary, though extremely harsh demands".

"He has announced to the world on a worldwide satellite broadcast that it was unfortunate that his Government had to use such extreme military force to cause some nations to conform to the environmental urgency that the earth faces".

"For that reason he could justify taking millions of lives to save our planet for continual billions of our citizens and all future generations to live and enjoy the bountiful resources of mother earth".

"During the past eighteen months, since the world leaders elevated General Mustaf Siki into his current position of Supreme Commander of the new earth, the most significant personal diplomatic achievements he has accomplished is, effectively bringing everlasting peace between the peoples of the nation of Israel and the Palestinian peoples, and removed the borders that separated these two neighbors for thousands of years". "For the first time in two thousand years, trade and commerce is flowing into and out of the Jewish state and from all its Arab neighbors".

"Siki was able to accomplish this by building the New World headquarters Temple Palace on the most holy site in all the Middle East, both to the Jews and the Muslims but first he had to remove all the structures that occupied the Temple Mount in Jerusalem". Including the Golden Dome of the rock shrine that housed the rock that all Muslims believe was the very rock upon which Father Abraham offered his son Isaac as a sacrifice to his God", and also the place they believe their Prophet Mohammad ascended into heaven". It is the Holiest place in the Middle East for both Jews and Muslims". "After many difficult days of negotiations with the leaders of Orthodox Jews and the highest leadership of the Roman Catholic Church which also reveres the site in their faith, a consensus was reached".

"The Muslim mosques on the Temple Mount would be carefully taken apart and relocated and restored to their original state and the Holy Rock would be carefully unearthed and moved into the restored Mosque". "The location in Palestine would be chosen by the Muslim leadership and must be somewhere inside their capitol city of East Jerusalem". "The Palace of the World headquarters would then be constructed on the top of the Temple Mount and would include a Jewish temple in facsimile to the original Solomon's Temple which would be occupied by the three religions, Jews, and Muslims, and Roman Catholics these three religions would combine to become one world religion".

"It has been eighteen months since construction began and it is almost complete, it is to be dedicated soon".

"The coalition of these three religions seemed to be working successfully, however in recent days a rift has risen between the three, the Muslims insist that their holy days be given priority throughout the world and that they and their Priests be allowed to commemorate the ascension of their profit, on the Jewish holy of Holies portion of the Temple".

"The Jewish Rabbi's and their High Priest refused to give that consent, the Jewish Priests believe that no other religion's Priests should have access to the part of the Temple where their Holy of Holies is located". "To do so they believe it would desecrate their holiest place which they believe is consecrated to their coming Messiah".

"The Roman Catholics are joining forces with them and against the Muslims, and there is a very heated debate within the Council of twelve over this issue". "Mustaf Siki will shortly make his ruling which will be final".

"The whole world is waiting for the final ruling on this matter and The Premiere has set 6:00 p.m. Middle Eastern time to telecast his decision to the world".

"All of the citizens here are anxiously waiting, it is now 5:55 p.m. the world leader will be speaking in five minutes, and after that, we will continue our broadcast".

CHAPTER 51

"CITIZENS OF THE WORLD, greetings from your Commander, as you know over eighteen months ago, when I was promoted to this office by your leaders from all over the world, I promised I would bring peace and prosperity to our world at any cost". "It was unfortunate that we have had to employ some extreme measures to bring some of the world's former governments into compliance with our plans and programs to assure that peace". "Now that peace has been obtained throughout the world we must work together to sustain a lasting peace".

"The destruction of our planet has finally been reversed by the environmental programs our scientists have introduced, and within the next three years we will achieve the prosperity we promised to all the people of earth". "The borders throughout the earth have been eliminated and the citizens registration is nearly complete". Citizens of our world are now free to move with their families anywhere they desire".

"When I was placed in this position I believed as you do, that religion was very important to all of us, therefore we brought together the three primary religions and created one world religion which would be controlled by the Council of twelve, in Jerusalem". "They would provide spiritual strength and guidance to all the citizens of the earth, and that seemed to be successful until recently". "There is now a cancer growing in that body and it must be removed".

"From this day forward there will be no religion recognized by the World Government, furthermore all Priests and spiritual leaders will be defrocked and become common citizens". "The new temple that is to be dedicated soon will be a Temple of the people where celebrations shall be held for all the citizens of the earth". "A throne will be erected in the Temple currently known as the Jewish Holy of Holies, and I alone will occupy that throne and govern the whole earth from there, I will in effect become the Jews Messiah, the Muslims Profit, and the Roman Catholics Jesus". "The citizens who identify themselves as Jews will be arrested and their rations will be given to others".

"This may seem to many to be cruel and extreme, but let me assure all of you it is necessary to take these steps to ensure lasting peace and prosperity for all the citizens of the earth".

"The Jewish people and their religion has been the cause of wars and destruction on our planet for thousands of years and will continue to be unless they are eliminated from our society". "Now I thank you for your devoted attention and your continued support, citizens of the New World".

"Citizens of the world as we resume our broadcast you have just heard your world leader announce that all religions are going to be banned from the earth, I know that this is just the beginning of destroying any personal faith that any citizen may have". "We have known for some time that all the Christians of this earth were taken out of this earth in what their Christian Bible refers to as, in our vernacular the rapture, and they are no longer with us". "So citizens of the earth those of you that have not and will not submit your allegiance to this New World Government and its Dictator, I urge you now if you have not been registered and received the implant of identification in your body, to rise up and gather together in groups, form coalitions of Jews and Muslims and Roman Catholics and all other faiths of this world and let us march with one voice and one goal to overthrow this Dictator and his Government, and take back our planet.

"We will continue to broadcast through this satellite feed as long as we are alive and we have access to all of the world". "Citizens can make contact with each other, and many of you have arms and ammunition and food supplies and all the resources that you need". "There is enough arms and supplies stored in all parts of the world, and can be used to overthrow this world government and its Dictator if we band together, putting all our previous prejudices aside and strive for one united goal".

"So I urge you now to stay tuned to this satellite feed, put aside your differences and let us develop an army that will be so massive that it will be impossible for us to be overcome or defeated, as we move on Jerusalem from the shores of every nation on earth to overthrow this Dictator and his government".

CHAPTER 52

Bill's cell phone rang in the studio in Washington, DC, "Bill? Erik, I have some sad news, our agents in the field have learned that your wife and daughter have both been killed". "I cannot begin to say how very sorry that I am we all thought they were hidden away in a safe place".

"We believe that they were able to gain information from your wife and daughter before killing them, the location of your studio in Washington". "It is therefore necessary and with extreme haste that you and your crew take whatever you need that is essential to continuing your broadcasting from another location and abandon your studio immediately".

"I am going to contact Karla and send her to the studio to remove her father from his quarters downstairs with all haste". "When they come for you they will surely have orders to arrest anyone and everyone that has assisted you and your broadcasting".

"Bill they are probably already on their way to the studio so I urge you, with all haste to dismantle the essentials for your broadcast and you and your crew leave at once, and when you have relocated you can reach me by way of our communicator". "Again Bill let me say how very sorry I am about your family's deaths".

The telephone rang at the office of the National Security Agency, and the receptionist routed the call to Karla's office, "hello this is agent Karla LeVanway". "Karla darling I don't have much time" Erik said, "the Colonel's men have located Bill's studio, and are probably on their way there now to arrest him, and everyone there including your father. You must get there before they do and get him out now". "I have already warned Bill of their coming but your father does not answer his phone". "Erik I'm about thirty minutes from there, I will leave at once, thank you for the warning goodbye my love".

Karla grabbed her automatic pistol belt and threw it over her shoulder and headed hurriedly out the door and down the stairs to her car in the parking garage.

How often she had thought this day would come, ever since her father agreed to let Bill set up his illegal broadcasting studio above his coffee shop. She knew it was going to be located sooner or later by The New World government, whose Intelligence service was searching diligently for it ever since Bill had moved it out of Moscow. They have placed a bounty on Bill's head and it was just a matter of time till they would locate his broadcasting facilities.

Her father offered his place after Erik asked him too, and he agreed without any hesitation, because he always loved his country and was a true patriot.

She was on her way to the coffee shop as fast as she could drive in the Washington, DC traffic. Only minutes away from her father's shop, as she turned onto his street, she saw a large pillar of black smoke, and heard a tremendous blast coming from the vicinity of the coffee shop building. Karla's heart began to race erratically. She saw the burned-out hull of what used to be a large van, the roof and one side was completely torn off from the explosion inside. The building that was her father's coffee shop had been completely destroyed. Both the ground floor and the second floor were burning out of control. Karla could not hold back the tears as she stopped her car about a half block down the street.

She waited to see if any rescue vehicles would come, they didn't, not even the fire department. She knew this was the work of the Colonel's men they didn't even have the decency to evacuate the patron's from inside the coffee shop. There were mangled and burned bodies of both men and women strewn about the debris. She left her car and walked cautiously up to the area where the building had collapsed from the explosion, thinking if her father was here when the explosion occurred then surely he was killed.

"Erik, did you hear what happened to Bill and his studio"? Sid said, "no! what happened"? "a van loaded with explosives was detonated in front of the building he was in and completely destroyed it". "Oh my God!

I just sent Karla there to warn her father to get out". "I also warned Bill to get out with his equipment but I don't know if I warned him in time". "I had no idea they would blow up the building, I thought they would arrest him and shut down his studio".

"Erik, it is too dangerous for us to stay in contact, you had better find some place to lay low, and I will do the same". "Some of my teams have joined up with a group of guerrilla fighters that call themselves the "Left Behind Army" they chose that name because they believe all the Christians were taken out of the world and they were left behind". "I'm going to join up with one of the groups in Germany, they have groups all over the world and they are well armed and have stockpiles of supplies hid in all the Countries".

"They intend to overthrow this Dictator and his Government". "The only criteria for joining one of these groups is that you're not registered in the World Data Bank and you do not have an implant in your body so you can be traced".

Then Erik asked Sid if he had heard anything from Little Lamb after the explosion. Sid told Erik he had not, and that all the Commanders in the field had been cautious about communicating with each other, for some time now the communications had been dead silence. Sid said, "now that we no longer have the satellite broadcasts from Bill's studio, we will have to communicate with each other, and that makes it too easy to trace our locations.

"Erik, this'll be the last time I can communicate with you, but we will get together again someday when all this is over, I love you my brother".

"Goodbye old friend and the best of luck to you go back to Minsk and marry your sweetheart and drop out of sight". "I will continue looking for my Karla if it takes the rest of my life".

Karla returned to her car, there were now hundreds of citizens pouring over the wreckage wringing their hands and wailing, many of them lost loved ones in the destruction. She was heading back to the National Security Agency building, and when she was in sight of the Capitol building and the White House she saw hundreds of New World government trucks, vans, and cars with their emergency lights flashing, surrounding both buildings. She saw men in uniforms escorting men and women out of both buildings in handcuffs and loading them into the trucks and vans. There were hundreds of Chinese and UN soldiers, armed with automatic rifles surrounding both the Capital and the White House buildings.

She turned her car around and headed toward her downtown apartment. She was sobbing over the loss of her father, and she was now unable to contact Erik, what could she do? She reached her apartment building and took the elevator up to her floor, and she hurriedly packed a suitcase, she did not know if the soldiers would come looking for those who were not in their offices ore not, but she couldn't afford take the chance.

Karla was heading out of the Washington, DC area, she did not know where she would go but she had to get away. She could hardly see to drive from the tears streaming down her face, *"is my father dead or wounded, lying somewhere in the wreckage? Did I do the right thing, when Erik asked my father for the use of his upstairs, or should I have resisted? Would my father still be alive now and how would it have affected my relationship with Erik"?* Her head was spinning so fast she could not think, as she continued driving in the direction of the state of Virginia. She would drive for about two hours and pull off the road to collect her thoughts and try once again to contact Erik . In Karla's apartment the phone rang, after several rings the answering machine picked it up, "Karla darling this is Erik, I am praying that you are alive if you are and you get this message please try and contact me on my private cell phone, you have the number, I love you darling and I will find you wherever you are, so go somewhere safe and I will come for you".

It was quiet in the mountains around St. Petersburg, Russia the Chinese and United Nations soldiers were too busy trying to control the anarchy in the cities of Russia to be concerned about any citizens that may be hiding in the mountains. Otto and Greta were sitting on the couch in the secluded cabin that belonged to Erik's father before he was killed. Erik told them they should leave Moscow and stay in his cabin. They were talking about the recent events that had taken place, the disappearance of millions of citizens from every part of the world and the explanation the Council of twelve and the Dictator General gave, and the Official Inauguration of General Siki, to be the imperial leader of the New World Government.

First it was Otto who thought he had heard a rustle in the dry leaves outside the cabin, and then Greta heard it. Otto got up off the couch and walked cautiously over to the window, he tried to see out but could not see into the dark then he motioned for Greta to turn out the light so he could see outside without being seen. There it was again, someone or something was walking up toward the back of the cabin. Otto walked over to the desk in the corner of the cabin, and slowly opened a drawer and gently lifted a pistol from the drawer, he checked to see if it was loaded, and it was. Being in the military Otto was very cautious and always kept a loaded revolver close by in case he ever needed it.

By this time who or what ever it was, was on the back porch at the door. Otto moved quietly and swiftly over to the door and stood very still with his weapon ready to fire at any unwanted intruder. Someone was trying the door knob, Otto now knew it was not an animal, but he could not see who it was. He knew there were a lot of people hiding out in the mountains, and had heard, when they no longer had food and supplies they would hunt down isolated cabins and they would forcefully take food and supplies from who ever and wherever they could find it even if it meant they would have to kill to get it. The door knob slowly turned and the small piece of wood that served as a fastener on the door was giving way under the pressure, the intruder was putting on the door. The door opened and Otto stepped in front of the intruder, with his gun pointed directly at their head.

"Whoa! my friend it's me, put that gun down" Erik said, "thank god" Otto said, "I nearly shot you, come in", "Greta" Otto called to his wife "it's okay it's Erik".

Erik told Otto and Greta what happened to Bill and his broadcasting studio, and he didn't know if Bill or Karla was still alive. He didn't have any way of finding out, President Brown called me, to let me know that he and all his staff of government leaders had been put under house arrest, or taken prisoner.

Erik told them about the call from Sid and what his plans were, Otto said they had heard of a resistance group of these "Left Behind" people, operating here in Russia, and he and Greta had been talking about joining them. Erik said he thought that would be a great idea, and he may do that himself, if only to use the group's network of communications to try and find Karla if she was still alive. After two days at the cabin Erik told Otto and Greta goodbye and said he would try to stay in touch with them.

Karla had driven as far as Virginia, and when she was unable to make contact with Erik, she continued on into West Virginia and into the mountains where she had heard that there were groups of resistance fighters that would take anyone in, who had not registered with the New World Government or had been implanted. She began to search for any group that would take her in, she would join a group now and become a resistance fighter against the New World Government.

CHAPTER 53

TWO YEARS HAVE NOW passed and the New World Dictator is firmly in control, his armies have destroyed the renegade satellite broadcasting of Bill Forney and now there was no way that the groups around the world that were resisting his government could contact each other. Now everything that was broadcast to the world citizens was propaganda, and only what he wanted them to hear, since he now controlled all the media. Since he had made that Satellite broadcast to the world, and said that all Jews should be eliminated from the earth the Jews had become a hunted people, and many of them have already been killed and many more that escaped from Jerusalem and Tel Aviv are now hiding out in the rocks and the caves in the area of Petra, in the mountains of Palestine. Many Jews from America have joined them there, and there are others coming from all over the world.

The armies of General Siki have stopped chasing the Jews because he knows that their resistance can't last much longer because their supplies and food is running out. When that happens they will either surrender to his armies, commit mass suicide or just die of starvation, anyway the world will be rid of them forever. He has already disbanded the world religion and its leaders and made it a crime of treason against the World Government for anyone who is caught practicing any form of religion.

The World Government has more problems with the groups of resistance fighters that call themselves the "Left Behind" people, because they are well armed and have been able to form a network all over the world and are wreaking havoc everywhere in his Government. One of these groups operating out of the United States, from the mountains in the State of West Virginia call themselves, 'The Little Lamb's Army", and are led by a woman. They are raiding the supply lines and food storage depots of the New World Government on a regular basis, and then they disappear back into the mountains. General Siki has posted a million Euro Dollar reward for their leader's capture, dead or alive.

Erik has managed to fly incognito to America where he has become a principal leader of a group of resistance fighters in Los Angeles, California, he has been training an army that has joined him in the desert. They're well armed, and with the expertise Erik has; in tactical guerrilla warfare, he has developed a formidable army.

He is known and admired throughout all the resistance movement worldwide and he uses the name "The Shadow". He just recently received a communiqué through the network that the leader of a group of resistance fighters in West Virginia would like for him to come to that area and assist them in the training of new recruits, which are joining their group everyday. Erik agreed to go and was planning on leaving shortly.

Karla was sitting in a small military tent that had been erected for a command post in the West Virginia mountains and she was watching and listening to a propaganda speech by Colonel Boris Chechnikov from World headquarters in Jerusalem, suddenly the screen on the small portable TV went blank, and then it came to life again and she saw a familiar face and heard an all too familiar voice.

"Good morning world citizens, and welcome to the new Bill Forney worldwide satellite program". "We will be bringing you all the real news of the world instead of the New World Government's propaganda". "We will keep you informed of the great resistance fighters and their progress and we will also inform all of you of the movements of the Premier's armies". "And through your private coded communicators we will plan and execute massive raids on food storage depots and supply lines until we have overthrown this Dictator and his Government". "Stay tuned to this channel".

"Thank God he got out", Karla thought, *"and maybe my father got out with him, I pray that he did and that he is somewhere safe and alive"*.

Erik also heard Bill's telecast and was so happy for his dear friend that he was alive and safe, he continued to wonder if Karla and her father were killed in the explosion. Every time he thought that his beloved Karla may be dead, tears would begin to flow uncontrollably down his cheeks. He could not help wondering if his call to her to warn her father may have caused her to be in the coffee shop when the explosion took place and killed both her and her father.

Erik was now in West Virginia at a small motel just outside the town where he was told to wait for a guy that would transport him into the mountains to meet their leader at their command center. A military jeep drove up to his door, occupied by two men carrying automatic weapons.

Erik stood with his gun drawn just inside the room that had been designated for him to meet his contact. One of the men got out of the jeep and left his rifle on the seat, while the other man kept his rifle ready to fire. The man approached Erik's door and knocked.

"Who is it?" came the voice from inside. "We have been sent to meet The Shadow", the man said, Erik opened the door and invited the man inside, "let me get my things, and I will be right with you".

Karla was waiting for her men to return with this mysterious stranger who the whole resistance movement knows only as The Shadow. She only hoped he is as good as all the resistance group's leadership says he is, and can train all their new recruits. She looked down the mountain trail and could see the jeep bumping along coming cautiously up the mountain road, and she turned and walked back into the command center and set down at her make shift desk, to wait for her men to bring the mysterious stranger to meet her.

The jeep drove up in front of the Command Center and stopped, the man on the passenger side of the jeep got out and motioned for Erik to get out of the jeep also. Erik got out, stood and stretched himself, looked around and said, "when will I get to meet your leader"? "She's inside the Command Center I'll take you to her now". Erik followed the man toward the Command Center tent, as he looked around at several hundred men going through what appeared to be training exercises, there were four armored vehicles with fifty caliber machine guns mounted on each of them, setting in a row, he thought, *this is a well armed group of resistance fighters*".

The man Erik was following pulled back the flap on the tent and Erik followed him inside. There were computers, maps, automatic weapons and boxes of ammunition lying in piles, on the tent floor. The man approached the desk where a woman in combat fatigues was sitting and said, "He's here" with her back against the tent door, the leader of the resistance group began to turn slowly in her chair to greet this mysterious stranger known as The Shadow.

As she turned Erik stepped forward and said, "They call me The Shadow, and it is a pleasure to meet you".

CHAPTER 54

SID HAD TAKEN ERIK'S advice and he had made his way back to Russia and to the city of Minsk. It had been a little over three years now since his fiancée had stood before the closed casket in Moscow which she thought held his dead body. He must be very careful how he approaches her, he looks so much different than he used to, his head is shaved and he wears a small goatee and mustache and looks rather sinister. He had heard that his mother had been living with his fiancée for about two years and she was taking care of her before she died a year ago. Sid was so sad that he could not attend the funeral of his mother because it would have placed the whole operation in jeopardy if he had exposed himself at that time. He wondered if he should call his fiancée before visiting her, he also wondered if she had found someone else, and perhaps was even married he just didn't know what to do.

He decided to just visit her at her apartment hoping that she was unable to recognize him until he wanted to reveal himself. He walked briskly down the sidewalk and stopped in front of the building where his fiancée's apartment was located. He climbed the steps of the porch, and walked over to the door, and tried it to see if it was open. He pushed it open and began walking up those familiar stairs that he and his fiancée had traversed many times. As Sid began to climb the stairs very quietly his heart was racing, he thought that it could be heard beating like a drum. What would he say to her he thought, *"what if she recognized him and fainted or worse yet died of a heart attack"*. One step at a time he climbed the stairs, when he reached the top he walked very slowly down the hallway to the door three B. He hesitated and then he knocked, he could hear footsteps coming toward the door and he was so nervous that his shirt was soaked with perspiration. The knob turned and the door opened just ajar there was a chain on the inside that prevented the door from completely opening. A small feminine voice said, "who are you and what do you want"? "If you're selling something I'm afraid you're wasting your time I have no extra money for anything".

"No ma'am I'm not selling anything I would just like to talk to you for a moment about a mutual friend". "And who might that friend be" the young woman standing on the other side of the door said. "Are you Kathy Ninski"? "Yes that's my name, who is this mutual friend"? "A very dear friend of mine and I think a very dear friend of yours also his name is Sydney Kichinski". "Where do you know Sydney from"? Kathy asked, "I was in the military with him we were both in the KGB during the old Soviet Union regime".

"I'm sorry Sir but you see Sid died more than three years ago in an auto accident outside of Moscow, he and I were engaged to be married but he died before we could go through with it, so you see we have nothing in common and further more during this time of turmoil I'd never let strangers into my apartment".

Sid stepped over to the opening of the door that was just ajar where Kathy could see him face to face and as he looked in he said, "Kathy look at my eyes and see if you recognize me", Kathy was startled and then she looked into this strange looking man's eyes, she could see exactly what Sergeant Daniel saw at the fishing stream in the mountains, there was no mistaking, she began to sob uncontrollably as she nervously released the chain on the inside of the door and threw the door open, and fell limp into the strangers arms. Still sobbing she looked up into his eyes and cried, "Sid how can it be you are alive"?

Sid held Kathy in his arms for what seemed like an eternity and then they both turned and entered the apartment and closed the door. They sat on the couch and Sid poured out his heart to Kathy and told her all that had happened, it was such a joyful time for both of them because Kathy had grieved over Sid's death and secluded herself with his mother in the apartment for more than three years.

She was so grieved over Sid's death that she never returned to her job, and the only time that she went out was to get food and supplies for her and his mother. She had worked most of her life and she had a few savings put away and she decided when they were all gone that there was nothing else to live for and she would just take her own life.

CHAPTER 55

AFTER ERIK LEFT THE cabin, Otto and Greta decided that it was time for them to leave and go into hiding and try and join the group of "Left Behind" people that was operating as a guerrilla army in the mountains of St. Petersburg Russia. It was difficult to find any of the guerrilla's, as they remained well hidden in the mountains. Unless you knew one of their members, and they would vouch for you, it was next to impossible to join with them. Otto took a daring chance, and contacted one of his old team leaders, via his communication device, knowing it may be traced. He had heard some of Sid's men were in this guerrilla army, and they were in this part of Russia.

Otto and Greta waited for two weeks, for a reply. While they waited they felt they may be in danger of being discovered, and were very nervous.

After two weeks Otto's communication device began blinking and He was very cautious in answering it, because other members of Sid's team members had been discovered, by the use of their communicators, and arrested by the Police.

He tapped in a special code, and was so relieved when the code came back, that only the team members knew.

Otto and Greta were introduced to the Guerrilla Chief and welcomed into the group. Because of Otto's military past, He was used to train new recruits which were coming in daily. Greta was useful for her administrative skills.

After joining the guerrilla's Otto and Greta began to take part in the Groups prayer vigil's and was introduced to God and The Christian Bible, and embraced Christianity, and was excited to find out that Jesus, The Son of God was going to return to the earth in the very near future, and take control of all the Government's on the earth, and they were excited.

CHAPTER 56

THE CHAIR IN THE Command Center tent in the mountain hideaway of West Virginia turned slowly to face the man the resistance movement called The Shadow. Greta could not believe her eyes.

The Beginning ?

EPILOGUE

E RIK AND KARLA ARE now man and wife, and they have established a very effective force of Guerrilla Soldiers that recruited men and women from all nations, to fight and cripple, or bring down the World Government.

Otto and Greta, along with Sid and some of his people are a significant equation of this force.

The world is in chaos, and General Siki has been unable to reign in these renegades. He has put a bounty on all of the "Left Behind" people. Many of the Jews have joined forces with Erik's soldiers, since The Council of twelve turned against them and began a systematic Genocide against them. Every Jew now has a bounty on their head, and are being hunted down and killed.

There is a movement throughout the earth, carried on by Jewish Evangelist's and many members of the "Left Behind" people, that is teaching the people of the earth that the World Government has a very short life span, and in seven years or less there is going to be a new Government established on the earth, by The Jewish Messiah returning to the earth and taking control.

This coming King according to the "Left Behind" Evangelists is The Son of God and His name is Jesus.